say yes to the mess

THE BAD DECISIONS DRESS
BOOK 1

JAX MCQUEEN

ISBN (paperback): 979-8-9948900-0-4

Cover Illustration: Claudia Bonet Morales

Cover Design: Torie Jean

Proofreading: Josie Cluney

This is a work of fiction. Names, characters, places, and incidents either are the product of the author's imagination or are used fictitiously. Any resemblance to actual persons, living or dead, business establishments, events, or locales is entirely coincidental.

For Debbie
I'm so fortunate and honored to have worked alongside you,
but seriously…RETIRE!

one

When Whitney Houston proclaimed that the children were our future, she likely hadn't experienced the chaos of returning to an elementary school classroom after Winter Break. The hyperactive six-and-seven-year-olds making up my first-grade class would be bouncing off the walls, waging biological warfare with illnesses that had hitched rides from visits with extended family, and just generally acting like they'd never attended a day of school in their young lives.

Teach, they said. It'll be fun, they said.

But it *was* fun. I loved the limitless creativity and imagination possessed by tiny humans, and I felt a deep sense of pride in helping them succeed and overcome challenges...at least, that's what I told myself as I cued up Taylor Swift's "Shake It Off" while getting ready on the morning of our first day back. I danced around my bedroom in my pajamas as brassy horns and upbeat drums spilled from the Bluetooth speaker on top of my dresser. Twisting my hips in time to the music, I froze in place and prepared to clap along with the chorus.

But the chorus never came. Instead of grounding handclaps, bass-heavy mumble rap filled the room.

Irritated, I rose from my squat and glared over my shoulder toward the bathroom. Geoff, my long-time boyfriend, stood in the doorway frowning around his toothbrush as he stared down at his phone. I tried not to get distracted by the hard planes of muscle converging in a well-defined V beneath the towel slung low on his hips.

"It's too early for that shit," he grumbled. "I've got my big meeting with Harrison today. I need to get in my zone."

And I'm about to spend several hours with twenty wild six-year-olds who would make a pack of feral hyenas look tame. I need to get into my zone.

With a sigh, I tamped down my annoyance. It wasn't worth an argument—not when I would need every last nerve to survive the day. And if it helped Geoff get the promotion, we could finally start the next chapter of our lives together.

I crossed the room, rose on my toes, and pecked him on the cheek. "You're going to do amazing. Harrison would be an idiot not to choose you. Once you become Vice President of Sales, there'll be nothing stopping us from planning a wedding!"

"Don't count your chickens before they hatch, Zee," Geoff said. "Besides, there's no need to rush into anything."

Another wave of frustration crashed over me like it had so many times over the course of our fourteen-year relationship. Who was rushing? Geoffrey Maurice Woods and I started dating a few weeks after meeting at a house party during our junior year of college. Among my friends, I'd been in a relationship the longest, but while others got married and had kids, I was still waiting for Geoff to find the "perfect moment" to propose.

At first, he suggested we wait a couple of years after graduation to focus on getting our careers off the ground, which made complete sense. After I had three years as a middle school language arts teacher at a local public school under my belt, and he was an Account Executive for an enterprise software company, I broached the subject again, at which point, Geoff explained he'd rather save and put the money toward a down payment on a house.

Two years after *that*, when my dad's tenants moved out of one of his rental properties and he gifted the townhouse to me, I was sure the time had come. Geoff, though, wanted to raise our kids in "something bigger, with a yard larger than the size of a postage stamp." He promised the wedding and life of my dreams would come after he worked his way up the sales ladder, but with every promotion, the goalpost seemed to move further away. Now that Geoff was in the running to become Vice President of Sales, there was a light at the end of the tunnel, and none too soon. On my last birthday, I swore to myself that if Geoff didn't propose by the time I turned thirty-five—six short months from now—I was done.

I already knew he'd purchased a ring; I found the navy blue leather box in the back of his sock drawer several months earlier while putting away his laundry. Unable to resist peeking inside, I found a large, round diamond set in a band made of two intertwining ribbons of white gold adorned with pavé diamonds. I couldn't have imagined a more perfect ring...but it didn't mean much when it remained hidden away.

I blinked back to the present, where Geoff had put on his slacks and was now buttoning up his shirt. After today, it would no longer be an issue; I felt it in my bones. Geoff would be home more often because he wouldn't have to work so hard to prove himself, or travel as much as in his current position as Regional Sales Director. I'd finally be able to give my family and friends the news they'd waited so long to hear, but after all this time, assumed would never come. More than once, I'd caught my mom and sister exchanging pointed looks with one another, or my friends rolling their eyes when they thought I wasn't looking. Even though our engagement was about our commitment to each other, it would feel damn good to flash the shiny rock on my finger and a smug grin at the haters.

God, I know I should be saving my prayers for my sanity in the classroom today, but if you have any mojo to spare, please, please, PLEASE let Geoff become VP of Sales. You know what this would mean to me. To us. I don't ask for much.

"Hey babe, can you help with my tie?" Geoff's eyes met mine in the mirror over the dresser as he held up a strip of emerald green silk.

I finished putting on my favorite pair of earrings, a set of cute strawberries given to me by a student years ago, before crossing the room and snatching the fabric from him with a playful frown. "How is it that you *still* haven't learned to tie a tie on your own?"

"Because you're so good at it," he said with a grin. After I expertly knotted the tie and made sure it was snug against his collar, Geoff spun me around and pulled me to his chest. Arms winding around my waist, he rested his chin on my shoulder. "When I get this promotion, I was thinking we could do something special," he whispered into my ear.

Hope blossomed in my chest. As I stared at myself in the mirror, safe and secure in his arms, I bit back a squeal of joy. *Finally.*

"We should host a dinner party for my work friends. Doesn't that sound fun?"

I shrugged off Geoff's embrace. A dinner party? *A dinner party?*

Wait, Zara—it might all be part of the plan. You prepare this dinner party to your standards, and then he springs the ring. You're essentially planning your own proposal.

"Nothing too big; just fifteen, twenty people," Geoff continued. "I was thinking we could do a theme. Maybe something *Mad Men*-inspired? Or a casino night?"

Neither of those sounded particularly appealing, but whatever.

"I'll provide a guest list, and you can coordinate with everyone." Geoff scrunched his nose up. "I don't think Trevor eats pork, and Brad's a vegan."

I swallowed, keeping a blank smile on my face. Trying to make conversation with Trevor and Brad made me feel like I was talking to the real-life Beavis and Butthead. This was sounding less and less like any kind of party I wanted to attend, let alone plan. Even so, I tried to keep hope alive.

"Alright, babe." Geoff pressed a quick kiss to my temple. "Wish me luck!"

"Good—" He was out the door before I even finished the phrase, leaving a cloud of Dior Homme in his wake. "Luck."

* * *

Half an hour later, I pulled into the school's rear parking lot, throat slightly raw from singing at the top of my lungs. I turned off the engine and cast a furtive glance around, finding only a couple of empty cars.

Perfect.

I cranked up "Single Ladies" even louder and went all in on the choreo—at least, as much as I could behind the wheel of my trusty Volkswagen—since my own days as a single lady were numbered.

Knock, knock, knock.

Startled by the sound of knuckles rapping on my window, I screamed and jerked my arm forward, unintentionally slamming the horn in the center of the steering wheel. I whirled around in my seat to find a man with a slouchy knit beanie pulled low over his forehead and neatly trimmed facial hair. He looked harmless enough, but I didn't see a child with him, nor had I ever seen him on campus before. My hand inched toward my phone where it rested in the cupholder to dial the school security office.

"I'm Caleb McMahon—the interim music teacher while Mariah is out on maternity leave," he said loudly enough to be heard over Beyoncé. Striking, pale green eyes twinkled with amusement, offering a cool contrast to the light brown of his skin.

Interim music teacher...right. Mariah had gone into labor over Christmas break and would be back in April. Vicki, the Director of Fallen Oaks Preparatory Lower School, had mentioned they'd found someone to cover for her, but the man in front of me was nothing like what I'd expected. I assumed Mariah's replacement would more than likely be a woman, and probably much closer to retirement age as most of our subs were.

Caleb stepped back from my door and tucked his hands in the front pockets of his dark jeans. "I was hoping you could point me in the direction of the office. I'm afraid I'm a bit turned around."

"Of course," I said sheepishly. I disconnected my phone from the aux cord, plunging my car into silence that seemed much louder than the music had been, and gathered my belongings.

When I emerged into the chilly January morning, bundled in my puffy coat and clutching my lunchbox containing last night's leftovers, Caleb beamed at me. "And you would be?"

"Oh, right. I'm Zara Whitmore. I'm one of the first grade teaching assistants." I extended my gloved hand, and he clasped it with a firm, confident grip, his penetrating stare locked on mine.

"Nice to meet you, Zara."

Was his voice this melodious a second ago?

Clearing my throat, I snatched my hand away. Of course his voice was musical—he was a music teacher.

I nodded toward the two-story school building and began

walking across the playground. "The front office is downstairs on the other side of the building. If you don't have a key, someone will have to let you in."

Caleb held up his empty hands in the air. "No key just yet. Guess I'm lucky I've got you."

I tucked my chin into my chest so he couldn't see the slight twitch of my lips. Was he actively flirting with me, or did he just have a flirtatious personality?

Should I tell him I have a boyfriend-almost-fiancé?

"How long have you been at Fallen Oaks Prep?" he asked.

"Five years. But I actually went to school here from sixth grade on." I held my breath, waiting for him to ask the inevitable follow-up questions people always did when they found out I was a teaching assistant: *But what do you* really *aspire to? Don't you want to be a real teacher?*

The joke was on them; I'd already been there and done that. After eight years of dealing with snarky attitudes from hormonal pre-teens and passive parents, I found my sweet spot in Susie Ellis's first-grade classroom. I didn't carry the heavy weight of responsibility that came with being a lead teacher, but I still got to have a relationship with the kids, and often received hugs from past students when they stopped by to visit younger siblings.

"Wow! You must really love this place," Caleb said.

I merely gave him a half-smile and pulled my key ring from my coat pocket. As only one of a handful of students of color attending the predominantly white Fallen Oaks Prep, my relationship with the school was a complicated one. But without my experience here, I never would have met my most cherished friends, with whom I still kept in touch almost a quarter of a century later. And in the time since my enrollment, the school had made a concerted effort to increase diversity and make sure Black and Brown students felt like valued members of the school community.

"Ah, Caleb, there you are!" Vicki waved at us from down the hall. Director of the Lower School for the last eight years—and the first Black woman to hold the role in the school's history—Vicki Nielsen fostered a positive environment for faculty and students alike. She got shit done. "I realized we didn't get your keys squared away, so I was just coming to see if you'd arrived. We can't have you stuck out there in the cold!" She turned to me with a sunny smile. "Welcome back, Zara. I hope you had a restful break. Did anything exciting happen?" She waggled her eyebrows and gave my left hand, still hidden in its fleece glove, a pointed look.

Swallowing around the embarrassed lump in my throat, I shook my head. I would've thought after how many times this same scene played out break after break, my colleagues would just stop asking. They always looked so hopeful as they hinted about an engagement, and every time, I let them down.

"Nope, nothing exciting in my neck of the woods." Vicki's brows furrowed slightly. Was there a hint of pity in her eyes? "Well, I should get to my classroom!" I added. "Welcome to Fallen Oaks Prep, Caleb."

"Thanks for getting me in. Maybe you can come guest teach the kids a few moves," he said with a wink, before following Vicki down the hall.

He winked *at me.*

Oh, he was definitely flirting. I'd have to set him straight the next time we ran into one another.

A glance at my watch told me I only had a few minutes before the kids started arriving. I sped down the hallway and took the stairs two at a time to avoid chatting with my coworkers about what didn't happen over the break. Stepping across the threshold of the classroom Mrs. Ellis had inhabited for thirty-three years, I breathed a sigh of relief.

The home-base of the Ellis Elephants, these four safari-themed walls were crammed to capacity with thirty-three years of memories—and stuff. So much stuff. Susie Ellis did *not* believe in throwing *anything* away. As a result, I often wondered how we managed to fit twenty tiny bodies and two big ones into the room every day…not to mention a forty-gallon fish tank and two hamsters.

But I wouldn't trade Susie for the world. Even at sixty-five, she was scaling playground structures at recess or chasing after students in a game of tag. She treated every child that walked through her doors as if they were one of her four grandchildren, encouraging them to learn, explore, and grow, and still made herself available to past families, even if the student she'd taught was now a senior in college.

"Hi honey!" She stood and wrapped me in a bear hug that melted away my lingering humiliation. "Did you have a good break?"

I sighed. "It wasn't long enough."

"Who are you telling? But I missed the kids."

"Of course you did, Susie. You won't know what to do with yourself when you retire."

She grinned. "Retire? I don't know the meaning of the word."

I crossed the large, oval-shaped alphabet rug where we gathered our students, and unzipped my coat, pausing at my desk when I spied the white, grease-stained bag awaiting me on top. I didn't have to open it to know there'd be a glazed, golden-brown apple fritter inside. I groaned. "Susie, you shouldn't have."

She waved a dismissive hand and returned to writing a morning message on the board with a red dry erase marker. "Hon, we both know we're gonna need a truckload of sugar, caffeine, and a favor from the Lord to make it through today. These children are going to act like they have no common sense whatsoever. Eat the fritter."

She didn't have to tell me twice. While Susie finished the

message and gave me a quick rundown of the day's schedule, I finished taking off my outdoor gear, then removed the pastry from its bag. My mouth watered at the aroma of spiced apples and cinnamon tickling my nostrils. Just as I opened wide to take that first divine bite, the classroom door flew open so hard it bounced off the rubber doorstop. A flood of small humans poured inside with cries of "I missed you, Mrs. Ellis!" accompanied by fierce hugs that would put a koala to shame, and excited chatter about the presents they got for the holidays.

At least, all but one.

Carissa Locke, a petite seven-year-old with a head full of springy, ginger curls, stood next to the fish tank with her hands on her hips, her blue eyes narrowed at me beneath sparse, red brows. When she started a determined march across the classroom, I bit back a groan, glumly slid my untouched pastry back in the bag, and greeted her with a smile. "Happy New Year, Carissa!"

"Are you married yet?"

The smile froze on my face as I tried to hide my confusion. While Susie was an open book when it came to sharing stories about her family and grandchildren with the class, I tended to remain close-lipped about my own personal life. "Excuse me?"

She raised her voice. "I said, *Are you married yet?* My mommy said you've been waiting *forever*. Like, since Hudson was in your class. She said lots of people get eng-eng—get married on Christmas Eve."

My chest tightened. Hudson was Carissa's older brother who'd been in our class two years earlier. Their parents—most of them around the same age as me—must have been talking about my relationship status at home. Great.

"My aunt's not married," the little girl continued, each sentence causing my throat to constrict a little more. "She has a dog and calls it her baby. Do you have a dog baby?"

"Carissa!" Susie's voice, uncharacteristically sharp, broke

through my thoughts. "Why don't you come over here and tell me what you did over break?"

"Okay!"

As Carissa skipped across the room, I glanced up and caught Susie's gaze. The compassion in her eyes nearly made me tear up. She'd never once made me feel less than or said anything about me getting married. When I eventually asked her why, she just shrugged and told me she knew I'd tell her whenever I was ready.

Thank you, I mouthed.

Eat the fritter, she mouthed back, before returning her focus to the crowd of little faces fighting for her attention.

Two cranky meltdowns, a yelling match over whose turn it was to feed the fish, and one escaped hamster later, I leaned my head against the brick wall in the faculty room and closed my eyes as blessed, steaming coffee dispensed from the Keurig and into my travel mug. With my hands full trying to diffuse arguments while chasing after Buttercup the missing hamster, I'd had little time to dwell on Carissa's pointed questions, but now that I'd dropped the class off at P.E. with a mumbled "Godspeed" to Coach Aaron, the punch of her words hit me full-force.

My mommy said you've been waiting forever.

If only we all had the audacity of a six-year-old busybody.

When the Keurig let out a final hiss, I opened my eyes, picked up my mug, and added a couple spoonfuls of sugar. I was bent over, searching the fridge for creamer, when my phone vibrated in my pocket. I grabbed the carton and straightened, then checked the screen.

GEOFF

Heading into meeting with H. This could be
it, Z.

Relieved excitement, warm and pleasant, coursed through me. I pictured Geoff in my mind's eye and aimed all my happy sentiments toward him, hoping he could somehow feel them in his office.

ZARA

Sending you all the winning vibes and luck,
even though you don't need them. You've got
this!

GEOFF

Thanks, babe.

Well-wishes sent, I slid the phone back into my pocket. I was reaching for my mug when I felt another text message come through. Puzzled, I fished the device back out. Geoff wasn't a huge texter; he'd rather send one long message than a series of short ones. He must've really been anxious.

Yet, as I glanced down at the screen, it wasn't a text; it was a notification about a direct message on Instagram. Since I didn't use the app frequently, I assumed it was some kind of bot, but because of my obsessive need to keep my inbox empty, I opened it up.

SWORDGYAL3

Do you and Geoff have an open relationship?

My name is Shantel btw.

I stared at the message in confusion. Who the fuck started a conversation like that, and then introduced themselves *afterward*?

Of course Geoff and I didn't have an open relationship. Once we started dating, we became exclusive almost immediately. And for the last year, he'd been so slammed at work that he barely had time for *me*, let alone an open relationship. Sword-Gyal3 clearly had my Geoff confused with someone else.

ZARAHW621

Sorry, but you've got the wrong person.

SWORDGYAL3

I'm talking about Geoffrey Woods. He's in sales at TaskTrac.

My mouth went dry as I clung to the edge of the counter like a lifeline, the only thing preventing me from being swept away in an undertow.

No way.

SWORDGYAL3

He has a small mole shaped like a teardrop on his inner thigh. The left one.

Oh. My. God.

The room spun around me. This had to be some sick prank —maybe a new scam I hadn't yet heard about.

SWORDGYAL3

I have receipts.

Screenshots rapidly populated the chat, one after the other.

And they didn't stop.

Hey. Your pics are fire. 🔥 🔥 🔥 😍 *What's your man think about you posting that* 🍑 *for the world to see?*

Last night was fun. When can we do it again? 😜

I can't get enough of you. You're the best thing in my life right now.

I was going to throw up on the faculty room floor. *My* Geoff couldn't be bothered to send anything more than a one-line text, let alone use emojis. I didn't recognize the person writing these messages.

The screenshots kept coming until I couldn't take it anymore.

ZARAHW621

Please stop.

SWORDGYAL3

I'm sorry. Honestly, I didn't even know you existed until last week. I ended things with him as soon as I found out.

My heart shattered into thousands of tiny splinters that lodged themselves in my gut.

I didn't even know you existed.

I scrolled back to the first message, which was dated last June. It had been a particularly stressful time for us. I was exhausted and beyond ready for the school year to end, while Geoff was frequently away for work, unable to answer my calls or send anything more than a brief text, but still somehow managed to post photos and videos of late-night club outings. There were moments I'd even thought about ending things for good, but I'd poured so much of my energy—so much of my *time*—into this relationship. Cheating hadn't once crossed my mind.

Seven months he'd been exchanging messages with this woman.

I thought about all the times he'd worked late or went on business trips over the last year. Was he with her? I glanced back at her first message. Shantel?

SWORDGYAL3

I just thought you should know. I'm happy to talk on the phone if you want.

She'd be *happy* to talk on the phone? *I'd* be happy to shove said phone right down her throat. With trembling hands, I emptied my travel mug into the sink; more caffeine was the last thing I needed right now. Still shaking, I typed out a reply.

ZARAHW621

I don't want ANYTHING from you.

I resisted the urge to throw the stupid phone on the ground, and instead, powered it off. Like a zombie, I made my way to the closest restroom, which was equipped for students. Normally I went to the adult one where the toilets and sinks were taller, but I knew I'd completely lose it before making it there safely. I couldn't handle a public breakdown on top of everything else; I could just imagine little Carissa going home and briefing her parents, then showing up tomorrow and asking about my anger issues.

I managed to hold it together right until I locked myself in a stall, and then the tears flowed like a busted dam. How could I not have known?

Was it something I did? Something I didn't *do?*

Geoff's myriad excuses for postponing a proposal cycled through my brain. Focusing on our careers. Building our own home. Being able to afford a dream wedding.

Or maybe I knew all along and just didn't want to admit it to myself.

The door to the restroom whined open, and I picked up my feet from the floor, balancing on the small toilet as I tried to quiet my sniffles.

"Who's there?" a suspicious, high-pitched voice asked. "My name is Seraphina. I'm in Mrs. Robinson's class."

Discovered, I put my feet back down and let out a noisy sniffle. "I know. We've met before."

Since my class and Mrs. Robinson's shared the playground twice a week during recess, I'd personally witnessed Seraphina's penchant for melodramatics, and often broke up fights between her and my kiddos over who got to decide what game they'd play or whose doll was prettiest. She loved to ask questions, but never gave anyone time to answer; it drove Blair, Mrs. Robinson's TA, up a wall. After the first time I encountered the talkative first-grader in the restroom, I'd dubbed her the "Bathroom Talker."

"Are you crying?" she asked.

I debated lying, then sighed. "Sometimes adults—"

"I cried when I fell off the monkey bars at recess today. Are you hurt?"

"No—"

"My brother hit me with the basketball he got for Christmas and it hurt really bad. Do you have a brother?"

"No, I—"

"Last night, his goldfish died, so we flushed it down the toilet." Seraphina finally paused for a breath, then barreled on again. "When I die, I don't want to go in the toilet."

Hysterical laughter bubbled out of me so hard I clutched my ribs. Just when I thought the day couldn't get any more damned ridiculous. As if on cue, Seraphina's small head appeared under the stall door, her two braided pigtails sweeping the floor. She blinked at me, her face a blend of curiosity and skepticism.

Sucking in a breath, I pulled myself together and rearranged my features into a stern frown. "Seraphina, go back to class."

She thrust out her lower lip. "But I haven't even used the bathroom yet!"

"Well, use it and go!"

"Hmph." Seraphina disappeared, but I didn't breathe again until I heard the stall next to mine lock.

I ripped a piece of paper from the roll, blew my nose, and left.

"You didn't flush!" the little girl called.

I groaned, then quickly flushed the toilet before the chatterbox could spread any rumors. At the sink, I hazarded a glance at my reflection. My eyes were red and puffy, my makeup smudged and streaked beneath them. Waterproof mascara, my ass. I looked like a waterlogged trash panda that hadn't had a decent night's sleep in months.

After splashing my face with water, I escaped the restroom before the Bathroom Talker could strike up another conversation and raced back to my classroom.

Susie looked up when I entered, her gentle features immediately softening in concern. She stood up from behind her desk, where she'd been organizing papers. "What's going on?"

Tears clogging my throat, I started throwing my things into my bag. "I don't feel well. I just need..." *A safe place to bawl my eyes out. To run into the forest and never come back.* I paused and sucked down a breath. "I just need to leave. I'm sorry, Susie."

She shook her head. "Honey, you've got to take care of yourself first. Go home, and I'll check in later, okay?"

My heart ached at her sweetness; Susie was the only person I knew who was so kind it hurt. I managed a nod and rushed from the room. In the hall and on the blacktop, I kept my head ducked in order to avoid accidental eye contact with anyone. Fat raindrops started to fall from ominous, gray clouds that blocked out the sun, mirroring my bleak mood.

"Zara!" called the velvety voice from that morning.

Ugh, the new music teacher.

I sped up, pretending I didn't hear him. He sounded far enough behind me that it was plausible.

"Zara!"

I made it to my car door, but fumbled with the key fob. My whole keyring fell to the ground. *Shit.*

When I knelt to pick it up, a pair of dirty white Converses entered my peripheral vision.

"Hey there," Caleb said. "I called out to you, but I guess you were too far to hear."

Heaving a sigh, I got to my feet and glared at him, ignoring the raindrops splattering on my face.

His forehead wrinkled. "Are you okay?"

"Do I *look* okay to you?" I snapped. "Just leave me alone!"

Stunned, Caleb took a step back. Embarrassed by my outburst, I got in my car and locked the door, before he could gather his thoughts.

As I peeled out of the parking space and made my way

toward the lot entrance, I looked in the rearview mirror to find Caleb staring after me in confusion. For the briefest moment, I felt bad; only one person was to blame for this mess. But just as quickly, the feeling abated. I'd reached my limit for the day, and no amount of Beyoncé or T. Swift could salvage it.

three

That evening, I sat on the couch in my living room with a fleece blanket draped over my lap, swirling a glass of merlot as the downpour outside beat a steady drum against the windows. With my free hand, I scrolled through SwordGyal3's Instagram feed, my masochistic side getting the better of me. Row after row of gym selfies and OOTDs showcased a statuesque woman with well-defined muscles and cleavage I'd kill for. In every photo, she posed in bright, form-fitting athletic-wear that accentuated her curves. I snorted. Suddenly, it made a lot more sense why Geoff had been religiously going to the gym as of late.

Just last week, she'd posted a picture of herself lounging by the pool in a yellow string bikini, peering down her nose over the top of a pair of giant white sunglasses. Talk about ridiculous —the temperature hadn't risen above forty all month! But it was the photo of a mixed bouquet of sunflowers and red roses in a frosted vase sitting on a spotless countertop that made a lump form in my throat. Posted only a couple of days earlier, the caption read, *Thanks for the dose of sunshine, Boo Bear.*

While I'd been running his suits to the dry cleaner and

applauding after listening to his promotion pitch for the sixth time, Geoff had been sending *her* flowers.

It wasn't fucking fair.

Disgusted, I tossed the phone aside, set my glass on the coffee table, and dropped my head into my hands. Though my eyes burned, I was all cried out; I hadn't been able to stop the flow of tears as I drove away from school. When Geoff left an excited voicemail about landing the position and getting home late because his coworkers wanted to take him out to dinner, I started crying so hard that I had to pull onto the shoulder of the road. Of course, I wondered if he was actually going out with his coworkers—or celebrating with the other woman.

I'd sat in my idling car as rain pummeled the windshield, typing out all kinds of responses. Messages full of loathing and hurt. Messages that started with me calling him every foul name I could think of. But I deleted all of them. I didn't want to give him any kind of advance warning or time to concoct some stupid story that magically excused his shitty behavior.

For a moment, I'd stared down at the bright screen, my vision blurry, and thought about calling my little sister, Jules, or one of my close girlfriends, but shame stopped me. I knew they would never say *I told you so* out loud, but they'd definitely be thinking it.

Eventually, I managed to calm down enough to drive the rest of the way home, but the minute I pulled into the driveway of the townhouse we'd shared for the last eight years, I lost it again. Technically, the townhouse was mine—a gift from my dad—but when Geoff's apartment lease was up, we discussed it and decided it made sense for him to move in; after all, at that point, we'd already been together for a long time. With his comfort in mind, I'd compromised on changing up the colors and decor. I even went so far as to convert the spare bedroom I used for crafting into his home office. I didn't want Geoff to feel like I was just squeezing him in; I wanted him to feel that this was just as much his home as mine.

And all for what? So he felt comfortable enough to cheat and stomp all over my feelings?

The pressure in my chest increased as blood rang in my ears. I prided myself on having patience to a fault—you had to in my line of work. I'd always taken comfort in the fact that every relationship required some measure of give and take. But I'd given away so much of myself for these last fourteen years, every sacrifice chipping away at my power, hoping someday, I'd be rewarded with the fairy tale wedding and happily ever after that was sure to follow—and that I so rightfully deserved.

Fury driving my every move, I leaped from the couch, snatched my wine glass, and stalked up the stairs to our bedroom. I glared at Geoff's bedside table cluttered with charging cables and supplements, then opened the door to my walk-in closet and rummaged on the top shelf in the very back. My hand closed around a sturdy, spiral-bound album.

Gotcha.

Settling myself on the floor of the closet, my fingers trailed over the silver letters I'd penned ages ago on the mint-green cover. *My Future Wedding.* After watching *The Swan Princess* for the first time as a kid, I'd been awestruck by all the elaborate preparations for the wedding of Princess Odette and Prince Derek. Though my mom no longer believed in marriage after divorcing my dad, she humored me and gave me an old album she'd bought for a project and never gotten around to using. I added to it throughout the years, stopping when I went away to college. When I finally worked up the nerve to show it to Geoff on one occasion, his teasing remarks prompted me to hide it away in the closet. I'd only brought it out a few times since—and always when I was alone—usually, during moments when Geoff and I were going through a rocky patch, and I needed a reminder of what the future held in store for me one day.

I flipped through the scrapbook's stiff pages, marveling at the grand vision I'd had for my wedding celebration. Cutouts of bridal gowns and bridesmaids' dresses were taped alongside pictures of the flowers I wanted in my bouquet, their names meticulously written in metallic marker beneath. Paint chips with names like "Cotton Candy Dream" and "Ballet Slipper Whisper" were glued in various combinations as I tried to figure out the perfect color palette. I'd listed venue ideas and the names of guests, annotations and random stickers embellishing the pages. I even dedicated a separate page to each bridesmaid, originally starting with a whopping fifteen but ending up with just five thanks to tightening my inner circle over the years.

I sighed and studied one of the few pictures I had of my mom and dad together, taken shortly after I was born. They'd separated for good when I was just six months old, and from the screaming matches and barbed insults that happened whenever they were in the same room when I was growing up, I'd realized co-parenting didn't work for them. I think the real reason I'd started my wedding scrapbook was because the only time I'd ever seen them happy and not ready to throttle one another was in photos in an album my mom stowed in her basement.

Tears welled and fell onto the pages, but these tears were different. I was crying for all the parts of me I'd hidden, the way I'd dimmed my light to be the perfect partner to a man who didn't give a shit about me or my feelings. Before I realized what I was doing, I gripped a page of potential first dance songs and tore it out of the book. I ripped another and another, shredding them into tiny pieces of confetti like a woman possessed. When only the pages containing my family and friends remained, I sat back on my heels, panting. Through the open door, my eyes landed on Geoff's closet, slightly ajar.

Shoving what was left of the scrapbook aside, I got to my feet and strode across the bedroom with purpose. I flung open the closet door, walked in, and put my hands on my hips as I stared at all the designer suits and expensive shoes. Before Geoff moved in, I'd kept *my* shoes in there.

I grabbed handfuls of fabric, yanking it from the hangers and sending them flying. When my arms were full, I marched downstairs and straight out the front door. Thankfully, the rain had calmed to a light drizzle. I deposited the heap beside the mailbox at the end of the driveway, where we put the trash and recycling bins out each week.

I allowed myself a few deep, gratifying breaths before returning to the house and grabbing another armful of Geoff's things, gleefully dumping them on the top of the first pile. Trip after trip, I repeated the process until nothing remained in the closet but empty hangers on the ground. When I entered the house again, the game console I'd bought for his birthday after months of squirreling money away caught my eye. Unplugging it from the wall, I hoisted it under my arm, swiped the controller from the entertainment center beneath the TV, and made my way outside.

I'd just started down the drive with it when Geoff's black Tesla turned in. He jumped out of the car without cutting the engine, his tie missing and the top buttons of his shirt undone. Immediately, my thoughts went back to SwordGyal3's Instagram feed.

"Is that my PS5?" he asked in disbelief. "Zee, what the hell is going on? Mr. Cornelius from across the street texted me, asking if we were having a garage sale, and if so, could he have my corduroy Gucci loafers!"

I inhaled deeply and stood up straighter. "We're not having a garage sale. I'm just making sure your shit is ready for trash pickup tomorrow." I relaxed my arm and let the game system fall onto the wet ground with a satisfying *thud*. The sick look on Geoff's face made me wish I could rewind ten seconds and do it all over again.

He clapped his hand over his mouth, his eyes on the pieces of his favorite toy. "Have you lost your mind?"

"You know what, Geoff? You want to talk about texts? Let's talk about texts." I glared at him, wishing my eyes had laser beams so I could fry his ass to a crisp. "I know you're cheating on me."

He dropped his hand and gave me an annoyed smirk. "Let me get this straight...you broke my PS5, a game system that costs *hundreds* of dollars, because you think I'm cheating on you?" He chuckled. "Do you realize how insane that sounds? I've been working above and beyond to get this promotion, Zara—which you didn't even congratulate me on, by the way."

"Don't you dare gaslight me!" I pulled my phone from my pocket and brandished it in the air. "I have receipts."

"I really don't know what you're talking about." Geoff scoffed, but I caught the nervous bob of his Adam's apple.

"I mean, you already know what they say *since you wrote them,* but apparently you need a reminder." I pulled up a screenshot and handed the phone over, then watched as his eyes darted back and forth, silently daring him to deny it.

He swallowed again, his guilty eyes flicking to me. I thought I'd feel powerful—like I finally had the upper hand in our relationship. In reality, I just felt worn down and ready to call it a night.

I snatched my phone back. "I think you get the idea."

"Baby," Geoff began, his voice soft like the crooner of a '90s R&B song as he reached for me. "I can explain."

I took a step back, a dark laugh tumbling from my lips, but the morbidly curious part of me won out. What on Earth did he think he could say to dig himself out of this? I crossed my arms over my chest and glared at him.

"I've just been so stressed with work, and then we weren't getting along...but that's all in the past, I promise. I got the promotion!" He grinned and waited for me to express my excitement. "You know what that means—we can get engaged! I already have the ring."

Surely, this can't be a proposal. If it is, it's the worst one ever. Actually, it's not nearly as bad as the one I read about online where the guy hid the ring in the kitty litter box for his fiancé to find. But it feels just as shitty.

"Fuck getting engaged," I said flatly. "And I found the ring ages ago."

Geoff's face went slack, his jaw opening and closing like a fish. "Zara, this isn't—"

"You can't stay here," I blurted out.

"What do you mean, 'I can't stay here'?" Geoff took a step forward, but I straightened my spine and blocked his path. He held his hands up in the air. "Okay, fine. A couple of days apart might do us some good, so you can cool down and we can discuss this rationally."

"I *am* rational, and there's nothing to discuss."

Geoff rolled his eyes. "Okay. At least let me pack—"

"I've already done it for you." I tipped my head at the damp pile on the curb.

"You're not really going to leave my stuff out here all night? People might think it's up for grabs."

"Well, then you better get moving." I turned on my heel and started for the house.

"Where am I supposed to go?" Geoff asked. He sounded more helpless than a six-year-old who still hadn't figured out how to tie their own shoes.

I shrugged. "Not my problem. Maybe your parents? Your brother? SwordGyal3?"

"Who?"

I closed the door on him and locked it. He still had more stuff upstairs—I hadn't cleaned out the bathroom or touched his office—and I would need to get the locks changed, but all that was for another day. Right now, I was just. So. Tired.

My bravado and strength leaving, I slid to the floor and burst into tears.

four

The next evening, I stared at the stupid "Moonlight Slate" walls through eyes that were practically swollen shut from all the crying I'd done. The color—originally a soothing pale green that reminded me of springtime—had been a compromise from when Geoff moved in. Now here it was, suffocating me.

My gaze drifted to the clock on my nightstand. When I first cracked my eyes open and glanced at it earlier this morning, it read *6:00*. Though I hated leaving Susie in the lurch—especially since we'd only just gotten back from break—I texted her and Vicki that I was sick and couldn't make it to school. Susie, bless her soul, told me not to worry about anything and said she'd take care of finding a substitute for the day. After handling that, I turned off my phone and went back to sleep.

Now it was twelve hours later, and I still hadn't made it out of bed except for two trips to the bathroom.

As much as I didn't want anyone to see me like this, it was time to call in help.

I powered my phone up, ignored the dozens of messages from Geoff, and sent my little sister a text.

ZARA

Hate to bug you, but SOS

JULES

Uh-oh. Where are you?

ZARA

Home.

JULES

Be there in 15.

With a relieved sigh, I set my phone back down and pulled the covers over my head. Technically, Jules and I were half-sisters, sharing a mom but different fathers. She was just eighteen months younger, and the two of us were extremely close, together adapting to ever-changing circumstances as our mom, Yvonne, moved us back and forth across the country from one spiritual community or energy vortex to another. Eventually we returned home to Fallen Oaks, North Carolina, to live with my grandma and grandpa when I was ten and Jules was nine.

Although our connection was strong, Jules and I butted heads regularly. Growing up, I often took on a mothering role while Mom was off on a shamanic journey or three-day vow of silence, and it was hard to let go of that, even though we were both grown women. At thirty-two, Jules's life should've had *some* semblance of stability, like a reliable job or decent living situation. Instead, she bounced from role to role, seeking greener pastures whenever she got bored, and changed residences just as often. Currently, she was a bartender and house-slash-pet-sitter, but next week, she might be working as a hand model or standing at an intersection, flipping signs for a mattress store.

Fifteen minutes later, my phone vibrated, triggering my anxiety. I couldn't walk around for the foreseeable future, jumping every time someone called or texted. Sucking down a deep breath, I peered at the screen through one eye to find a text from Jules saying she was downstairs. Quickly, I blocked Geoff's number, then dragged myself out of bed and to the front door, where Jules waited on my worn-out welcome mat in her usual festival-ready, boho chic attire. Today, she wore flowy, wide-leg pants with a gray Fleetwood Mac shirt knotted over her midriff, and her long, natural hair was coiffed in a soft, sculpted updo.

She scrunched up her nose. "You look like shit."

"Thanks for the confirmation," I said. Leaving the door ajar, I retraced my path toward the stairs.

"Um, where are you going?" she asked.

"Back to bed."

"Oh, no you don't!" Grabbing hold of my arm, Jules dragged me to the couch and plunked me down. I promptly slumped over. "Have you eaten anything today?" When I shook my head, she sighed and produced a brown paper bag from the tote bag slung over her shoulder. "Eat and then tell me why I'm here. Did you even go to school? You never miss school."

As I dejectedly unwrapped my favorite Italian sub loaded with meat and cheese, she looked around the living room, pausing at the entertainment center. "Where's the PS5? And Geoff's framed Jordan jersey?" Eyes widening, she let out a gasp. "Did he die?"

I licked my parched lips and shook my head, feeling slightly better with each bite of food. "No. But he *is* dead to me. He cheated."

Jules's mouth dropped open. "I'll kill him—no, first I'll chop off his balls, *then* I'll kill him. Where's he at now? It'll only take me twenty minutes to run to Mom's and grab her garden shears."

I laughed weakly. "Please don't get sent to prison on my account."

There was no love lost between Jules and Geoff, and this would absolutely throw gasoline on the fire. No matter how much of a tornado her life was, one thing remained constant: from the moment they met, she had despised Geoff with a passion...all because he joked that her fake lashes were so big she could take flight if she fluttered them hard enough.

Her expression softening, she leaned over and rested a hand on my shoulder. "In all seriousness, how are you doing?" She gestured at my swollen face with her other one. "I mean, not well, obviously."

"I'm..."

How am *I?*

I was numb, unsure which emotion should take priority. Anger? Betrayal? Grief? I felt all of them so deeply it was just easier to lock them away in a box and push it to the furthest recesses of my mind. My entire world had been upended overnight. For fourteen years—all of my twenties and nearly half my thirties—we were Geoff-and-Zara. I couldn't tell where I ended and he began.

Now it was just me.

"I'm a little lost," I said, a tremor in my voice.

She nodded. "Anyone would be."

"Jules, I'm serious." A tear slipped down my cheek. How I had any moisture left in my body was beyond me. "I don't even have a dog baby to love."

Her eyebrows knitted in confusion. "I don't know what that means, but okay? I'll put *Find Zara a Dog Baby* on tomorrow's to-do list."

I held my breath, waiting for the "You know, I told you so" that she was dying to say, but it never came. Instead, she followed up with, "What happened? How'd you find out?"

Sniffling, I melted into the couch. "His side piece sent me

screenshots of their convos while I was at school yesterday. He had the nerve to try and deny it."

"That asshole," Jules muttered. "You want me to help you get rid of his stuff?"

One corner of my mouth quirked up. "Already taken care of. I dumped a lot outside last night."

Jules's almond-shaped eyes grew big. "You didn't!"

"I did."

"Atta girl!" She surveyed the room again. "I bet everything in this place reminds you of him. You really changed stuff around for him."

Groaning, I hid my face behind a throw pillow and debated screaming into it. When I felt a gentle but persistent tapping on my leg, I peeked one eye out and found Jules's face inches away from mine.

"We're getting you out of here," she said.

I dropped the pillow and stared at her warily. "What are you thinking?"

* * *

"Jules, this isn't at all what I had in mind. I was imagining something more like you rubbing my back while I sobbed into a pint of Neapolitan ice cream and hate-watching *Vanderpump Rules* at your place," I whined, looking around the wine bar that currently employed my sister.

After forcing me into the shower and into real clothes, she'd shoved me into her car without telling me our destination, only for us to arrive at Cork & Vine. Ever since our tastes for wine matured beyond grabbing the cheapest bottles we could find at the grocery store, Cork & Vine had been the go-to place for myself and my friends to gather. Over the years we'd celebrated all sorts of things here—birthdays, promotions, general life check-ins—or commiserated...at least we had, until everyone got so busy we mostly kept in touch through a group chat. Although I adored the place, I wasn't up for being out in public, let alone being social. What if I ran into someone I knew? Someone *Geoff* knew?

"Cozy" and "rustic" were the words that struck me as Jules and I navigated our way through overstuffed armchairs and tufted couches creatively arranged around a massive, reclaimed wood bar in the center of the space. An alcove on one side of the room was lined with large, open bookcases filled with paperbacks, hardcovers, and board games. Opposite us, watercolor images for sale formed a small art gallery on one wall. People were scattered about the bar, typing away on laptops or quietly chatting in pairs.

Jules didn't speak again until we'd plopped down on a plush, purple loveseat within view of the entrance. "Sis, I'm just one person. I had to call in reinforcements."

"You told The Six?" I asked, insides twisting.

Obviously, I was going to tell my close girlfriends—or as we'd started calling ourselves while bonding over being the few girls of color attending a predominantly white private school, the Sensational Six—about the breakup at some point, but I wanted to lick my wounds in private for a little longer.

"Ding dong, the dick is dead!" a voice rang out across the wine bar, right on cue.

Mortified, I shielded my face with one hand as heads turned toward the entrance where Max Baldwin shimmied in place. The resident rebel and fashionista of our friend group, she commanded attention in a black leather jacket layered over a polka-dotted dress, holey fishnets, studded black ankle boots, and oversized sunglasses even though we were indoors and the sun had already set.

"This isn't happening," I said.

Looking just as pained as I felt, Stevie Newkirk—Max's best friend and another of the Sensational Six—hung back near the door, trying to create some distance between them. Even from this far away, the death grip on the cellophane-wrapped gift basket in her hands was evident.

Max swept across the room with a self-assured stride. For the near quarter of a century we'd been friends, she continually cycled through distinctive phases, experimenting with—and getting in trouble for—altering her clothes, before completely transforming herself through wigs and makeup in her teens, and finally embracing more permanent changes like tattoos and piercings.

It made sense that after graduating high school, she'd hopped on the first available flight to study drama and design at NYU, eventually becoming a professional wardrobe designer for TV and film. It was odd to see Max back in town given her strained relationship with her parents and older sister, but she'd taken a leave of work and raced home when her Great-Aunt Cecilia had suffered a heart attack three months earlier. No one was quite sure when Max would pick up and leave again, but one thing was for certain—when she was around, life spiraled into a whirlwind of unpredictability.

Stevie, however, was on the opposite end of the chaos spectrum; you always knew what to expect from her. She exuded poise and didn't hesitate to rein us back in when we got a little too rowdy. Though she and Max both enrolled at Fallen Oaks Prep the year after I did, the two of us didn't become really tight until we roomed together during our years at the University of North Carolina at Chapel Hill. A super-organized, lifelong over-achiever with an affinity for lists and spreadsheets, she'd used her strengths to build a thriving lifestyle photography business here in town.

Basically, the two women were the epitome of "opposites attract," with the rest of us falling somewhere between.

"High-five, friend!" Max said by way of greeting. Half-heart-edly, I slapped her palm with mine.

"Max is on-time for once. Has hell frozen over?" Jules asked.

Stevie tossed her immaculate ponytail over her shoulder. "All my doing; she was assisting me on a shoot." She turned to me with a sympathetic smile. "This is for you. Sorry about your breakup."

I accepted the beautifully wrapped gift as Jules scrunched up her face. "Y'all really came in here like two of the Three Wise Men. What's in there? Frankincense and myrrh?"

Stevie's dark eyes narrowed. "*Zara*, inside you'll find a three-wick stress relief candle, bath salts—"

"For bathing, *not* ingesting," Max cut in, sliding her sunglasses off and adjusting the red bandana in her short curls.

"—a couple of face masks and aloe-infused fuzzy socks," Stevie continued as if Max hadn't spoken. "A notebook and pen set to journal about your feelings, and a gift card to Bella Cucina, which I know is your favorite restaurant."

"This is really sweet, Stevie." While prickly and aloof on first impression, once Stevie warmed up, she revealed a supportive and thoughtful side of herself. She had a knack for recalling even the smallest details about your interests or preferences, whether they were mentioned months or years earlier. "Thank you."

"Oh look—another gift basket," Rosario Díaz said drily, strolling up to the group.

They managed to get Rosario out of the house, let alone out of Durham? I thought, unable to mask my look of disbelief.

As a stay-at-home mom of two little boys living the next city over, Rosario was now almost as rare a presence as Max. Despite being the oldest, and therefore, our fearless group leader by default, she was seldom around these days. Once a jet-setting Global Events Designer, she'd traded her passport for pacifiers, her tight, sexy clothes for leggings and oversized tops, and an extensive collection of stylish stilettos for slip-on sneakers and Uggs. This evening, her sweater hung off one bronze shoulder, accented by a faint milky stain near the collar.

After Max plucked a random spaghetti noodle from her hair, Ro kissed me on the cheek, then claimed the armchair beside mine. "Which one of you finally had the guts to pull the plug?"

"Ro!" Jules glared at her, while Max grimaced and said, "Yikes!"

After all these years, was anyone really surprised? Rosario had never been afraid to say aloud what we were all thinking. Even so, the question was a hot dagger in my gut. How long would Geoff have continued to let us live a lie if I hadn't called it quits? Would I have actually walked away on my thirty-fifth birthday like I'd promised if there'd been no proposal?

Before I could reply, Amber Vadsaria-Washington, the final member of the Sensational Six, hurried over—well, as fast as a five-month pregnant woman could—her long, black hair streaming behind her. "Hi, hi, hi. Sorry, sorry, sorry. My last parent conference ran late. C'mere, sweetie."

Stepping around Jules, Amber tossed her purse in Rosario's lap and embraced me in a tight hug. I sagged against her, finding comfort in her familiar aroma of vanilla and coconut. Fiercely protective of her loved ones and almost too sweet for her own good, it was only fitting that our mother hen was finally becoming an actual mother in just a few short months.

After Amber released me and took the remaining chair next to Ro, she noticed the gift basket in the middle of the table. "Nice one, Stevie."

Stevie sniffed and brushed off an imaginary speck of dust from her jeans. "At least someone appreciates my hard work."

"We *all* do, Stevie," I quickly said to stave off an argument. "We know how busy you are."

Satisfied, Stevie reclined on the loveseat opposite me, the corners of her mouth lifting ever so slightly.

"Okay," Ro said, leaning forward with her elbows on her knees. My eyes tracked the spit-up stain as it moved beneath her collarbone. "Enough talk about Stevie's fucking baskets; I need the tea. Jules just sent some drier-than-hell text saying you and Geoff called it quits."

"Jesus, Rosario," Stevie hissed.

I blinked rapidly, checking back into the conversation. Wait a minute—did the girls have a group chat I wasn't a part of besides our regular one?

Jules clapped her hands. "Ladies of the Sensational Six, we are gathered here today—"

"Fucking hell, is he dead?" Max looked back and forth between us. "Jules, you didn't say anything about him being dead!"

"I would have made a completely different basket if I knew that was the case," Stevie muttered.

"No one's dead!" I snapped in exasperation.

"If you dingbats let me finish, I'll explain," Jules said loudly to be heard over everyone. "We're here to support Zara in her time of need." She looked at me and raised her eyebrows. "Do you want to say anything?"

"You seem to have it all under control, Radio Jules. Why don't you just go ahead and give them the details?" I raised my hand overhead and waved frantically to catch the attention of a passing server. If this was the way the evening was going, I'd need a bottle of wine all to myself to make it through.

"Here's the gist: some thot DMed Zara that Geoff was cheating and had the receipts to back it up. Last night, Zara dumped his stuff on the curb and kicked him out," Jules announced with the confidence and enthusiasm of a late-night talk show host. "Our good sis is free!"

Rosario snapped her fingers in the air. "Yaaas, bitch! Can I just say I am *so* glad you didn't marry that jerk? It felt like you were trapped in some kind of hostage situation. I was ready to tell you to blink twice for help."

I frowned as Max snorted. Surely, things hadn't appeared *that* bad?

"I never liked the way he spelled his name. Who freaking spells Geoff with a G?" Stevie asked.

"To be fair, he had no control over that." Leave it to Amber, great at seeing all sides of an issue, and frequent peacemaker, to attempt to quell the Geoff hate.

Max leaned forward and slapped the table. "Fuck that! We're blaming his sorry ass for *everything*. It rained today? Geoff with a G's fault. Power outage in the neighborhood? That's all Geoff with a G."

"UNC lost to Duke—thanks a lot, Geoff with a G!" Ro chimed in.

"Can we go *one night* without Duke slander?" Amber pleaded, the only one of us who'd gone on to become a Blue Devil.

"Amber caught a stray," Max said. "You're the *worst*, Geoff with a G."

Everyone but me dissolved into giggles. I desperately wanted to join in, to find humor in the absurdity of it all, but it felt like it was me—not Geoff—who was the butt of the joke. It was me who'd put up with hundreds of empty promises and being strung along. It was me who'd made excuses for Geoff's comments and given explanations for what was causing him to drag his feet when I, myself, didn't even understand.

"Oh, come on, Zara. You know it's funny," Max said when she could breathe again.

Rosario nodded in agreement. "We've been telling you for *years* that the man was playing in your face and wasting your time."

"I'm not sure this is exactly what she needs to hear right now," Stevie said, noticing the tight-lipped expression on my face. I flashed her a slight smile of gratitude.

What they didn't understand was that it was easy to judge when you were part of the starting lineup. When you were watching from the sidelines like me, waiting to be put in the game, you held tight onto every tiny scrap of hope, praying one day to get your turn on the field. I longed for the security and assurance that accompanied a partner whose actions not only aligned with their words but demonstrated just how lucky they felt to have you in their life—and I wanted to be that person for someone else.

I wanted the same fondness that colored Rosario's voice every time she talked about Edgar taking the boys so she could have a "Mommy Me-Day." The adoration that lit up Amber's face whenever she spoke about her husband, Dwayne, who insisted on talking through their day every night before bed, or surprising her with flowers just because.

I even envied the women without partners, who seemed to flourish by themselves. I wished I could be more like Max, unafraid to strike it out on my own, or less attached to outcomes and able to reinvent myself like Jules seemed to do every five minutes. At this point, I'd gladly even take Stevie's backbone of steel.

"He just kept painting this beautiful picture of what our future would look like when all the pieces fell into place. I really thought it was only a matter of time," I finally said, looking down at my lap. "If I was patient and waited it out, I'd get my happily ever after, like Rosario or Amber."

"Happily ever after?" Ro snorted. "If Edgar leaves his dirty underwear beside the hamper one more time, you might see me on an episode of *Snapped*."

Amber nodded. "And while I'm head over heels in love with Dwayne, I could tell you things about him that would make your skin crawl."

"Please don't," Jules said.

I took a deep breath. "I couldn't face the idea of having to start over...or worse, ending up alone."

"Maybe you're *supposed* to start over," Amber said. "Maybe your person has been patiently waiting for you to learn everything you needed to from this relationship, and for Geoff to move the heck out of the way."

"And isn't being alone better than being with the wrong person?" Stevie added.

I swallowed the lump in my throat as I considered the question. It only then dawned on me that, for all intents and purposes, I was now unattached.

I was on my own.

As if sensing the dark spiral of my thoughts, Amber left her chair and perched on the arm of the loveseat. She grabbed my hand and squeezed it. "But she's not alone—she's got us."

Stevie caught my eye and gave a firm nod, while Max flashed me a thumbs-up, and Rosario rolled her eyes with a, "Duh!"

Jules tackled me from the side. "Even when the zombie apocalypse happens, we'll still have your back—we know you can't fight for shit."

Who would have thought that the six of us, thrown together as kids by circumstances we didn't have a choice over, would forge a bond so strong it was unshakeable almost a quarter of a century later? As teenagers, we'd hung out in Aunt Cecilia's sunroom, feeling sophisticated as we drank mocktails and daydreamed aloud about where we'd be twenty years on. I think if we knew then what awaited us in adulthood, we probably wouldn't have been in such a hurry to grow up. And yet, despite each woman having her own busy life—Stevie running her photography business; Max taking care of Cecilia; Rosario wrangling Mikey and Mateo; Amber adjusting to newlywed life and a preparing to become a mom; and Jules being Jules—they'd made a point of showing up for me tonight.

"Zara," Max said suddenly. "I'd go to jail for you. All of you actually...well, maybe not Ro."

"Hey!" Rosario flipped her middle finger at her.

"She already said she doesn't want to be responsible for anyone doing time," Jules said.

"I could always send a gift basket with a file in it. Maybe a grappling hook and rope? A map of the surrounding area?" Stevie caught my eye and winked.

"You've been holding out on us, Steev. How do you know so much about escaping the clink?" Max asked.

Stevie mimed zipping her lips and throwing away the key.

Shaking my head, I burst into laughter. For the first time since my life fell apart, I felt like maybe, just maybe, I just might be okay.

five

"Hadleigh, I don't understand how you leave here fully clothed each day when I'm always finding piles of clothing beside your desk." At the door of the classroom, I stuffed a rainbow tutu, striped leggings, and a pink sweatshirt emblazoned with a giant kitten face into her bookbag. "And don't even get me started on all the dirty socks."

Hadleigh shrugged. "I like to play fashion show with Carissa. Bye, Ms. Whitmore!" she called over her shoulder as she raced into the hallway.

I shook my head; a Max in the making.

Aside from Walker breaking off a pencil tip in his ear, it had been a good, uneventful day back at school. I'd woken up with a happy hangover from spending time with my girls and hadn't even shed one tear when I spied Geoff's empty side of the bed. Sure, I felt a pricking sensation behind my eyes, but not actually crying was progress, right? Confident I'd turned the corner and could make it through the day without falling apart, I got dressed and came to work.

The kids were thrilled to see me when they entered the classroom that morning and behaved impeccably, even though

Susie left early for a doctor's appointment. Clearly, the universe knew I needed a break.

Once all the students were gone, I finished wiping down desks and putting things away so I could head to the first faculty meeting of the new year…where I was bound to run into Caleb, the interim music teacher. Groaning, I grabbed an emergency Dr. Pepper from the fridge and uncapped it. Now that the shock of Geoff's infidelity had ebbed, I couldn't help but remember how rude I'd been to Caleb the other day. I'd managed to avoid him thus far, but I owed him an apology.

After I packed up, locked the door, and took a few more fortifying sips of caffeinated sugar to get me through the conversation, I walked up to the music room, conveniently located in the same building as the school auditorium where our meetings were held. I put the cap back on the soda, took a deep breath, and knocked on the door.

"Come in!"

Caleb, seated behind a pile of recorders with a pen and clipboard in hand, looked up with an easy-going smile when I entered. If he was surprised to see me, he didn't show it.

"Hi," I said, walking awkwardly into the room.

"Hey, I was just doing some inventory." As he stood up, I got my first look at him, unencumbered by layers of winter clothing. His dark brown hair was cropped close to his head, accompanied by neat sideburns and a couple days' worth of stubble along his jaw. He'd accessorized his patterned, short-sleeve button down with a wooden mala looped around his neck, and beaded bracelets on one wrist. I swallowed as my eyes traveled along the inside of one toned, brown forearm, where an inked treble clef dissolved into a flock of birds just below his elbow.

Girl, what are you doing?

I cleared my throat. "Hi," I said again, fiddling with the strap of my backpack. "I, uh, came to apologize for snapping at you the other day. I was…having a moment."

Caleb shrugged. "All is forgiven; no one's one hundred percent one hundred percent of the time. When Susie brought them to class yesterday and not you, I thought, *Wow, I must have made the worst first impression.*"

Blood rushed to my face. "No! No, I was out sick."

I didn't want any bad blood between us—not when I'd be seeing him regularly since one of my duties included ferrying the kids to their enrichment classes.

His light eyes scrutinized me, as if he was trying to determine whether I was telling the truth. Uneasy, I shifted my weight from one foot to the other. "Well, I'm glad to hear you're feeling better."

"Thanks. Um, anyway, I just wanted to clear the air."

Caleb placed the clipboard on his desk and slid those fit arms into his wool overcoat. "Consider it cleared after you accompany me to the faculty meeting." He slipped the strap of his messenger bag over his head, lips curling in a subtle smile.

Ugh, why do attractive men always feel entitled to make demands?

I wanted to tell him no just to wipe the smug look off his face, but I'd only just extended an olive branch. Besides, the auditorium was all of ten feet away—if this wiped the slate clean, fine.

"Okay," I said with a shrug.

I waited as Caleb switched off the lights and locked up. We fell into step next to each other as we started down the hall.

"How have your first couple of days been?" I asked.

He let out a noisy exhale and shook his head. "Like I got thrown into the deep end without a life vest. Mariah didn't leave many notes for the spring music program, several instruments need repair or are missing, and the students are...well, you know how they can be coming back from break. Your class, in particular, is very...spirited."

I grinned despite myself. "That's a nice way of putting it. We tend to get the kids who need a little extra love placed in our class."

"I'm not surprised. Susie's incredible; she's like a fairy godmother from a Disney movie."

Caleb opened the door to the auditorium and gestured for me to go ahead. With minutes to spare until the start of the meeting, faculty and staff filled the tiered seats. In the middle of a row near the top, Susie waved her hand overhead and gestured to the single open seat next to her. "Do you want—"

"Looks like Susie needs me!" I cut in. "I'll see you around."

Caleb's brow furrowed ever so slightly. "Oh. Okay."

Leaving him at the entrance, I nabbed an apple from the snack table, and headed up the steps to Susie and the other first-grade faculty.

"How'd your appointment go?" I asked, dropping into my seat.

"Fallen Oaks won't be rid of me anytime soon." Susie paused in working on the crocheted scarf she'd begun during the last meeting and looked at me over the reading glasses perched on the tip of her nose. "I see you've gotten acquainted with the new music teacher. He's nice."

"Just welcoming him to the neighborhood," I said breezily.

"Uh-huh. How'd the afternoon go?"

"Not too bad. After Trisha fished the pencil tip out of Walker's ear, I didn't hear a peep from him the rest of the day. And I sent Hadleigh home with a laundry load's worth of clothes."

"That tracks," Susie murmured.

"Everyone, attention up here," Vicki said from the stage. Though she'd spoken into a microphone, her voice was barely audible over the chatter in the auditorium. "Uh, hello? Is this thing working?"

A piercing whistle sliced through the air. The room went silent as heads whipped toward Aaron, who leaned against a wall in his customary track pants.

Vicki nodded at him. "Thank you."

"We need him in the classroom," I whispered. Susie snorted and looped a piece of yellow yarn over her crochet hook.

As Vicki delivered her opening remarks, I, along with everyone else, zoned out, retrieving my phone and opening the Sensational Six group chat. Since we weren't able to get together often, the chat let us stay connected, whether we were in Fallen Oaks or halfway around the globe. It had been quiet all day, which was odd for us. The conversation was ongoing, with no need for greetings or goodbyes, and filled with a decade's worth of inside jokes, advice, encouragement, and more information than I ever wanted to know about the spread of pink eye and ringworm at Rosario's son's daycare.

ZARA

Terrible idea to meet at the wine bar on a weeknight. I didn't want to get out of bed this morning.

MAX

Dammit, Geoff with a G!

JULES

[Shirley Temple giggling gif]

A chuckle slipped past my lips, but I covered it with a cough. Susie elbowed me in the arm as a few curious glances landed on us.

"Sorry," I whispered. Pasting on a contrite expression, I set my phone in my lap, screen down, and made a show of paying attention while Vicki went over expectations for the new semester. Once enough time had passed and people resumed their own distractions, I picked up the device again.

ZARA

You guys are going to get me in trouble. In a faculty meeting and I literally LOLed.

STEVIE

Shouldn't you be paying attention? You're responsible for educating the world's future leaders.

I thought about a tearful Walker tugging on his ear, and Duncan, who I'd found playing with an unwrapped tampon beneath his desk not once, but *twice*, and shuddered.

MAX

Only if the asteroid doesn't take us out first.

AMBER

Way to bring down the chat. 

MAX

Whatever. Bring your asses to Summit Square Food Court at 6.

After a full day of school *and* a faculty meeting, Max wanted me to go to the mall, where I was bound to run into at least five of my students and be forced to reassure their parents that it was completely normal for Little Baylee to pretend to be a cat, but not so much that she wanted to use a litter box? No thanks.

ZARA

Nah, I'm tired as 💩. I'm just gonna head home.

JULES

Booooo.

MAX

[Tomato throwing gif]

STEVIE

You're no fun.

Stevie "Fun Sponge" Newkirk telling me *I* was "no fun"? Were we in some kind of alternate dimension? I sighed.

ZARA

If it shuts y'all up, fine.

AMBER

[Tigger hugging Eeyore gif]

ZARA

Are you calling me an Eeyore?!

While I waited for a reply, I yawned and stretched my arms high over my head. Maybe I was going to have to start stocking the classroom fridge with actual energy drinks because Dr. Pepper just wasn't doing it for me anymore.

Beside me, Susie tutted, her eyes wide behind her reading glasses. "Are you sure?"

Confused, I frowned at her. "Sure about what?"

"Zara"—my head snapped to the stage where Vicki was beaming at me—"thank you for volunteering."

Volunteering? Alarm bells screeched in my head as colleagues in close proximity shot pitying glances my way. I plastered on an uneasy smile.

"Exactly what did I just volunteer for?" I asked Susie out of the side of my mouth.

"Helping Caleb plan the spring music program," Susie said matter-of-factly.

I just volunteered for what?

"Why didn't you stop me?!" I hissed.

She dropped her crochet hook in her lap, tilted her head, and gave me a look that said, *I tried, you big dummy.*

I took a couple of deep breaths, trying to stave off the panic building in my chest. My life was crumbling down around me. I was only just barely holding it together, and now I had something else added to my plate.

Just freaking great.

I scanned the rows of seats ahead of us, locating the back of Caleb's head and glared at it. As if sensing my gaze, he turned around and smiled at me, a mischievous twinkle in his eye.

six

"Want some?" My sister extended a large soft pretzel toward me.

"No, I don't want any pretzel. Will someone tell me what the heck we're doing here?" I planted my hands on my hips next to the Auntie Anne's storefront in Summit Square Mall, glaring at Jules, Amber, and Stevie. "Thanks to you bozos, I have to help with the stupid spring concert."

Amber leaned back in her chair and rested her hand on her slight belly. "Aw, that'll be cute."

Caleb's good-looking—but annoying—face flashed in my mind's eye. I'd spent the rest of the meeting fuming, sinking low in my seat as I tried to think of a way to get out of volunteering without ruffling feathers. After Vicki dismissed us, I booked it through the stairwell at the rear of the auditorium and sped to my car to avoid another run-in with him.

"Then you come and organize it," I grumbled. "I repeat, what are we doing here?"

Stevie exchanged a nervous look with Amber. "Max can explain when she arrives. It was her idea."

I glanced at Jules, who took a huge bite out of her pretzel

and glanced away guiltily. Max's ideas—typically off-the-wall, like dressing up and crashing a wake for the free food, or registering all of us in a chili pepper eating contest for the prize money—were enough to induce anxiety on their own, but the reactions of my friends had me concerned.

"So, have you heard anything from Geoff?" Amber asked brightly.

No, since blocking him, I thankfully had not. And he hadn't tried to reach out through any other means. But frustratingly enough, my thoughts kept straying to him. Where had he ended up staying? With the woman who messaged me, or someone else? Did I ever cross his mind? Did he understand how much his betrayal hurt me? Did he even care?

"Radio silence, and I'm just fine with that," I said.

Stevie frowned. "But doesn't he still have stuff at your place?"

"He has the essentials—I'm sure he'll manage for now."

"What up, losers." Max sauntered up to the pretzel shop in a faded "Not Today, Satan" t-shirt tucked into a black-and-white plaid skirt with a wide red belt. Red pumps and a red rose tucked behind her ear pulled the whole look together.

Stevie rolled her eyes. "So glad you could make it—especially since you're the one who set it up."

"Will someone *please* tell me what *it* is?" I pleaded.

Max's hand darted forward with a quickness that would make Mr. Miyagi proud, snatched a piece of Jules's pretzel, and popped it in her mouth.

Jules scowled. "Get your own! I don't know where your hands have been."

"And you don't want to." Max wiggled her eyebrows.

"Gross," Amber muttered.

Max looked around. "Where's Ro? She's been MIA all day."

"The kids," Amber and Stevie said simultaneously.

"A convenient excuse."

"She's a stay-at-home mom!" Jules exclaimed.

Max waved a dismissive hand in the air, then gestured for us to follow her out of the food court. The others complied, but I remained rooted to my spot and crossed my arms over my chest.

"I'm not going anywhere until someone tells me what the hell is going on."

Max stopped and eyeballed Stevie and Amber. "Ladies."

Each firmly took hold of one arm and started tugging me down the mall.

"This is ridiculous," I said, between giggles. "Why all the secrecy?"

The girls only released me when we stopped in front of a window display featuring an array of mannequins wearing stylish party dresses, hundreds of black, pink, and gold balloons at their feet.

"Um, why are we at a bougie clothing boutique? Does someone need a dress for a party or special occasion?"

Max spun around, looking very pleased with herself. "*You* do."

"Me?" I asked, bewildered. "What for?"

"I told Aunt Cecilia about your breakup," she said.

"You told Cecilia?" I glared at the group. "Is there anyone y'all *haven't* told? At this rate, the entire state of North Carolina is going to know within a week!"

"The woman's been married four times. If anyone knows how to navigate a breakup—or a makeup—it's her." Max shrugged. "Besides, it took the old lady's mind off of her health woes."

"Not old—*mature*," Stevie said. "She'd kill you if she heard you were using her name and the word 'old' in the same sentence."

"She had the *best* idea," Max continued.

Muscles tensing, I waited for the other shoe to drop.

"We're throwing you a breakup party!" Amber blurted out, shooting her hands in the air like she just won a game of Bingo.

Max frowned. "Way to steal my thunder."

A breakup party? My gut instinct was that I wanted no parts. Just what would we do? Play Pin the Tail on the Asshole and the target was a picture of Geoff? On second thought, I could get behind that.

"See?" Stevie said hesitantly. "I told you she wouldn't be excited about it."

I shrugged. "I just don't see the point."

"Uh, to give you some closure?" Jules said.

"To mark the end of one chapter and usher in your Single Girl Era." Max moved her hands in front of her face as if setting the scene.

"At the very least, it'll be a positive distraction," Amber said firmly.

"I don't need a positive distraction." My voice bordered on frantic. "I have enough going on already!"

"Sweetie, your shirt's inside out." She pointed to my waist.

I looked down at my striped sweater and saw the visible tag and seam. Good grief—it'd been that way all day and no one at school had said a word.

"You don't have to do anything but show up; we'll take care of the rest," Max said, inching forward into the shop.

"Just try on one or two dresses, please," Jules begged.

Max pushed her sunglasses up on her head. "Cecilia always says when you look good, you feel good."

I made a face. "I think we've had enough advice from Cecilia today."

But maybe the girls were right—I could use some light-hearted fun right now. Even if I didn't buy anything, at least I wouldn't be moping alone in the townhouse. I entered the store and ran my hand along a rack of garments made from shimmery, metallic fabric.

Amber held up a glossy, black body-con number. "Something like this would bring men to their knees."

With a shake of my head, I jumped away from the rack. "I broke up with Geoff only two days ago; I don't even want to think about men right now—bringing them to their knees or otherwise." My jaw went slack as a new thought occurred to me. "Oh my God, you guys—I've been with the same man for a decade and a half. I haven't seen another dick in forever. *I'm going to have to find and learn a new dick!*"

I sank to the floor of the store, ignoring Stevie's horrified gasp, which had an equal chance of being caused by my vulgarity or sitting on the well-trod ground. Having survived five years in a first-grade classroom and lived to tell the tale, the germs here didn't stand a chance.

"Girl, that's the fun part!" Max exclaimed. "Now you get to try them on for size...kind of like these dresses. That one's too small? Upgrade to a bigger fit. That one's got some weird lumps in places we don't want? *No gracias.* That one's too big? Next... but slip me his number." She licked her lips.

"Max!" Stevie scolded.

Amber giggled. "This sounds like *Goldilocks and The Three Bears.*"

"More like *Goldilocks and the Three Cocks.*" Jules grinned. "And I'm ninety-nine percent sure that porno already exists."

Stevie made a disgusted noise and drifted away into another part of the store.

"I'm with her," I said, jerking my thumb in her direction. "I'm glad *y'all* are enjoying this. Meanwhile, I'm down here freaking out."

Amber, at least, had the decency to look sheepish. "Sorry, Zara. The whole point of this was to get you to have some fun."

"Fun? Do I look like I'm having fun right now? Nothing about this is fun," I said. "My life as I knew it was completely upended. How am I supposed to start over at my big age? I don't even know what apps to use." My eyes widened, and I looked at Jules. "Do people still use apps?"

"I mean, what's the alternative? Talking with someone out in the wild?" She shuddered.

"Enough," Max declared in a no-nonsense voice. Grabbing me by the arm, she hoisted me to my feet and pressed a hanger holding a short dress covered in rainbow beaded fringe into my hand. "Try this on."

The weight of the dress made my wrist droop. I looked at the multicolored monstrosity and tried not to let my dismay show; it wasn't my style at all. In fact, I downright hated it, but I was a team player. My friends were trying to help me in the best way they knew how. Not only that, but they'd carved out time for me two evenings in a row; the least I could do was put on a dress.

I sighed. "Fine."

Amber squealed and clapped before taking a seat in a plush armchair near the fitting rooms. Reassured I wouldn't bolt from the store, a satisfied Max squeezed onto half of the chair Stevie had claimed. Jules continued to browse through the racks.

In the fitting room, I took off my work clothes and stepped into the dress, grimacing as I pulled my shoulders through the armholes. The hundreds of thousands of beads made it ridiculously heavy, not to mention they were noisy as hell. I'd barely be able to leave the fitting room without muscle fatigue, let alone wear it out to a party. But maybe this would make them see what a silly idea this was. Stiffly, I walked out to where my friends waited, the straps of the dress digging into my shoulders, each step setting off another round of muted clattering.

The four women stared at me as the dress settled, then, as if cued by one of those live TV audience signs, all erupted in laughter in unison.

"Sorry," Stevie said, struggling to catch her breath. "It's just —you look like a cone of melted rainbow sherbet."

Amber winced and tucked a throw pillow behind her back, attempting to find a more comfortable position. "Yeah. That would fit perfectly in Max's closet."

"Rude!" Max said, a wounded look on her face.

One corner of my mouth lifted in a grin. "I'm glad we can all agree this isn't it."

"Definitely not." Jules pushed another dress at me. "Try this one. Ruby red is your color."

Obediently, I returned to the fitting room. The new dress—a sparkly, knit mini of deep red with a high neck, long sleeves, and feathered hem—was a little better than the first, but still not something I'd choose for myself. And Jesus, it itched. When I walked back out, the expressions on the girls' faces echoed my sentiments.

"It's not *bad*," Amber said.

Jules wrinkled her nose. "But it's not good."

"Maybe we're in the wrong store?" Stevie suggested gently.

"Hi ladies, sorry for the delay!" A young woman looking effortlessly chic in bottle green slacks and a cream blouse greeted us with an apologetic smile. "My name is Hilary. Can I help you find anything today?"

I opened my mouth to tell her no, but Amber cut in. "Yes, please. Our friend is newly single and she wants the perfect dress to celebrate."

Scratch a week—all of North Carolina was bound to hear about me and Geoff in forty-eight hours max.

"Oh!" Hilary blinked in confusion, her helpful salesperson mask slipping momentarily. "Congratulations?"

My cheeks burned. "Thanks."

"She needs a dress for a breakup party," Jules piped up. "Something that says, 'I am woman, hear me roar.'"

"And it should be comfortable," Amber added.

"Something bordering on slutty," Max said.

"But we don't want her to get mistaken for a sex worker." All heads turned to Stevie. "What?" she asked defensively.

"If you had it your way, she'd look like one of Martha Stewart's long-lost Black granddaughters—just like you do," Jules muttered.

Stevie scowled and pulled her oatmeal-colored duster tighter around her body. "Don't bring Martha into this."

"Guys, this is a lost cause," I said, stuffing my hand down the back of the dress to scratch my shoulder blade. Who would make a dress of this material with no lining? A sadist, that's who. "Let's just go."

Hilary shook her head, biting her lip in concentration. "Lost cause? No such thing. What I'm hearing is: fierce, comfy, and sultry…but not so suggestive that she'd arouse attention from local law enforcement."

"Damn, you're good," Max said, an impressed look on her face.

"I have my work cut out for me, but I'm always up for a challenge. Let me see what I can do."

Bless Hilary. If I were in her position, I would've said it was above my pay grade and kept it moving.

"I'm taking this off," I announced, retreating to the fitting room for a moment of peace.

My skin thanked me as I peeled off the itchy dress and put it back on its hanger. Worn out, I perched on the edge of the velvet ottoman in the corner that held my discards, wanting nothing more than to go home and collapse on the couch. Since Hilary was already off on her mission to find a dress that checked all of my friend's boxes, I'd try on just one more. That would hopefully be enough to placate everyone, and we could leave. I'd tackle convincing them there was no need for a breakup party another day.

The rap of a fist sounded outside. "It's Hilary. I brought a couple of dresses you might like."

With a weary sigh, I cracked open the door and accepted the three hangers the woman held out. "Thanks."

Closing the door, I reviewed her selections.

The first was a form-fitting, gunmetal gray dress with a long scarf attached to the neck. *I'd look like a sausage stuffed into a casing in this. Not to mention the scarf is a serious safety hazard; it'd be just my luck to get it caught somewhere.*

I didn't even bother taking it off the hanger.

The second dress was a stark contrast, its bright pink and orange color blocks reminding me of a tropical cocktail. A flowy halter neck with cut-outs on the sides, the dress revealed way too much skin for my liking. It was perfect for spring break in Miami, but not winter in Fallen Oaks.

I moved it to the ottoman, ready to try on the last outfit and be done. When I turned around and saw a ruby red, satin slip dress hanging on the back of the door, my entire mood shifted. Delicate spaghetti straps looped over the hanger, and the neckline dipped into a soft V, elegant with just a hint of danger. I yanked it down and put it on, reverently twisting back and forth in front of the mirror to admire myself from all angles.

The slippery satin rippled over my body like water, flowing with me as if it were quietly alive, before settling mid-calf, a length that felt more sophisticated than scandalous. And maybe my eyes were playing tricks on me, but now that I was actually wearing the dress, the color seemed to have deepened. Instead of the bold jewel tone from before, the fabric held the smoldering warmth of red wine in candlelight, setting my complexion aglow.

Gathering my hair on top of my head, I straightened my spine and lifted my chin. The woman staring back at me was glamorous, mysterious, and sexy; she knew exactly what she wanted out of life and how to get it. The woman in the mirror was a total bad-ass.

"What's going on in there?" Jules called. "You didn't run out the back, did you?"

"Coming!" I yelled, my eyes still locked on my reflection.

With a deep breath, I exited the fitting room into the store. All the girls—Hilary included, now resting her elbows on the back of Stevie and Max's chair—gasped.

Amber brought her hands to her chest. "Zara, it's gorgeous. *You're* gorgeous."

"Bitch, you look like you could make a lot of bad decisions in that dress," Max said. "Get it, then let me borrow it."

"I had a bad decisions dress in my twenties." Amber let out a wistful sigh and gave her pregnant belly a pat. "Those were the days."

Stevie frowned. "She does look great, but should we be encouraging her to make bad decisions? Especially when she's so"—she dropped her voice to a whisper—"fragile?"

"She's not an antique vase, Stevie," Amber said.

Click.

My head whirled in my sister's direction. "What was that sound?"

"A picture," Jules said. "Now turn to the side and gaze over your shoulder off into the distance."

"Why?" I asked suspiciously.

"I'm taking your profile photo for the apps, obviously."

I covered my face with my hands. "What? No! I literally just broke up with the man I thought I'd be spending the rest of my life with."

"We were talking about Goldilocks and cocks five seconds ago," Max reminded me.

"Where was I for *that* conversation?" Hilary asked.

"The fastest way to get over Geoff is to get under somebody else. I mean, *he* already did," Max said.

Stevie's mouth dropped open while my heart dropped to my feet. Max's words knocked me right back into the reality of the situation—the girls brought me here to pick out a dress for a *breakup party*.

My breakup party.

"Too soon, Max," Amber hissed. "Too soon."

I turned my back on them and stared at myself in the three-way mirror. There was no way the bad-ass staring back at me would let a man string her along or put up with unacceptable behavior; if she even caught a whiff of anything amiss, she wouldn't give Geoff another thought.

She was everything I wasn't, but who I longed to be.

"Zara?" Jules said softly.

"I wasted so much time," I said to my reflection. "I spent my entire twenties and nearly half of my thirties trying to make myself indispensable to a man who clearly couldn't care less. Even worse, I missed out on making the dumb mistakes you can only get away with when you're young."

The saleslady shook her head. "There are no age limits on anything. Everyone's life path is different."

We all looked at her. Blushing, she excused herself and started straightening clothing on a nearby rack.

"She's not wrong," Max said. "Look at me—I'm the same age as you and I'm having the time of my life...well, when I'm not in Fallen Oaks."

The difference was Max thrived on chaos and spontaneity, purposefully seeking new experiences. That wasn't me at all; I *needed* security, stability, and a clear path forward with a goal in sight.

"I hate to say this, but Max is right." Stevie grimaced.

Max pulled her phone from her purse and extended her arm so the device was near Stevie's mouth. "Can you say that again, but a little louder? I want to make it my ringtone."

Rolling her eyes, Stevie batted the phone away. "Zara, your life isn't over just because your relationship is."

"Nope." Amber scooted to the edge of her chair. "What are some things you wished you'd done?"

As Jules, Amber, Max, and Stevie stared at me expectantly, I swallowed. "I...I'm not sure. I just know that everyone talks about their twenties with so much fondness—how fun and free they were. That wasn't my experience at all. I feel robbed."

Geoff and I might not have had the ceremony or official documents saying so, but we'd definitely lived like an old married couple. After college, we rarely had wild nights out; the only reason he'd even been at the house party the night we met was because he needed to borrow a book from his friend. When Geoff was in town, ours was a life of routine: trips to the Farmers' Market and grocery shopping on Saturday mornings; brunch with Geoff's parents and sister every Sunday; having dinner and going to bed around the same time each night. School shenanigans aside, the messages from his side piece were the most unpredictable thing that had happened to our lives in more than a decade.

"If it makes you feel better, I wish I could forget some of the crazy shit I did back then," Max said. "Honestly, I don't even know how I'm still alive."

"We don't either," Stevie added.

Jules bounced on the balls of her feet, face brightening. "I have an idea—the *best* idea."

"I don't know; the breakup party was pretty damn good if I say so myself," Max said.

Jules ignored her. "We're going to help you make the mistakes you missed out on in your twenties."

Max stood up. "Ooh, I do like your idea better."

"Come again?" I said uneasily.

"Stay with me—I'm just thinking out loud," Jules said. "We'll each choose one of our favorite experiences from our twenties and help you make it your own...but you get to reap the benefits of maturity and lessons learned."

Amber heaved herself out of her chair. "I kind of love this. What about Ro?"

"We'll ask her too!" Jules said.

Amber grinned. "Rosario got into some *freaky* stuff back in the day."

Stevie made a face. "'Back in the day' makes it sound like we're old."

"And that's exactly why this is an awful idea," I said, before it could go any further. "We *are* old. I sneezed yesterday and pulled a muscle in my neck."

Stevie snorted. "Speak for yourself."

"Look, I'm responsible for keeping twenty six-year-olds alive every day. Amber's having a baby. Rosario is a *mom*. Stevie's an unstoppable boss lady." I gestured at each woman in turn. "Jules is...well, we'll come back to Jules. And Max—wait, where's Max?"

"Right here," she said triumphantly. She walked out of the hall of fitting rooms wearing a dress identical to the one I currently had on.

"Seriously?" Jules asked.

"Wow, Max! It looks great on you, too," Amber said. "Maybe I should try it on."

I wagged my finger at her. "Absolutely not. We are *not* all getting the same dress."

"Max, put it back," Stevie snapped.

Max scowled. "Fine." She stomped into her fitting room.

"Okay, girls, here's the game plan," Jules said, trying to corral us back to the topic at hand. "Each of us will come up with *one thing* to help Zara reconnect with her inner twenty-something and move on from Geoff with a G."

I bit my lip. "I don't know."

Jules placed her hand on my shoulder and stared into my eyes. "Big sister, you deserve this. You *need* this." She looked at Amber and Stevie. "I think we all do. And it'll be fun!"

I looked at my reflection again, wondering what my alter-ego would say. *Hell yeah! What's stopping you?*

What *was* stopping me? Now that Geoff and I were over, all the time I devoted to keeping our life running smoothly was freed up. This could be my chance to find joy again. To rediscover the essence of Zara Harmony Whitmore and explore what that looked like now. This was my time to make twenty-four-year-old Zara proud.

I turned to my sister. "Okay. I'm in on one condition."

Crossing her arms over her chest, Jules narrowed her eyes. "And that would be?"

"No one chooses anything that lands us in jail," I said.

Max burst out of the fitting room with the dress back on its hanger and flashed us a devilish grin. "I make no promises."

seven

JULES

Get ready, bish. We'll be there in 5.

I set my phone down on the bathroom counter and finished blending coppery bronze eyeshadow across my lids, adding a soft gold highlight to the inner corners. The flashy makeup pushed me out of my comfort zone, but that was the whole point, wasn't it?

When the girls had floated the idea of throwing a breakup party, I didn't realize they meant two days later. True to their word, they'd kept me in the dark and planned everything themselves, only making three requests.

One: I keep my Saturday evening free (Jules's ask).

Two: I wear the Bad Decisions Dress (as Amber had taken to calling it).

Three: I look "fierce as fuck" (Rosario's directive).

The joke was on them—since I'd kicked Geoff out, all my evenings were free. I filled my time with mindless reality TV, and even tried to organize more of Geoff's stuff so it was ready for him to take, but every time I opened his office door, I felt the hurt all over again.

I glanced over at the second sink in the bathroom, where Geoff's face wash, shaving cream, and toothbrush patiently waited for his return, my buoyant mood deflating.

Aht, aht. We're not doing that anymore, my bad-ass alter-ego whispered. *This is your brand new chapter, and you are a brand new bitch, Zara Whitmore.*

Zara 2.0, as I'd named her, was right. I was determined to have fun tonight, even if it killed me…though I hoped it didn't get that far. But with Max and Rosario in control, all bets were off.

I was putting the finishing touches on my makeup when another text came through, no doubt Jules, telling me they'd arrived. I'd told her I could meet them wherever, but she insisted they pick me up—probably to make sure I couldn't bail if I thought things were going south. It was a tactic we'd used with Stevie the first—and only—time we all ever went camping.

The more I tugged and smoothed the dress, the more it seemed to answer—lifting here, hugging there, sliding and shifting until my waist was snatched and cleavage I didn't even know I had made an appearance. More than satisfied, I flicked off the light, grabbed a pair of strappy gold heels, and ran downstairs. When I hit the bottom, I heard a series of honks outside.

"Good grief," I muttered.

Why did we always spend twenty minutes or more waiting for Max, but the one time I took two minutes to walk down the stairs, it was the end of the world?

I pulled on my heels and buckled them quickly, then grabbed my coat and purse from the back of the couch. Opening the front door, I pulled up short. "What the hell?"

A small, hot pink bus with tinted windows idled at the end of my driveway. The door swung outward and Jules hopped off in a flowy boho maxi dress. It was only when she threw her arms wide that I noticed the beauty pageant sash and tiara in her hands. "Welcome to your breakup party!"

"Um…thanks." I pointed to the rose gold satin and plastic tiara. "Please don't say those are for me."

"Oh, but they are!" Beaming, Jules slid the sash over my head, then used the combs at the bottom of the tiara to secure it in my hair. "There! You're the star of the show tonight."

I looked down at the sash now draped across my front. *Boy Bye.* Beside the two words, a sparkling, glittery hand flipped the bird. There was no way I'd be inconspicuous now.

That's right, Zara 2.0 said. *Bask in it, bitch. It's* our *show.*

"Come on," Jules said.

She shooed me up the bus's three short steps, where a bored-looking man behind the wheel greeted me with a curt nod. When I came into view of the Sensational Six—everyone present and accounted for—a chorus of screams, cheers, and catcalls broke out. Involuntarily, a grin stretched across my face. The girls were extra, but their actions were driven by love—and at the moment, all of that love was focused on me.

"Now we can really get this party started!" Max shouted, raising a Solo cup in the air from her seat behind a shiny silver pole. Her sleek, off-the-shoulder black dress covered in red roses was par for the course, but the headband with two red horns perched in her pixie cut set off alarm bells in my head.

To distract myself from whatever nefarious activities she had planned for the night, I glanced around the interior of the bus. Pink-and-black leather seats formed a horseshoe around the chrome stripper pole. Bright, color-changing LEDs lined the ceiling, making me feel like I was at a rave and large, mounted flatscreens cycled through videos of…giraffes and zebras on the savannah? The hell?

As for the girls, they already seemed to have gotten the party started. Stevie sat in the corner, wearing a high-necked black dress with ruffles on the shoulders, legs crossed demurely at the ankle. On her right, you couldn't miss Amber's baby bump in her form-fitting cobalt blue halter dress.

Rosario brought a plastic shot glass to her lips, knocked it back, and jumped up, surprisingly agile while wearing four-inch stiletto ankle booties in a moving vehicle. With her hair falling in perfect waves, blood-red lips, and one-shoulder snakeskin minidress, she looked light years away from the bedraggled mom at the wine bar.

Her gaze swept over me. "That dress is killer. You have to let me borrow it sometime."

"Of course." I slid between Jules and the seat Rosario had just vacated. Jules handed me a Solo cup filled with a sweet-smelling red liquid that nearly singed my nose hairs and conjured up memories of drinking booze from trash cans during college.

"After me—I'm first! I wanted to get one too, but they wouldn't let me." Max pouted.

Rosario placed one hand high on the pole and began a slow, sultry walk around it. "But I'm the one who rented the bus."

"But the party was *my* idea," Max shot back.

"Ladies, my dress is your dress," I said, one eye on Rosario's ankles as the party bus rolled down the streets of Fallen Oaks. "Everyone chipped in for it—it's the least I can do."

I truly didn't mind sharing—especially if it kept the peace. We didn't need a repeat of the Corn Dog Incident of 2008, which caused Rosario and Max to stop speaking for three months and forced the rest of us to take sides. I shuddered at the memory.

"But back to this rented bus situation—you seriously did all this just to go out dancing?" I asked.

"Better than cramming into an Uber," Amber said.

I held my breath as Rosario hooked one leg around the pole and used her momentum to spin. "Until someone gets injured."

Rosario bent over and locked eyes with me, her head

between her legs. "I'll have you know, Zara Harmony Whitmore, I am *incredibly* limber. How do you think I ended up with Mikey and Mateo?"

"No one wants to hear that," Jules said, at the same time Amber and I exclaimed, "Ew!"

Stevie just frowned.

Max rolled her eyes and let out a bored sigh. "Put your cooch away, Ro."

"It's not like you all haven't seen it before." Rosario reached for the top of the pole again, but the bus hit a speed bump at a fast clip. I watched in horrified slow motion as Rosario flew from the pole and landed in a heap at Amber's feet with a loud *thunk*. She let out a pained groan and placed a hand on her tailbone. Jules and I darted forward to help, but she waved us off.

"I knew this was a bad idea!" Stevie exclaimed, a hint of smug righteousness in her voice.

"Not now, Stevie," Amber snapped. She turned concerned eyes on Rosario. "Ro, are you okay?"

"I'm fine," she squeaked. She crawled on her hands and knees across the bus before climbing up into the seat beside me. "Nothing's broken...just my pride." She rubbed her left shin where the purple stain of a bruise was rapidly blooming.

"Seems like a fine time for a shot," Max declared, passing out small, neon-colored cups. "Ro and Amber, yours are apple cider."

"Why do I have cider?" Rosario whined.

"Because I refuse to track down a shopping cart, stuff you in it, and wheel your ass around again." Max leveled a stern stare at her. "You are *not* ruining Zara's night."

Ro mulled it over, then shrugged. "Fair enough."

Max raised her plastic shot glass high in the air. "To the Sensational Six!"

We all raised our glasses. "To the Sensational Six!"

* * *

Twenty minutes later, the party bus came to a stop, thankfully without further incident. I let the girls chatter about their day and trade teasing barbs, content just to be among friends. The tinted windows made it hard to see where we'd ended up, so when we piled off the bus and I found myself standing outside Dusty Spurs Saloon—a country-western bar nowhere near the nightclubs of downtown—I glanced around in confusion. Women crowded the sidewalk in groups, and there were two lines of them waiting to get inside. This was becoming more curious by the minute.

And then I looked up at the marquee.

Alphas Unleashed All-Male Revue SOLD OUT.

My jaw dropped open. "What exactly is happening right now?" I asked, unable to drag my eyes from the sign.

"You were worried about learning a new dick, so we thought we'd help you out," Max said proudly.

My mouth snapped shut as I glanced at Jules. Blinking innocently, she shrugged.

Despite all of Jules, Rosario, and Max's attempts to drag me out, I'd never visited any kind of strip club—and it wasn't just because Geoff was opposed to the idea. I'd barely been able to sit through a showing of *Magic Mike* in the theater because of overwhelming secondhand embarrassment. I covered my face and watched most of the movie through the gaps between my fingers.

Fully recovered after her tumble and remarkably coherent for the amount of drinks she'd consumed, Rosario reached into the quilted leather bag over her shoulder and pulled out several neat, banded stacks of cash and waved them in the air. "One final contribution to tonight's festivities."

"Whoa! I'm not complaining, Ro, but did you rob a bank?" Jules asked.

Rosario fanned herself with one stack. "Just the Bank of Edgar."

Stevie frowned. "Does your husband know you're spending his hard-earned money on exotic dancers?"

"Yup," Rosario said. "Besides, he'll do a BBL and make it back like that." She snapped her fingers. "Spend it wisely...or don't."

She gave each of us a stack of money like she was merely handing out samples to passersby at Costco. Using the pad of my thumb, I flipped through the bills, estimating I was holding at least a hundred dollars. I wondered what they'd do if I made a run for it and parked myself at Cook Out for the next few hours. One hundred dollars would buy a lot of milkshakes and chili-cheese fries.

"And here are your tickets." My phone vibrated in my purse as Max sent them electronically.

"Ooh, *VIP*," Amber read.

"Nothing but the best for our Za-za." Max pinched my cheek.

"Time is ticking, bitches," Rosario said. "I'm child-free for the next five hours, and I intend to make the most of every one of them." She sauntered toward the shorter of the two entry lines marked with a laminated VIP sign.

Laughing, Amber and Max followed close on her heels. I stared at the marquee once more, then at the stack of ones in my hand.

"I know what you're thinking," Stevie whispered. "And I already looked it up—the closest Cook Out is ten minutes away by car. Just say the word and we're gone."

I smiled. On the outside, Stevie could be as abrasive as sandpaper, but after she kept me hydrated and comfortable during a nasty bout of the flu during our freshman year at UNC, I'd cemented her in my mind as a well-guarded softie.

"How'd they even get you to agree to this?" I asked.

She rolled her eyes. "Y'all act like I'm the world's biggest party pooper."

"Well, you *do* act like one sometimes," Jules said. "A lot of times, actually."

"One of us has to make sure we stay out of trouble—and to remind Rosario she can't risk it all; she has a whole husband at home. A good one." Stevie shook her stack of ones at us for emphasis. "Besides, I still have needs. If you're up for it, I'm ready to make it rain. You two in?"

"Zara?" Jules raised her eyebrow in question.

My sex-positive little sister loved this kind of thing. Not only did she see every *Magic Mike* movie opening weekend in the theater, but she held a viewing party of *Chocolate City*, complete with gray-sweatpants-and-dick-print cookies. It wouldn't surprise me if, sometime in the future, she ended up hosting at-home parties where she sold sex toys.

I looked at our resident fuddy-duddy, less uptight than usual, her dark eyes shining. If Stephanie Renee Newkirk was up for this, so was I.

"Let's do it."

I linked arms with her and Jules and walked to where Rosario was frantically waving us over at the front of the VIP line. After exchanging our tickets for neon green wristbands, we made our way inside.

Dusty Spurs Saloon was an interesting choice for a strip show, but what did I know? On weathered wooden walls, cowboy hats and cracked leather saddles hung alongside framed sepia photos of cowboys on horseback and the American South-west. A scuffed hardwood floor took up most of the room, dotted with circular tables draped in black cloth. In the corner to our right, denim-and-plaid-clad bartenders mixed cocktails in mason jars and poured beer from a tap in front of a well-stocked bar. Back in the far-left corner sat a dejected-looking mechanical bull with an OUT OF ORDER sign around its neck.

But the pièce de résistance had to be the giant chandelier made of antlers. I wasn't sure exactly what animal they'd come from, but they were huge and there were a lot of them. Even more numerous were the bras hanging from it in all sizes and shades of the rainbow. I looked down at my boobs, sitting high and perky thanks to God's favor and the magic of the Bad Decisions Dress. How many women had walked through these doors wearing a bra, but exited with their titties flopping around like one of those inflatable men at a car dealership? And why? Who put the bras up there?

The abandoned bras quickly became the least of my problems as Ro stomped past table after table and my nerves grew. To my horror, she didn't stop until we arrived at a table right in front of the stage with a RESERVED placard sitting right in the middle.

"Welcome, all you ladies and nasty women," a deep bass voice that would make Barry White proud boomed through the speakers. "Take your seats and hold on to your hats 'cause we're getting this show on the road in just a few minutes."

Swallowing my apprehension, I pulled out the furthest chair from the stage. It wouldn't make much difference, but every inch counted.

"No ma'am." Rosario narrowed her eyes at me and pointed one coffin-shaped black nail at a chair on the other side of the table...and *maybe* three feet from the stage. "You're the guest of honor."

Reluctantly, I slid into the seat just as a tall, *jacked*, dark-skinned man holding a microphone swaggered onstage to catcalls and excited shrieks. Seriously? He still had all his clothes on and everyone was already going crazy.

"How y'all ladies doing tonight?" he asked. More screams ensued, and the guy chuckled. "Sounds like we've got a lively bunch...just like I like it."

"I love you," screamed a woman at the table next to us.

"Have some respect for yourself," Stevie muttered, seated in the chair I'd tried to claim.

Amber gave her a warning look. "Behave."

"Shhh! I'm trying to focus," Jules hissed, eyes glued to the stage.

"Thanks, sugar. I love you, too, but you should probably know my name first. I'm Hershey, as in Hershey's Kiss 'cause I'll melt right in your hand." He blew a kiss in the direction of the woman who'd called out. "I'll be your emcee for the evening."

Max snorted in her chair on my right. "Hershey?"

On her other side, Rosario looked over her shoulder with a worried expression. "Something about that feels a little racist. Am I allowed to call him that?"

"I swear to God I will change tables," Jules growled on my left.

"She takes her male stripping very seriously," I whispered with a straight face.

"Let's go over a few rules before we start."

"*Booooo!*" someone shouted from the back of the bar.

Hershey shielded his eyes from the spotlight and squinted, a mock stern glare on his face. "And *she's* the reason we have the rules."

The audience giggled.

Hershey adopted a serious tone. "This is a sexy, fun, and *very* adult show; we want you to be part of it, but we also want everyone—performers and the audience—to feel safe. Our entertainers reserve the right to kick anyone out because of disorderly conduct. You hear that back there, miss?"

Once he got a sound of agreement, he continued his spiel, telling us how the performers might interact with us—well, with everyone else because I was going to redirect anyone who might come near me with a polite "No thanks"—and which parts of their body we were allowed to touch. Practically every-thing but eggplant—his words, not mine—was up for grabs.

"Now that we've got that out of the way, we can get to the fun." He shielded his eyes again and looked out over the audience. "I see we've got some bachelorette parties…a couple of divorcées…"

I shrunk down in my seat as the emcee's gaze landed on me with curiosity. The corner of his mouth quirked up as he read the stupid sash across my chest. *Damn you, Jules!*

"We're all gonna have a good time tonight," Hershey contin-ued, planting his feet in the center of the stage and cupping a hand around one ear. "What do you think, ladies? Is it time to bring out my boys?"

The noise level in the room reached deafening levels. Winc-ing, I surveyed the table to gauge the other girls' responses. Jules was clapping enthusiastically like one of those circus monkey toys with the cymbals while Max cupped her hands around her mouth and hooted. Rosario was on her feet, waving her hands in the air like she just didn't care.

"Men of Alphas Unleashed, come on out!"

Without warning, the spotlight cut off and the room plunged into total darkness. As a low, pulsating beat started up, white lights at the back of the stage blinked on in time to the music. I held my breath as a long row of men in camouflage cargo pants, ribbed black tank tops, and gold masks covering their faces came into view. They stood with their heads bowed, hands clasped down in front of them. Fog crept along the floor from the wings and obscured their feet.

"Oh *my*," Jules breathed, leaning back and gripping her chair with both hands.

I had to agree—it was an impressive sight.

In perfect unison, the men executed a complex choreo-graphed routine with formation changes and floor work.

"When are the clothes coming off?" Max complained.

In answer to Max's plea, each man grabbed the sides of his tank top and tore it off, revealing oiled-up torsos that gleamed beneath the lights.

"You have to wonder what their wardrobe budget is," Stevie said. "That can't be sustainable in this economy."

In unison, they all bent over, ripped the pants from their legs, and tossed them to the side.

"The breakaway pants have velcro. See? They're doing their part for the environment," Amber said.

Stevie harrumphed.

Hungrily, my eyes devoured the taut, glistening bodies and skimpy, well-endowed, bright red speedos. I felt guilty objectifying them, but I couldn't help but appreciate what the Lord had made.

Without warning, the barely dressed men jumped off the stage and danced through the audience, stopping and grinding on random women. I kept my gaze on the floor so I didn't make eye contact and prayed they'd bypass us. It was one thing to ogle them while they performed a choreographed routine onstage, but completely different when they planted a combat boot on the table and humped your face.

When the song came to a close, the men returned to the stage, and the lights went out. I barely had time to relax before the show continued with a solo number by an entertainer dressed as a sexy pirate who had a penchant for body rolls. After the pirate, a man clad only in a black bowtie, white cuffs, top hat, and speedo printed to look like a tuxedo performed several silly magic tricks. There were a couple more duo and trio acts, and by the time Hershey, the emcee, announced a "Best Abs Contest," I was actually enjoying myself.

Once all the dancers lined themselves up, Hershey explained how the contest would work. The men would show their goods, and one at a time, he'd hold his hand over their head. We'd clap as loud as we could for our favorite.

The pirate was the first in line. He flung the tails of his burgundy waistcoat jacket with a flourish, revealing a bare chest and abs on which I could wash a load of laundry. "Shiver me timbers," he said into Hershey's microphone.

"Take my money!" Stevie screamed. She used a folded napkin to dab the perspiration beading at her hairline.

The other girls and I exchanged amused looks. None of us had witnessed her behave so brazenly before.

"Guess we found out Stevie has a pirate kink," Amber joked.

"No wonder you made me watch *Pirates of the Caribbean* so many times," Max said.

I didn't blame her—the pirate obviously took good care of himself—but I was more drawn to the third man in line, a cowboy. I wasn't into country music or the aesthetic, but there was something about him that intrigued me. Even though he was only one of two men on the stage whose face was obscured, he exuded confidence and charm.

In addition to the leather half-mask with a long fringe hiding his mouth and falling to his collarbone, Cowboy wore the requisite hat and boots, a vest of black leather that exposed a smooth stomach, and matching chaps. When Hershey told us to make noise, Cowboy flipped around, where the back of his leather pants featured two strategically placed cutouts. The two round, brown globes of ass jiggled as he held his arms above his head and gave it a shake, sending the crowd into a wild tizzy—me, included.

Max nudged my shoulder with hers. "Do we have a cowgirl on our hands?"

I stuck my tongue out at her. "You know what they say—save a horse, ride a cowboy."

"Ayy! That's what we like to hear," she said.

The emcee continued down the line, but my attention stayed on the cowboy. Though I couldn't make out his expression because of the mask, he seemed to enjoy himself, clapping and dancing with the other men onstage. Once Hershey had gone through everyone, it was clear Cowboy had won by a landslide. When Hershey grabbed his right hand and thrust it high in the air, proclaiming him the winner, I foolishly felt a smidge of pride, as if I'd had something to do with it.

"And now your winner is going to grace us with a performance. Take it away, Colton!"

The lights came up as the intro to a hip-hop/country hybrid began to play. Cowboy stood in the middle of the stage by himself, one hand on the brim of his hat, the other limply holding a whip down by his side. With unexpected swag, he strolled around the stage and moved through a series of precise steps as the song built to the chorus. I'd assumed the whip was just a prop, but without warning, he gripped the handle and snapped it forward, sending a sharp crack reverberating throughout the room.

"Good God. If I'd worn underwear, I'd have to change it now," Jules said, wide-eyed.

Being that I *was* in fact wearing panties and they were damp, I completely understood where she was coming from. My entire body flushing with warmth, I licked my lips. A tiny voice in my brain whispered I should be ashamed, but screw that, it was just human nature.

When Cowboy carefully descended from the stage and started toward our table, I held my breath. Instead of trying to make myself invisible like I had earlier, I arched my back and lifted my chin. But like many a man and woman, he only had eyes for Max. I watched, feeling some type of way as he straddled her lap and she ran her hands over his stomach before slipping a few bills beneath his giant belt buckle.

You're being silly. The man is a stripper. You'll forget all about this and him by the time you walk out of here.

As if he could sense my thoughts, Cowboy looked over at me and his green eyes—all I could make of his face—widened. He faltered for a moment before finding his groove again and returning his attention to Max.

Weird.

He dismounted her moments later and danced on a few more women, vaulting back onto the stage just as the song ended. Before I had time to miss him, a man with a topknot and face paint marched onto the stage, a flaming baton spinning in one hand. I remained on the edge of my seat throughout his number, partly because I was in awe of his skills, and partly because I worried the baton would fly out of his grip, sail through the air, and catch the bra chandelier on fire.

"Are you having fun?" Jules asked, her face aglow. While Max and Ro had been ready to throw themselves at the performers every five seconds, Jules had sat gripping her chair, eyes riveted to the action.

I held up the few dollars I had left, one corner of my mouth lifting in a half-smile. "What do you think? I'm almost out of money."

Max leaned over. "Don't worry, we gotchu."

"What does that mean?" I asked.

Onstage, Hershey announced it was time for the Grand Finale, and the dancers lined up folding chairs in a row with ample space between them. Before he could even finish speaking, women pushed and shoved as they raced for the stairs at the side of the stage.

Max stood and pulled me up with her. "It means I saw how jealous you got when the cowboy danced on me earlier. It's your turn."

"Oh no—that's really not necessary," I squeaked, as Max dragged me behind her toward the horde of women waving orange tickets, waiting to be seated onstage and manhandled by the entertainers. Helplessly, I glanced back at the table, where only Stevie and Amber remained. Rosario and Jules had eagerly followed us and gotten in line. "I don't even have a ticket."

Max pressed a piece of orange cardstock into my palm. "Now you do."

Biting my lip, I looked down at the ticket. There were a hundred reasons why I should've given it right back and reclaimed my seat. I didn't do things like this. A student's parent might be in the audience and recognize me. I might find I actually liked it and turn into some kind of sex addict who couldn't get enough.

My eyes traveled to where the entertainers were grinding on the first group; every single woman's face displayed some degree of delight. I felt the slippery satin from the Bad Decisions Dress beneath my fingertips. What would twenty-four-year-old, Geoff-with-a-G-free Zara do?

She'd strut across the stage, sit down, and let the man in front of her make her feel damn good—and she wouldn't think twice.

The line moved pretty fast; the guys were only grinding on the women for about a minute and a half, then Hershey would thank the ladies and send them on their way while a new group took their seats. All too soon, my friends and I made it toward the front of the line. Max counted the chairs onstage and the number of women waiting ahead of us.

"Perfect! You'll end up with the cowboy." She waggled her eyebrows.

"It's not that serious—"

"Ladies, take your seat quickly. As soon as Hershey says, 'Thanks,' exit on the other side of the stage," an overly made-up woman in a leather miniskirt and cropped *Alphas Unleashed* t-shirt instructed us. She stopped the line after Rosario, leaving Jules to wait in the group after ours.

Instead of a confident strut, I shuffled across the stage through the confetti scattered on the floor from the last group number, my anxiety at an all-time high. At least I couldn't see the audience because of the bright-ass lights shining at me. God, I hoped I didn't look as petrified as I felt.

"Have fun, kid!" Max called.

I opened my mouth to reply, but before I even realized what was happening, I was sitting in a black folding chair with Cowboy straddling my lap, no longer wearing his vest. I could barely breathe as I stared into the playful green eyes above the red fringe. Despite my unease, something about the man currently rubbing his sweaty body against me felt familiar.

"What's your name, darlin'?" he asked in an exaggerated Southern drawl.

"Z-Z-Zoey." It was the name I'd used when I went clubbing in college and didn't want to share my real information.

"Nice to meet you, Zoey. So what's the deal?" He nodded at my sash before leaping up, spinning around, and bending over. He planted his hands on the ground, giving me a clear view of his ass-less chaps, and shimmied.

"Um, my ex ch-cheated on me, so I broke up with him," I stammered loudly, unable to take my eyes off the smooth, jiggling tush in front of me. Would it be weird to ask if he shaved it or used one of those booty masks? "We were together for fourteen years."

"That's a long time. What an idiot." Cowboy stopped his wiggling for a second. "Him, not you."

"Right? I didn't think you meant me, by the way."

He stood up, then reclined in my lap, his back against my front. "Some guys just don't know what they have in front of them." He grasped my wrists and guided my hands down his sweat-slicked torso. Sure, I could do without the bodily fluids, but this was nice.

"Thank you!" *See? Cowboy gets it.*

"Hold on tight," he said.

"What?"

I screeched as the cowboy hooked his arms under my knees

and hoisted me into the air, frantically smoothing my dress down so I wouldn't flash him or anyone else. I ended up on his shoulders with his head between my legs. Face inches away from my vagina, the masked man stared up at me, only the fringe and a couple layers of fabric separating us.

"You okay up there?"

Well, I wasn't dead, and he hadn't flipped me upside down or tried to motorboat me like some of the other guys. "I think so?"

"Thanks, ladies. Exit on this side," Hershey's voice said over the blood pounding through my ears.

With exquisite gentleness, Cowboy lowered me to the floor, quickly extricated his head from my nether region, and took a step back, wiping his palms together.

"Good luck, Zoey," he said with a wink. Only when his left hand flicked my sash did I notice the tattoo beneath his elbow crease.

A tattoo I had seen before.

A tattoo of a large treble clef evaporating into a flock of birds.

eight

C aleb McMahon—Caleb, the new music teacher from school—*is the cowboy I've been drooling over all night.*

In a daze, I glanced over my shoulder as I made my way off the stage. Caleb's sole focus was on the woman who'd been quick to take my chair when I got up. I faced forward and accepted the arm of a security guard waiting to help me down the steps.

Was it possible that it *wasn't* Caleb? That someone else could have the same tattoo as him…in the exact same place? No, not when paired with those unique green eyes. How hadn't I realized it sooner?

When I reached our table, Rosario grabbed my upper arms and shook me. "How was it? Every time I looked over, you and the cowboy were having one hell of a discussion."

Max frowned. "I paid for a lap dance—not a talk therapy session."

"I mean, it sure looked like she was getting some sexual healing up there," Amber said. "Did you see when he had her on his shoulders?"

"Did you at least get a vagina tingle?" Max cut in.

"Max, you can't just ask someone if they got a vagina tingle," Stevie said.

Caleb from school is a stripper.

Oh my God.

He sat on my lap. I felt him up. I had a conversation with his ass.

I. Had. A. Conversation. With. His. Ass.

How would I ever be able to look him in the eyes again? I was supposed to meet with him after school on Monday to talk about the concert. This had to be some kind of HR violation.

"Uh-oh, I think Zara's glitching," Ro said.

Max sighed. "Fuck. We broke her."

"No, I'm good," I squeaked.

"I know someone whose vagina is definitely tingling." Amber pointed to the stage. "Jules is living her best life right now."

The rest of us followed the aim of her finger. Sure enough, Jules sat in a chair in the center of the stage, captivated by the magician, her hands full of polyester-clad ass. Involuntarily, my gaze went back to Cowboy—Caleb. His hat perched on the head of a woman who clung to him like a koala, her ankles locked around his lower back as he bounced her up and down.

"That's what Stevie needs," Max said. "Get up there, girl!"

She shook her head. "I'm good. My eyes feasted on a beefcake buffet tonight."

"'Beefcake buffet?' What are you—sixty?" Max laughed and turned to Amber. "What about you? Baby's first lap dance?"

"I don't think so," Amber said. "Acrobatics aside, it just feels disrespectful to Dwayne."

Rosario rolled her eyes. "It's all in how you spin it. Edgar loves it because I always come home horny."

"When are you *not* horny?" Stevie asked.

"Huh...that's an excellent point," Ro said, her face thoughtful.

"Zara, seriously, you look traumatized." Amber's brows furrowed in concern. "Are you okay?"

Okay, it made sense that I wouldn't have known it was Caleb until I'd seen the tattoo—he was wearing a mask that covered most of his face, and I'd had my fair share of drinks. But he'd been able to see who *I* was. Fuck, I needed to process this, but it wasn't the time or place. The flashing lights, shrieking women, and booming music were completely overwhelming my senses.

Fanning myself, I grabbed the bottle of water Stevie held out and took a long swallow before nodding. "Yeah, I'm fine...just a little tired. Can we go?"

"Works for me." Stevie looked around the table, eyebrows raised.

Ro hid a yawn behind her hand. "The show's pretty much over, anyway."

Finished with her dance, Jules joined us at the table. "Jesus Horatio Christ, that was amazing! Zara—it seemed like you really hit it off with Mr. Yeehaw." She did a little gallop and spun an imaginary lasso above her head. "What were you two doing over there? Exchanging IG handles?"

The water I'd just sipped shot out of my mouth.

Jules made a disgusted face. "A simple 'no' would have sufficed."

"The party girl is ready to head out." Max grabbed her clutch from the center of the table.

"Boo. Blake told me the guys are going to an afterparty downtown," Jules said.

"Who the hell is Blake? And *you* are more than welcome to go, but my bed awaits." I shouldered my purse, hating the fact that my eyes once again sought out Caleb onstage. He faced the woman in his chair, his ass on display for the audience again. Those cheeks would forever be burned into my memory.

"Nah. I came with you, I leave with you." Jules smiled and

slid an arm around my shoulders. "There'll be other parties with sexy, sweaty strippers."

Rosario made the sign of the cross. "From your lips to God's ears."

We filed out of Dusty Spurs and waited only a couple minutes for the pink party bus that brought us. As we collapsed on the seats, I reflected on the night. Except for learning my new colleague might have been an extra in *Magic Mike*, I'd actually enjoyed myself.

"Thanks for a fun night," I said with a smile. "I was skeptical at first, but I think it was the perfect start to my new chapter."

"Yay!" Stevie said.

Max grinned. "That's what we like to hear."

"This seems like a fine time to circle back to the idea I had at the boutique." Jules looked around at all of us. "How are we going to help Zara embrace her inner twenty-something?" When Max opened her mouth, Jules quickly added, "Max, the breakup party was yours."

She scowled. "I know what you're doing, and I don't like it."

Jules shrugged. "Amber?"

Amber stuck her tongue between her teeth and squinted like she did when she was thinking hard. "I'm going with speed-dating."

"*Speed-dating?*" Max scrunched up her face. "When the hell did you go speed-dating?"

"Dwayne and I took a short break when I was twenty-six—and when I say short, I mean, like, two weeks. A friend dragged me to a speed-dating event. I went on dates with a bunch of guys, and in that hour, I realized just how good I had it."

I raised my eyebrows. "So, you want *me* to go speed-dating because...?"

"Because you never know. You might meet someone special," Amber said. "The odds are pretty good with so many single men in one room."

Meet someone special? Ha! If speed-dating went anything like tonight, I might wind up on a mini-date with Coach Aaron.

"Speed-dating, it is!" Jules said. "Stevie?"

Stevie pursed her lips. "You know how I feel about this."

Jules leaned over and poked her in the ribs. "I thought you were being fun tonight."

"I *am* fun," Stevie protested.

"Sure you are," Amber said sweetly.

Stevie crossed her arms over her chest. "Fine. I think Zara should go on solo dates. She doesn't need a man for romance; she can romance herself. Romanticize her life, if you will."

Romanticize my life? That didn't sound like such a bad idea.

"I've gone on so many dates with mediocre men that it made me realize I can love myself better than anyone else can," Stevie continued. "So, I built up my self-worth and took myself out on dates. For example, I once bought myself roses and a small charcuterie board and had a solo picnic in the park. Another time, I had dinner and went to one of those candlelight concerts."

"But that's not a mistake," Max pointed out.

Stevie shrugged. "It's what I've got. Take it or leave it."

Jules held up her hands for peace. "It's fine; my choice counteracts Stevie's anyway. I think Zara should have a one-night stand."

Max slapped the seat. "That's more like it!"

I glared at them both. "Jules, come *on*."

"We're promoting STDs now?" Stevie asked.

Jules clapped her hands twice. "Silence, Big Sister. Your only condition was that we didn't end up in jail."

Amber nodded. "You did say that."

"It's on the list. I will be taking no comments or questions at this time." Jules cleared her throat and narrowed her eyes at me. "Now, what's one thing you've always wanted to do?"

I'd been mulling the question over ever since Jules first came up with the idea two days earlier.

"I want to get a tattoo."

I'd always admired the way Max expressed herself through the artwork on her body. I loved the idea of believing in something so much that you committed yourself to it permanently. My mind strayed to Caleb's treble clef tattoo. I wondered if it signified anything in particular.

"Love it." Max trailed the fingers of her left hand over the delicate tattoos decorating the fingers and back of her right one.

Jules gave a firm nod. "I approve." She frowned at Stevie, who'd pulled her phone from her purse and was frantically typing on the screen. "Who are *you* texting?"

"I'm not texting." Stevie paused and looked up. "I'm compiling a list of what's been said. *Speed-date. Go on Solo Dates. Catch an STD. Get a Tattoo.*"

Max rolled her eyes at her best friend, then turned to me. "Zara, are you ready to make your first mistake?"

I chewed on my lip. Tonight had been fun and twenty-four-year-old Zara would certainly approve, but could thirty-four-year-old Zara keep up?

"We don't have to do everything all in one weekend," Amber said quickly. "We need time to bounce back; we're not as young as we used to be."

"Seriously. Just look at Ro," Jules added.

Our attention shifted to Rosario, who was slumped over on the seat, mouth open as she snored softly.

"Maybe it doesn't have to be in one weekend, but it's gotta be soon," Max said. "When I'm sure Aunt Cecilia will be fine without me, I am *outta* here. I believe the saying goes, 'I'm here for a good time—not a long time.'"

Jules twisted her lips in a smirk. "We'll keep that in mind."

The party bus slowed at the end of my driveway, exactly where the night began. I stood and stretched. "Ladies, this is my stop."

Each of the girls—even Rosario, who Amber had managed to

rouse from her slumber—gave me a hug. After thanking the bus driver, I hopped down and started up the driveway.

"Hey!" Jules shouted.

I sighed, knowing my neighbors were no doubt less than thrilled with our late-night shenanigans. I could already imagine the passive-aggressive post Mr. Cornelius from across the street would leave on the neighborhood message board. When I turned around, the girls were all crowded in the doorway of the bus, waving and blowing kisses.

"We love you!" Amber yelled.

Happiness bubbled up in my chest at seeing them all excited to let loose and have fun. For a few mischief-filled hours, we weren't thirty-something-year-old moms or girl bosses or tasked with not fucking up the children who would one day run the world—we were carefree women doing whatever the fuck we wanted and enjoying life to the fullest.

Jules was right. We needed this.

"I love you all, too," I shouted, not giving a damn about the neighbors. "Let's make some mistakes!"

nine

R*ing. Ring.*

The Monday after the breakup party, I met Susie's eye across the classroom and frowned. Our students were at art, so we'd been sitting in blissful silence, appreciating the moment of peace—at least, until my desk phone rang.

Susie froze, a piece of dark chocolate halfway to her lips. "Well, what are you waiting for?"

"I never get calls." I stared down at the ringing phone like it was an alien lifeform.

"All the more reason to answer it." She popped the chocolate into her mouth and returned to grading phonics worksheets.

I picked up the handset. "Hello?"

"Hi Zara, it's Kimiko. You just received a delivery," a chipper voice said on the other end of the line.

A delivery? I'd never gotten a delivery at school before. Susie, on the other hand, had all of her packages delivered to the school because of the porch bandits in her neighborhood.

"Um, okay. Be right there." I hung up and looked over at my lead teacher, whose eyebrows raised in expectation.

"Kimiko says there's a delivery for me."

"Then you should go get it."

As I walked down the hallway, my thoughts returned to the day before. I'd slept in until Jules arrived with her locksmith friend to change the locks, then spent the rest of it relaxing... until I got an email from Geoff that annoyed the hell out of me. Since I'd blocked him on pretty much everything else, it was the only way he could contact me. He'd felt "compelled" to write to me after hearing from a friend that his wife "saw me at a strip club," and attached a blurry photo she'd snapped of me with my hands on Caleb's bare stomach. Instead of responding, I marked the message spam, smug at the idea of Geoff being irritated enough to resort to sending an email.

Unfortunately, the smugness was only a temporary reprieve from stressing about what would happen when I finally came face to face again with Caleb later on today. The kids didn't have music class, but on Friday afternoon, he'd caught up with me in the parking lot and asked if we could meet to discuss the music program. Still unable to come up with a single legitimate reason to get out of helping, I reluctantly agreed.

But that was prior to his face becoming well-acquainted with my crotch.

I considered asking the group chat for advice, but I didn't want to sound the alarm until I confirmed it was Caleb McMahon behind the mask that night. Lots of people had musical tattoos and light green eyes. I might have even imagined them, or the lights in the bar were playing tricks with my vision. One thing was for sure—I'd find out either way in about four hours.

When I walked into the front office, Kimiko Nakamura, the Lower School administrative assistant, greeted me with a sunny smile. "You've got flowers!"

She gestured to a bouquet sitting on the corner of her desk

like a model showing off a game show prize. Pretty pink lilies were nestled among white roses, sprays of berries, and green foliage in a simple, square vase with a mint bow affixed to the front.

"From who?" I asked, my forehead wrinkling. They were beautiful, but who could've sent them? My friends?

Kimiko giggled. "Geoff, I'm assuming."

Oh, right. That makes a lot more sense, I thought, the yogurt I'd eaten during snack curdling in my stomach.

Kimiko let out a wistful sigh and looked longingly at the flowers. "He did so good! I need him to give Howard some pointers."

Though I laughed uneasily, I was boiling on the inside. How dare Geoff have the nerve to send flowers to my job! He knew I couldn't avoid them here *and* it would get everyone talking.

What a jackass.

I inspected the flowers again, tempted to offer them to Kimiko, but that would *really* give people something to talk about. Thanking her, I picked them up and walked back down the hall, fuming.

"Ooh, pretty flowers," Susie said when I entered the classroom.

"Take them. Please." I placed the vase on my desk and opened the card that had been perched in the middle of the bouquet.

Dear Zara,

I'm here when you're ready to talk. I've loved you for 14 years, and I'll love you for the rest of my life.

Yours,
Geoff

What the fuck? Where was the apology? In the days since I called Geoff out, he'd said everything *but* the words "I'm sorry." *Yours?* Ha! What a load of bullshit.

I ripped up the card and dropped the scraps into the trash can under my desk. Eager to get the stupid thing out of sight—and Geoff out of mind—I carried the vase across the room to the desk Susie rarely sat at, cluttered with thirty-three years' worth of student artwork and creations made especially for her. Carefully, I cleared a spot and plunked it down. "Seriously, they're yours if you want them."

Susie absently tapped the purple marker she'd been using to grade against her cheek. "Zara, I know I always say this, but I mean it—if you need anything, *anything at all,* I've been told I'm a good listener."

I thought about the millions of people already depending on Susie, always claiming pieces of her so that she rarely had time to do anything for herself. Not wanting to add to her burden, I pasted a smile on my face. "Thanks for the offer, but I'm fine."

* * *

By the time I raised my hand and knocked on the music room door that afternoon, I still didn't know where to start with navigating the OMG-Caleb-is-a-stripper situation.

Oh, hi, Caleb. Do you happen to own a pair of ass-less chaps?

Hey, Caleb…funny story—I think you picked me up on your shoulders and put your face in my crotch two nights ago!

The man in question opened the door with a pleasant smile. My eyes dropped to his left arm resting against the door-frame, his sleeve rolled up to reveal the telltale treble clef.

It's the same tattoo.

"You're a stripper," I blurted out.

Caleb's cool-as-a-cucumber facade fell. He hastily poked his head around the door, looked up and down the deserted hallway, and then pulled me into the music room. His fingers around my forearm reminded me of how he'd maneuvered my hands over his dewy body on Saturday night. I sucked in a breath and took a giant step away from him, casting a nervous glance at the door he'd just closed.

Folding those toned arms over his chest, he narrowed his eyes at me. "And your name isn't Zoey."

"You knew it was me!" It was my turn to cross my arms and glare back. *There we go! Indignation is good.*

He snorted. "Of course I did. *You* weren't the one wearing a mask. That was a nice dress, by the way."

"Thank you," I said, feeling my face flush. I couldn't believe I was the one ready to melt into a puddle on the floor while he was standing here, completely chill, like he didn't bare his ass to me and most of the women in town.

"Can I take your coat?" Caleb extended his hand toward me, but I pulled the coat tighter around myself.

"Um, I think I'll keep it on for now."

He shrugged. "Okay." He motioned to two folding chairs in the middle of the room.

I had a direct flashback to Saturday night, filled with jitters as I crossed the stage before he'd launched himself in my lap.

"Zara?"

I snapped back to the present and daintily sat on the chair closest to the door, while Caleb sat on the other one.

"Wanna talk about it?" he asked nonchalantly.

"No."

We stared at each other in awkward silence. After a moment, I said, "I—you—" I took a deep breath and tried again. "Does Vicki know you're a stripper?"

Caleb leisurely crossed a leg over his knee and reclined back as if we were having afternoon tea and not discussing the fact that his second job comprised taking off his clothes and shaking his butt for money. "I prefer the term 'entertainer,' and to answer your question, no—no one here does." His gaze pinned me to my seat. "Except for you."

I gulped and looked at the floor, overwhelmed by the intensity in his eyes.

"I'd like to keep it that way, if it's cool with you. I feel that whatever I do in my time away from school is my personal business as long as I don't put the school's reputation in jeopardy," Caleb said.

I lifted my gaze to meet his. "Is that why you wear a mask? Or are you embarrassed?"

"I think you're projecting, *Zoey*."

The smirk on his face irritated me, but I refused to take the bait.

"I'm not embarrassed in the slightest. I keep my face covered so I can maintain a separation between my professional and personal lives," he continued calmly. "Colton the Cowboy is just a role I play. Like Tom Holland playing Spider-Man. Or Joaquin Phoenix as the Joker. When they leave the set, they're just Tom Holland and Joaquin Phoenix. Being an entertainer supplements my income and gives me time to focus on my music."

Was I projecting? Caleb was totally at ease while talking about this. He'd clearly thought it all through.

He raised an eyebrow. "Any other questions?"

Chastened, I shook my head.

The easy-going smile returned to his face. "Good. Maybe we should talk about the actual reason we're here?"

"Right—the spring music program," I said, more so to myself than him.

As we talked through logistics, like the ideal length of the show—thirty minutes was developmentally appropriate and would get parents in and out—and which classes to pair up together—it made sense for my students to be paired with Mrs. Alvarez's third grade class since several had siblings there—my mind gradually shifted from thinking of Caleb as "Caleb the Stripping Cowboy" to "Caleb the Music Teacher." During our conversation, it became clear that he had a strong passion for both music and working with children.

After about half an hour had passed, he stood up and grinned. "I have a good feeling about this. I think we're on the right path."

Was he talking about us, or the music program?

"Me too." I grabbed my coat from the back of the chair, unsure at what point I'd removed it.

"Oh! Before you go, here's a list of songs Mariah suggested." Caleb passed me a piece of paper. "I'm still making a shortlist of show themes, but do any of these stand out to you?"

I looked over the list and frowned. I recognized some songs from previous shows—basic and boring. Had *any* of these been penned this millennium?

"Not a fan?"

I glanced up to find Caleb studying my face. I hesitated. "It's just...why can't we do *fun* songs? You know, *real* music?"

He chuckled. "*All* music is real music. Have anything particular in mind?"

"Nothing specific. But, I mean, practically everybody likes Taylor Swift, BTS—"

"Beyoncé?" A smile played on Caleb's lips.

I cringed as I remembered our first meeting at my car.

"Just kidding," Caleb said, shrugging on his coat. "I love T. Swizzle and BTS, by the way. Taylor is a premier songwriter. And BTS makes banger after banger."

My eyes narrowed in suspicion. "There is no way you're an Army. What's your favorite song?"

"Hmm, that's a hard one. It's a toss-up between 'Mic Drop' or 'Save Me.' What about you?"

"'Butter,'" I answered without hesitation.

Caleb hummed the chorus and moved through the choreography. Apparently, country wasn't his only specialization. I felt the faintest of flutters in my stomach…a different kind of attraction than when I saw him perform over the weekend.

"Oh my God, *stop*," I said, even though I wouldn't mind watching him dance all afternoon.

He laughed and grabbed his messenger bag. "I may play in a reggae fusion band, but I listen to everything. What kind of musician would I be without an open mind?"

"What instrument do you play?" I asked as we walked across the blacktop.

"In the band, I play bass. I've also been known to tickle the ivories, and while I'm decent on drums, they're not my favorite."

I stared at Caleb with fresh eyes, intrigued by the new information. A stripping multi-instrumentalist who had an affinity for K-pop choreography and teaching small children about music. Talk about multifaceted.

"Do you play anything?" he asked me.

"That would be a negative. I can't even sing; the closest I get is shower karaoke."

Caleb scoffed. "If you have a voice, you can sing."

"I don't know about that," I said skeptically. On more than one occasion, I'd sang along with the radio while riding with Geoff and he'd asked if I was trying to communicate with dolphins.

We stopped next to my car door, and Caleb gently rapped on the window. "But you can dance."

I shook my head. "So can you…and I'm not talking about K-pop choreo."

He rewarded me with a hearty laugh that sent the butterfly wings in my stomach flapping again. How could I be feeling flutters for someone when it hadn't even been a week since I split from Geoff? It didn't make sense.

He's a colleague, and a stri—entertainer—who knows how to turn on the charm. It's not you; it's him.

I turned down the wattage on my smile, tipped my head at him, and opened the door. "Have a good evening, Caleb."

"You too, Zara."

ten

With trepidation, I stared up at the nondescript brick exterior of Heart of Ink Tattoo Studio. It looked like a perfectly normal building; you wouldn't even know people got stabbed and pricked for the fun of it if *TATTOOS & PIERCINGS* wasn't graffitied across the large tinted windows. Slowly, I backed away, jumping when I bumped into my sister.

After receiving the flowers from Geoff at school the day before—and sending him a sternly worded email when I got home—I felt called to do something big and new. I spent a couple of hours online researching tattoo shops, along with images for inspiration. If I was going to have something inked on my skin for the rest of my life, I wanted it done by an incredible artist, and I wanted it to mean something. Under the influence of booze and fun on the night of the breakup party, and irritated beyond belief the evening before, getting a tattoo seemed like a great idea. But stone-cold sober on a Tuesday evening, and much less furious than the previous night, I was having second thoughts.

"Maybe I didn't think this all the way through," I said. "If I show up at school tomorrow with a tattoo, the kids are going to run home and blab to their parents. They'll think I'm a delinquent or something."

"What is this? 1956?" Max flashed a wicked grin. "It's an easy fix—just get it somewhere no one'll be able to see unless you're wearing lingerie."

Swallowing, I cast a nervous glance at her, Jules, and Amber. "Or maybe I should just wait until summer break. It's probably a better time for it, anyway; my skin is so dry during the winter."

Jules put her hands on her hips. "You can't wimp out on us now."

"And actually, I did some research and found out that winter is one of the best times for a tattoo. Your skin is less exposed to the sun, and you sweat less, so it's more comfortable as the tattoo heals," Amber piped up.

"How very Stevie of you," Max said.

"You're just scared because you've never done this before. But *we* all have tattoos and we're still here to tell the tale," Jules stated. "You know I have four."

Amber held up two fingers.

"I lost count of how many I have," Max said with a shrug. "I've got the designs on the back of my hand, the garter on my right thigh, and the cow skull with flowers on my left one. The lotus on my ankle, the crescent moon on the back of my neck." She pointed to the various parts of her body. "I've got a couple that are for private viewing only, and—oh! The dancing taco from the Casa de Tacos logo so I could get free tacos for life."

Amber frowned. "Didn't that place close down last year?"

"Did it?" Max asked. "Well, shit."

"See? It's a rite of passage!" Jules said.

I raised one eyebrow. "Then why doesn't Stevie have one? Why isn't she here?"

Amber gave me a look. "We all know the answer to that one. If Stevie was here, she'd be quizzing every employee in the building about sanitation practices and asking to see credentials. You wouldn't get tatted until *next* January."

"Rosario has tattoos, too," Max added. "Stevie's an outlier."

"Zara, this was *your* idea. Why pick it and then bail?" Jules asked.

This *was* my idea. And I didn't want to bail. Just...maybe... *postpone* things until I'd had a chance to think them through with a clear head. At the same time, did I really expect my life to change for the better by staying in my comfort zone?

"Let's do it. Quick, before I change my mind!" I strode toward the doors as Jules let out a whoop behind me.

The inside of the studio had a modern industrial feel, made warmer by the bold, colorful geometric patterns and funky neon signs on the walls. The muted buzz of tattoo machines and the whiff of antiseptic gave me an empty feeling in the pit of my stomach.

"Hi, can I help you?" asked a short guy with a buzz cut and glasses. He stood behind a transparent counter containing lotions and creams, body jewelry, and merchandise like stickers and enamel pins advertising the shop.

"We want to get a tattoo," Max declared.

The guy looked us over, stopping when his eyes landed on Amber's baby bump. "Um, we don't tattoo pregnant people."

"Just here for moral support." Amber pointed at me. "It's for her."

"Got it. Hold on a sec; I'll let Tank know you're here."

Tank?

The name didn't instill me with confidence. In fact, it conjured up an image of a big, burly man covered from scalp to sole in ink, maybe with a forked tongue and metal implants, who owned a pit bull.

While I fretted about meeting Tank, Max and Jules flipped through laminated sheets filled with flash artwork.

"We should FaceTime Ro," Amber said. "She really wanted to be here."

Max made a tsking noise. "That's what happens when you have crotch goblins; they suck all the joy from your life." She looked over her shoulder at Amber and gave her a sweet smile. "But I'm sure yours won't."

Amber rolled her eyes.

"Hi! I'm Tank," a silky, feminine voice said.

I spun around to find a short, pixie-like woman with both arms covered in tattoos, cotton-candy pink hair, and a pierced eyebrow. "*You're* Tank?"

She jutted out her hip and made a *ta-da* gesture with one hand. "The one and only. Ready to come on back?"

"Yep." Jules nudged me forward.

I placed one foot in front of the other, keeping my eyes trained straight ahead as we walked past people reclining or sitting on tattoo chairs while the tattooers did their thing. I knew if I saw one drop of blood, one grimace, I was *out*.

"Who's Zara?" Tank asked once we'd made it to an empty station in the back of the shop.

Hesitantly, I lifted my hand.

Tank grinned, revealing a pink gem on one of her front teeth. "Don't worry—I don't bite." She looked at my friends hovering nearby. "I see we've got quite the audience."

"We're all here to welcome Zara into the Tattooed Lady Club," Jules said.

"It's a great club to be part of." Tank perched on the corner of the tattoo chair and swung a leg back and forth. "So, Zara, why did you decide today was the day?"

"Well, um, I'm kind of going through a transitional period, and bangs never look good on anyone, so…"

Jules stuck a finger in the air. "Zooey Deschanel would like a word."

"So, you decided to go with injecting permanent ink into your skin instead?"

Oh, geez, Tank has a point. This is a terrible idea.

She grinned and hopped down. "I'm just kidding. Have an idea for me?"

"Um, yeah. I looked online." I pulled up the pictures I'd saved and handed my phone over.

"You're the chosen one; you're the only person she's shown," Max said, winking. "She wouldn't let anyone else see."

Was Max flirting with my tattoo artist? I wouldn't put it past her, but I also needed Tank's mind fully focused on the task at hand.

"I didn't want anyone to question my choice or offer any 'constructive feedback,'" I said. "This is going on *my* body, so my opinion is the only one that matters."

"I don't know why you're worried about that; Stevie's not here," Jules muttered.

Eyes still on my phone screen, Tank made a sound of agreement. "Black and gray? Color? Where do you want it?"

"Black and gray. I was thinking the inside of my wrist?" That way, I could look at it whenever I needed a reminder.

Tank tapped a pencil against her lips. "Gimme a sec to whip up a drawing. Don't miss me too much." She fluttered her lashes as she walked away.

And now my tattoo artist was flirting with Max. Great.

"Gather 'round, girls. I'm calling Ro," Amber said. We crowded around her to squeeze into the FaceTime frame.

"What's up? What's up?" Rosario filled the screen, her face makeup-free and hair in a sloppy side ponytail. We got glimpses of the ceiling and then the side of the bathtub as she set the phone up. "I'm bummed I had to miss it, but it's bathtime in the Díaz household. Mateo, do *not* eat the soap!" She leaned out of view briefly. "What are you getting, Zara?"

"It's a secret, but you'll see soon enough," I teased.

Onscreen, Rosario held up her hand to shield her face as she dodged a splash from her three-year-old son, Mikey. "Can't wait! And speaking of things I can't wait for—I've come up with my mistake for you to make. Well, all of us, actually."

"We're all ears," Max said.

"A weekend girls' trip! I *loved* getting a change of scenery and hoeing it up in different area codes in my twenties. Imagine Saturday night, but for an entire weekend," Rosario said through gritted teeth. She gripped her infant's arm and wiped his face with a damp washcloth as he struggled against her. "My family has a vacation home in Wayside Beach, so we've got a hook-up."

"Yes! The sooner the better!" Max exclaimed.

Jules glanced at me, a question in her eyes. "Zara?"

I shrugged. "I'll never turn down a trip to the beach."

"Jules's birthday is coming up soon, so maybe we can combine it," Amber said.

"A weekend celebrating *moi*?" Jules shimmied her shoulders. "I'm here for it."

A high-pitched wail emanated from the phone.

"I have to go, but I'll start planning the trip and get you guys the details. Mwah, love you, bye!" Rosario said in a rush before blowing a kiss at the camera.

"Bye!" we chorused.

"Mikey, *Mikey*, splash your brother one more time and see what happens," she growled just before the call dropped.

"Couldn't be me." Max shuddered.

Jules looked at us with pleading eyes. "Can I make just one request? Please, for the love of God, don't let Ro plan the whole weekend. We might not make it home alive."

Amber made a face. "Don't worry; we'll rein her in."

"Hey, Zara," Tank called. "Wanna take a look?"

I gulped. In all the bathtime-we're-going-on-a-girls'-weekend excitement, I'd almost forgotten why we were there. Joining Tank at her desk, I looked down at the crisp line drawing. The design felt strong, but still feminine. I imagined what it would look like on my skin—how I would *feel* seeing it there.

Resilient.

Sexy.

Bad-ass.

"It's perfect."

Tank smiled. "Cool. I'll make a stencil, and we'll get started."

Seeing the design lessened some of my nerves, but I still worried about the pain. Needles and I didn't get along. I only got my ears pierced because Jules begged Mom to get hers done, and there was no way I was going to let my seven-year-old-sister do something before me. I couldn't even watch when I had to get bloodwork done at the doctor's office.

Quicker than I thought imaginable, Tank created a stencil of the design. I watched with morbid curiosity as she prepped my skin by wiping down my wrist with rubbing alcohol and running a disposable razor over it. Carefully, she transferred the paper stencil, then lifted it off and confirmed the placement. From a safe distance where she couldn't see the design, Jules filmed the entire thing with her phone.

I frowned. "Is this for my non-existent dating profile, too?"

"Nah. Just my personal amusement," she said.

I stuck my tongue out at her.

Tank finished organizing her little pots of ink, then smeared some ointment over the stenciled image. "I'm going to get started. Just breathe, okay?"

Catching sight of the needle in her hand, I gulped. "Okay— *ow. Ow, ow, ow.* Holy crap, that hurts!"

Jules let out an evil laugh.

No amount of online anecdotes had prepared me for the

pain. Tank may as well have been carving the alphabet into my flesh with a rusty razor blade. Jules, Amber, and Max tried to distract me by rehashing Saturday night and thinking up shenanigans that might happen on the girls' weekend. I sat with the sweaty fingers of my free hand digging into the side of the chair for what felt like forever—but in reality, was probably only about an hour.

Tank rolled away on her stool. "All done!"

I looked down at my angry, burning wrist. The core of the design was a sturdy anchor with bold lines and shading, a singular rope winding around the shank. A delicate butterfly perched on the top, its patterned wings extended outward as if preparing to fly away at any moment. It was everything I wanted, like the message had been patiently waiting in the ether, ready to be summoned when I was finally prepared to receive it.

"Can we see it now?" Jules begged.

"Sure," I said.

The girls all came over and immediately began gushing over the fresh tattoo.

I smiled down at it. "Butterflies are the ultimate symbol of transformation. If they can make it through being an ugly caterpillar, and then that icky, uncertain stage when they're literally *goo*, they evolve into this bright, beautiful, *bold* creature that has wings to rise above it all. As for the anchor—it's a reminder that I can always come back to myself."

"Seriously poetic," Tank said.

"Thanks." I couldn't tear my eyes away from my newly inked skin. The dress was amazing, but this—this would be with me until my dying day. Whenever I needed to remember how capable I was, I could just look down at my wrist. I could have used it while dating my ex. "Geoff hates tattoos. He says it's like putting bumper stickers on a Porsche."

Tank's lip curled. "I don't know who Geoff is, but he can go fuck himself."

"Hear, hear!" Max exclaimed.

Jules snaked one arm around my shoulders. "I'm proud of you, Big Sis."

I smiled at her. "I'm proud of me, too."

eleven

Two days later, I walked into Bella Cucina with my head held high, still on cloud nine from getting *my first—and last—tattoo*. I resisted the urge to scratch it. No one mentioned anything about tattoos being so damned itchy beforehand, but the girls assured me it was a normal part of the healing process.

Since it had been a wonderful couple of Geoff-free days and things were going well at school—the kids were pretty chill and Caleb and I were on good terms—I decided to follow Stevie's recommendation to romanticize my life by going on a solo date at my favorite restaurant using the gift card she'd given me.

"Good evening," the host said. "How many are in your party tonight?"

"Uh, it's just me?" I hated the way my voice went up at the end. Where was the Zara from a minute ago who'd walked in ready to kick ass and take names?

"Table for one…okay."

Did I detect a hint of disdain, or worse, *pity*, in the man's tone? He studied the iPad in his hands with a creased brow. Was he going to tell me the restaurant didn't allow solo patrons?

Stop it, Zee. You're being irrational.

The host looked up and gave me a pleasant smile. "Right this way."

I stuck close as he wound through the dim interior of the busy Italian restaurant. My stomach tightened as we stopped beside a table with a burgundy tablecloth and two place settings, right in the center of everything.

They couldn't sit me somewhere—anywhere—less conspicuous?

"Your waiter will be with you in a moment." The host placed a menu in front of me and departed.

Feeling overly exposed, I picked up the stiff cardboard and pretended to study it even though I practically knew it by heart. Because Geoff thought the portions were overpriced for the size and refused to eat here, I regularly treated myself to takeout when he was away for business. I risked looking up from the menu, glancing around to see if anyone was watching me.

"Hi! I'm Alan, your waiter for the evening," a lanky man with reddish hair and freckles scattered across his face said in greeting. "Are you expecting someone?"

I shook my head, trying not to cringe. "Nope. Just me."

"No problem!" Alan said cheerily. When he quickly swept up the second place setting, my face and neck grew hot. And I'd thought I felt conspicuous before. "Can I get you something—"

"I'm ready to order now," I blurted out. The faster I got my food and ate, the faster I could leave and stop feeling like an animal on display in a zoo. "Caprese salad—extra balsamic and add fresh black pepper—and shrimp fra diavolo. Extra saucy, please."

"I'll put that in for you and be right back with a water," Alan said.

After he left, I pulled out my phone and listlessly scrolled through my social feed. I found the usual posed family portraits complete with golden retriever, wedding and/or honeymoon photos from college classmates, pictures of babies laying on a blanket displaying their age in months.

Exactly what I needed right now. Increasingly anxious, I called the person whose idea this was in the first place.

"Hey there," Stevie answered on the second ring. "What's up?"

"I'm on a solo date like you said." The words came out in a rush.

"That's great! How's it going?"

"Horribly. That's why I'm calling you!"

"Uh-oh, what's going on?" Stevie asked, sounding concerned.

"People are looking at me," I hissed, my eyes darting around.

"I'm sure they're not. But if they are, let them." I could picture the slight crease between her brows and the what-do-I-care shrug. "This isn't about anyone else; it's about *you*. You shouldn't *just* be comfortable with your own company—you should enjoy it. The next guy who comes in has to be so amazing that he's worth giving up your peace."

I looked down at the butterfly wing peeking out from beneath the sleeve of my sweater.

"Zara? Are you still there?"

"Yeah." I scanned the restaurant again, and when my eyes landed on the entrance, they went wide. Caleb and another guy who looked awfully similar to Hershey, the emcee from the Alphas Unleashed show, were chatting with each other as they approached the host's station. "Oh *shit*."

Before I even had time to process what I was doing, I straightened my legs and slid down my chair in one fluid motion, careful not to bump the back of my head on the way down.

"What's going on?" Stevie asked.

"I'm under the table." It was dark thanks to the thick burgundy fabric, and I could only make out a golden glow.

"What? Is that new slang?"

"No, Stevie. I am *under the table*," I said through clenched teeth. "I saw someone from school."

"So? Did you not just hear a word I said?" She blew out one of the exasperated breaths usually reserved for Max or Rosario into my ear.

I scooted forward and carefully lifted the tablecloth, my head hovering above the polished wood floor. I couldn't see much—just the legs and feet of the other restaurant patrons—but three walking pairs of feet entered my line of sight. Hastily, I let the fabric fall and scooted back. "Shit. Shit, shit, *shit*."

"Are you still under the table? You can't stay there all night!"

"You think I don't know that, Stevie? Jesus."

A shadow stopped outside the tablecloth. I froze as it moved, holding my breath and praying to God, the Universe, *whoever* may have been listening, that it wasn't Caleb. In the next instant, light poured under the table. I blinked as my vision adjusted, relieved to find Alan the waiter in a crouch, peering at me with a baffled expression.

"Um, your food's ready. Would you like it on top of the table, or…"

I brought the phone to my chest. "Can you just box it up and let me know when it's ready? Oh—did you remember my extra sauces?"

"Uh, sure." Alan started to stand, then dropped back down. "And just to clarify, food above or below the table?"

I frowned at him. "Above. What do you think I am? A groundhog?"

Alan's face turned so red it gave his hair a run for its money. "No, ma'am…this is just…a little out of the ordinary."

"For you and me both, Alan. You and me both." I handed him my gift card, sighing when he dropped the tablecloth and darkness surrounded me once again. I put my phone back up to my ear. "You there?"

"Yeah," Stevie said after a beat. "I have no idea what I just heard."

"That was the sound of every last shred of my dignity disintegrating."

"And I'd be correct in assuming you're *still* under the table?" Even without Stevie in my presence, I knew she was squeezing her eyes shut and pinching the bridge of her nose. I'd seen it a million times during college when she got a call from Max asking her to bail her out of some kind of trouble.

"Yep."

"You do realize that probably no one was looking at you before, but now…"

I groaned and massaged my temples with my free hand. "Trust me, Stevie, I know." God, this evening was such a bust. I was silly to think getting a tattoo changed anything; I was still the same old Zara. "I'm going to hang up now."

"Call me if you need to hide in a bush somewhere on your way home," Stevie said, her voice tinged with amusement.

"Ha ha ha, you're so funny."

I ended the call just as Alan moved the tablecloth aside again. "Food's on the table. Anything else?"

"Actually, yes." My self-respect was already shot to hell; what else did I have to lose? "Can you tell me if an attractive guy with light green eyes and a jawline sharp enough to cut steel is anywhere nearby? Or is he looking this way?"

Alan leaned back on his heels, gripping the top of the table as he looked around. God bless him. "Nope. There's a guy matching that description, but he's sitting at the bar talking to someone."

"Perfect. Cover me!"

"What?" Alan sputtered.

Without hesitation, I shot out from under the table, grabbed the handles of the paper bag containing my order, and ran for the restaurant's exit without looking back.

twelve

The day after my disastrous solo date, I paced up and
down the hall just outside the music room while
Caleb finished up his lesson with the Ellis Elephants. I
felt just as nervous as I had last Monday after the breakup party.
If he hadn't seen me sitting alone, or somehow miraculously
missed my peculiar dining spot, there was no doubt he'd seen
my speedy exit from the restaurant. I'd lucked out that Susie
volunteered to drop the class off, but since she was currently in
a grade level meeting with the other first-grade teachers, I had
no choice but to pick the kids up.

*So what if he saw you last night? What's the worst that could
happen?*

I stopped beside the classroom door and peered through the
slim glass pane that offered a prime view of what was going on
inside without interrupting. Caleb sat at the piano, a grin
stretching from ear to ear as his fingers danced over the keys.
My students, each standing inside an individual hula hoop and
holding some type of instrument, watched him with enraptured
faces, trying to keep up. Suddenly, Caleb jerked his hands back
from the keys, his eyes huge as his mouth formed an "O." The

kids dropped their instruments, stepped out of the hoops, and scrambled around the room like ants whose pheromone trail had been disrupted. After they all found a new hoop and instrument, they eagerly waited for Caleb to play again. A tiny smile tugged my lips upward.

Buzz.

I ignored the vibrating phone in my jeans pocket as Walker tried to insert the end of a drumstick in his ear. When I rapped on the glass, he glanced over, and I narrowed my eyes at him. He quickly dropped the stick and gave me an angelic look.

Buzz.

I turned my back on the lesson, moving out of view and fishing out my phone to find the Sensational Six group chat abuzz.

MAX

You're supposed to eat ON the table. Not UNDER it, Z.

ROSARIO

Girl, you were under a table??

I narrowed my eyes at the screen and sent up a silent curse in Stevie's name.

ZARA

Can ANYBODY in this group keep their trap shut?

STEVIE

I didn't know it was a secret!

JULES

You realize you can never ever show your face
there again, right?

AMBER

That's a shame. Their carbonara is to die for.

MAX

I love their tiramisu.

I massaged my temples as I contemplated muting the chat for a
while.

STEVIE

Back to the topic at hand, please.

ROSARIO

Babe, you need a win.

JULES

And a dick.

AMBER

How do we always end up talking about dicks?

I shook my head at the screen. How *did* we always come back to
dicks?

Without warning, the classroom door opened, startling me.
My grip on the phone loosened, and it slid out of my palm.
Heartbeat thundering in my ears, I watched in horror as my
phone journeyed to the tiled floor below as twenty unruly six-
and-seven-year-olds streamed into the hallway. The clatter as it

hit the ground made my stomach flip. I could just imagine the spiderweb of cracked glass I'd find when I flipped it over. I'd just freaking replaced the screen a couple of months earlier when I knocked the phone off my kitchen counter.

"Whoa, guys. Let's help Ms. Whitmore," Caleb said, parting the crowd of small humans. My heart climbed into my throat when he crouched down and reached out a muscled forearm to pick up the fallen phone.

A phone that had fallen amid a conversation about dicks.

"No! I've got it," I screeched, diving for the device.

Eyebrows raised, Caleb got to his feet. "*O*-kay."

Rising, I turned it over and inspected the screen. Miracle of miracles, it only had a couple of slight scratches. I let out a relieved sigh. "It's fine."

"Glad to hear it," Caleb said. Stuffing his hands into his pockets, he inclined his head at my wrist. "Nice tattoo, by the way."

"*Tattoo?*" Hadleigh asked, her cornflower blue eyes nearly bugging out of her head.

"My mom has a tattoo right here." Bronwyn turned around and pointed at her lower back. "My dad said it's a stamp."

"I want a tattoo, but *my* mommy says I have to wait 'til I'm a grown-up," Duncan said, pouting.

I yanked the sleeve of my sweater down over my itchy wrist, staring daggers at Caleb. I'd managed to keep the nosy snoops from noticing for the last couple of days, and he'd gone and blown it all up in sixty seconds.

Sorry, he mouthed, ducking his head. The cheeky quirk of his lips said otherwise. I was *not* amused.

Ignoring him, I addressed the class. "Alright, Ellis Elephants, single-file! Who's line leader today?"

"I am!" Cooper raced to the front of the line and lifted his chin in the air. "Everybody behind me."

I tried to calm my frazzled nerves as my students formed a crooked line, but it was all for nothing when Caleb sidled over.

"Sorry," he said under his breath. "I figured they'd seen it."

I shrugged, keeping my eyes on a developing situation between Duncan and Rory toward the end of the line—and attempting to avoid breathing in the faint patchouli aroma surrounding Caleb.

"Speaking of seeing things—did I see you at Bella Cucina last night? Around seven?"

My blood froze in my veins even though I kept my face a cool mask. Sure, I'd *assumed* he saw my mad dash for the door, but my mortification reached another level to have him confirm it.

"I'm not sure what you're talking about," I mumbled, turning on my heel and striding toward the door leading outside. Cooper and the rest of the class followed like a brood of restless baby ducks.

"But Ms. Whitmore, Baylee is in the bathroom!" someone exclaimed.

"She can catch up," I said, not slowing my pace.

"Have a good long weekend, Ms. Whitmore! See you next week," Caleb called through the open door.

I waved a hand over my head in response. It wasn't lost on me that my current escape from his presence mirrored my sudden departure from the restaurant the night before.

* * *

As I sat behind the wheel for the drive home, I wondered if there'd ever be a point in time in which I wasn't anxious about seeing Caleb or fleeing from his presence in utter humiliation.

But once I turned onto my street, the familiar black Tesla parked in front of the house made my interactions with Caleb seem like the least of my problems. Slamming on the brakes, my fingers clenched around the wheel in a vise that would have been extremely useful earlier, and every muscle in my body tensed. What the hell was Geoff doing here?

"Lord, I know you're testing me, but I'm *tired*. Seriously, I'm not up for this today," I said, frustration coloring my words. I debated putting the car in reverse, getting the hell out of dodge, and hiding out at Amber or Stevie's for a couple of hours, but screw that—this was *my* home.

As the townhouse came into view, so did Geoff. He sat bundled up on the porch stairs, head tucked, and shoulders around his ears. I swallowed as a wave of hurt caught me off-guard. I hated how he still had such a visceral effect on me.

I purposely avoided looking at him as I pulled my car into the garage. I could always lower the door, go inside, and pretend he wasn't out there. Change into some comfy clothes, pour myself a glass of wine, and disassociate in front of the TV for a few hours.

No.

If I really wanted to move on, I needed to deal with this— now. With a sigh, I turned off the car, took my time getting out, and made my way to the porch.

Geoff's face softened with a hesitant smile as I approached. "Hi."

"Can we skip the pleasantries? What are you doing here?" I asked bluntly.

I took satisfaction in the way his smile faltered. "I see you're still mad—actually, I gathered that from you changing the locks."

"This isn't your home anymore, Geoff."

The smile slipped completely. "Zara, don't you think you've taken this far enough? You won't respond to my calls or texts—I have to *email* you, for God's sake. I learned my lesson, okay? Shantel"—he made a show of wiping his hands clean—"she's out of the picture."

My pulse began to race. "She should have never been *in* the picture to begin with."

Geoff stood up, grimacing as he stretched his legs. I wondered how long he'd been sitting here on the porch. God, I would have let Tank tattoo my entire back if I could've seen his reaction when he tried his key and couldn't get inside.

"You're right," he said. "You're so right, and I realize that now. That's why I'm here—to talk."

I shook my head. "Well, I don't want to talk to you now; we can talk when *I* feel ready. You don't call the shots anymore." I pushed a piece of hair out of my face.

"*A tattoo?*" Geoff's face registered his shock before his lip curled. "Please tell me that's fake."

"It's not," I chirped, not bothering to hide my pleased smirk.

Geoff steepled his index fingers and brought them to his nose like he did when he was trying to figure out the best way to deliver one of his backhanded compliments. "Zara, you're a beautiful girl; why would you ruin that by doing something in a fit of anger?" He lowered his voice, despite no one else being outside. "Are you on your…*period*? That would explain *a lot.*"

Why the hell didn't I put the garage down and go change into my comfy clothes when I had the chance?

"Goodbye, Geoffrey."

When I stomped back in the direction of the garage, he hurried down the steps. "Wait, wait. Can I at least grab a few things? With the promotion, I have some really important meetings coming up."

I stopped and spun around. "No, you cannot."

"You can't just hold my stuff hostage!" Geoff snapped, his face furious.

I folded my arms over my chest. "I can leave it on the porch if you'd like."

Geoff's face went slack. "That's okay," he said hurriedly. He raised his palms in the air as if surrendering. "Sorry for coming over unannounced. I'll wait for when you're ready to talk."

Instead of answering, I hit the button on the garage wall to close the door. Geoff stood frozen on the other side, like I might take pity and invite him in. Normally, I would have gone inside as soon as the door started to descend, but I didn't trust my ex not to drop and roll under it like Indiana Jones. Bit by bit, Geoff disappeared until only his shiny dress shoes were visible, and soon—but not soon enough—even those were gone.

Inside the townhouse, I closed the door and leaned against it, waiting for the far too familiar sting that preceded the inevitable oncoming tears.

It didn't come.

thirteen

And he had the audacity to accuse me of holding his shit hostage! Like I need any more reminders of that asshat. I wish I could wipe every trace of him from the townhouse, but that's hard to do without burning the whole thing down.

Sounds like you're ready to move on!

I wouldn't go that far.

It's been almost two weeks.

She dated him for 14 years. Compared to that, two weeks is a drop in the bucket.

I was thinking about getting a pet. Like a pug. Or maybe one of those cute orange cats.

JULES

AHA! A dog baby.

[Shaq facepalm gif]

AMBER

Dog baby?

ROSARIO

If you want an actual baby, I've got one you can take for free.

STEVIE

Maybe you should start with a plant. A pet is a big commitment.

AMBER

Seriously, no one's gonna explain "dog baby"?

ZARA

I'll fill you in later, Ams.

AMBER

How about this evening? At El Ranchito? My treat.

I chewed on my lip as I mulled over her offer. After my failed solo date a couple evenings earlier, I was a little hesitant to venture back out in public, but I wouldn't be alone this time. And I was a sucker for a free meal.

MAX

Hiya. Just got back from a coffee date. Catching up on convo now.

JULES

How'd it go?

MAX

Meh.

El Ranchito, I wanna go! Treat me too, Amber. What time?

AMBER

[Little girl wagging finger no gif]

I want some QT with Zara.

My chest filled with warm fuzzies. Because of Amber's recent marriage and volleyball coaching after school, we hadn't hung out one-on-one in ages. I cherished the moments when it was just the two of us. Without the other girls competing to be the center of attention or offering unsolicited judgment, I could rely on Amber as a sounding board to get a level-headed take on things.

Like why I found myself on edge whenever Caleb was near.

MAX

Booooo!

ROSARIO

Come spend QT with me, Max.

STEVIE

Stop trying to dupe people into unpaid childcare, Ro.

ZARA:

I'm in.

For hanging with Amber. Not babysitting.

AMBER

Wear the Bad Decisions Dress.

STEVIE

We're seriously calling it that?

JULES

[Yasssss gif]

* * *

"What the fuck is this?"

The déjà vu was *strong* as I stood next to Amber just inside El Ranchito Mexican restaurant, wearing the freshly dry-cleaned Bad Decisions Dress and looking around warily.

Ahead of us was a long, rectangular table covered with name tags, manned by two beaming women beckoning us over with the enthusiasm of someone trying to find new recruits for their MLM. Behind them, instead of the typical scattered arrangement, the tables were organized into two rows, each with two chairs sitting opposite each other. At the far end of the room, a large digital timer with bright red digits displaying *5:00* sat on a stool.

Men and women milled around—most of them dressed to impress in blazers, button-downs, and cocktail dresses.

"I have the strange suspicion we're not here for dinner," I said, turning my narrowed eyes on Amber.

She twisted the end of a long lock of hair around her index finger so tightly I worried about her circulation. "Um, because we're not—at least, not just yet."

I felt my blood pressure rise. "What does that mean?"

"We're going speed-dating."

"*Speed-dating?*"

I looked around the room again. Name tags. Nervous-looking guys leaning against the bar. Women surreptitiously using selfie mode on their phone to primp. The timer. Suddenly, it all made sense.

"*Et tu*, Amber? I told y'all I wasn't ready." Amber's deception was surprising. Out of all the girls, I would have pegged her as the least likely to pull something like this. "I'm starting to notice a pattern here."

She released the death grip on her hair. "We find you're less likely to say no to things when it's an ambush."

I really had to work on this people-pleasing thing.

"At some point, we need to have a Come to Jesus meeting about boundaries," I said firmly. "Did the other girls know about this?"

Amber's sideways glance was all the confirmation I needed.

"Of course they did," I muttered.

"C'mon, it'll be fun." She gave me a hopeful, earnest look. "And I didn't really get to take part in the breakup party festivities."

I stared at her, aghast. "*I* wasn't the one who got you pregnant!"

She waved her hand in the air. "Tonight's not even really about the outcome. It's about dipping your toe back into the waters of the dating pool."

I glanced around the restaurant and wrinkled my nose. "It looks like the dating pool is filled with pee and that guy might be getting ready to take a dump."

"Don't judge a book by its cover, Za-Za," Amber scolded. "Think of this as an opportunity to not only gain clarity on what you do or don't want in a partner, but to work on exercising discernment. You don't want to meet the perfect guy and screw things up because you haven't dealt with your mess."

"Which is why I need more time."

"And I get that...but I know you. You'll read a million self-help books and hoard all the knowledge about what you *should* do in that big brain of yours. It's another thing entirely to put it into practice; there's only so much you can do alone, Zara."

Damn Amber and her perceptiveness. While it felt entirely

too soon to be thinking about a new relationship, I didn't want to drop a flaming bag of crap on my future partner's doorstep, ring his doorbell, and head for the hills.

Two attractive guys wearing name tags walked past us toward the bar. The taller of the two glanced back over his shoulder at me with an appreciative look. Heat rose to my cheeks as I looked away, but more of my reservations melted away with the small boost to my ego.

I didn't have to find the love of my life tonight; I probably wouldn't. But if I wanted to give myself a fighting chance of finding my forever person, at some point, I had to let down my guard and open myself back up. *Surrender my heart*, as my mom would say.

"I'll stay," I said. "But you still owe me dinner."

"Deal." Amber sounded relieved. "I had to prepay online, and not everyone's got money to throw around like Rosario."

"Amber, Dwayne's a software engineer. You're not exactly strapped for cash either."

She waved the comment away and propelled me to the check-in table. "Hi, I'm Amber and this is Zara. I purchased our tickets online." She held her phone out to a lithe woman with feline eyes. The woman's name tag read *Meghan*.

"*Our* tickets?" I asked in confusion. Meghan's eyes flitted to Amber's stomach before a judgmental crease settled between her brows.

"Yes, *our* tickets," Amber said as if it was the most normal thing in the world for a happily married and five-months pregnant woman to go speed-dating. "I'm your wingwoman."

"Uh…" I gestured at her bump.

Amber placed a protective hand on top of it. "It's not stopping me from sitting on a chair and vetting these guys. And think of it this way—you're getting two wingwomen for the price of one."

"Two wingwomen—" I broke off, eyes widening as Amber's

meaning dawned on me. I jumped up and down with joy before throwing my arms around her. "Oh my God, you're having a girl!"

Beaming, Amber nodded. "You and Ro are the first people we've told besides our families. We found out last week. I know we said we were going to wait and be surprised, but I just couldn't."

"I'm *so* excited for you! But, you know…you could sit on the side and watch," I said gently.

Amber wrinkled her nose. "Well, I *could*, but where's the fun in that?"

"You sound like Max."

"This is the *only* time I won't take offense to that. Besides, every now and then, I need a little reminder of why I should keep Dwayne around."

"Please find your name," Meghan finally said. "We'll get started in just a couple of minutes."

I found my tag and stuck it to my chest while Amber did the same. When she finished, she fussed with the straps of my dress. "Remember my number one piece of dating advice?"

I stared at her, curious. What kind of advice could she possibly have after being out of the dating game for so long? But Amber had a great head on her shoulders and a relationship anyone would envy—it seemed in my best interest to listen.

She leaned forward like she was about to reveal she had prime knowledge of the goings-on at Area 51. "Never trust a man with a dangly earring, a pinkie ring, *or* a ring on every finger. If he has two of the three, *run*."

That's *the advice? I'm doomed.*

When Meghan handed her post over to another well-dressed woman and made her way toward the timer at the front of the room, Amber and I followed.

"Attention, attention." She clapped her hands and waited for the chatter to die down. "Welcome to tonight's speed-dating event! Is it just me, or is there a frisson of love in the air?"

Definitely just you, Meghan, I thought, unable to keep my jaded thoughts at bay. *I'm just getting suffocated by Drakkar Noir and desperation.*

"Whether you're looking for your forever person or a wedding date, you're in for a good time. For you newbies, here's how it works: you'll have five minutes to chat with the person sitting across from you. When the timer goes off, the women will remain seated, and the men will move on to the next table." Meghan rambled off the instructions like one of those voiceovers listing all the potential side effects on a pharmaceutical commercial. "We've provided each person with a feedback form so you can collect your thoughts and mark your interest. At the end of the event, you'll turn that form in to me, and we'll contact you with any mutual matches."

I kind of wished I'd grabbed a glass of wine, but a larger part of me didn't want to lean on anything that would cloud my judgment; I needed to go through this experience with a clear head.

"And that's it! Just relax, be yourself, and have fun. Easy peasy, right?"

Easy peasy...sure.

"Ladies, take your seats, and let the speed-dating begin!" Meghan announced, throwing a hand in the air.

Amber wrapped me in a hug. "Knock 'em dead."

I was pretty sure that was the opposite of what I was meant to do here, but okay.

As the first guy—your average thirty-something white guy from Fallen Oaks wearing a name tag reading *Keith*—plopped into the empty seat across from me and the timer started its countdown, I wiped my clammy palms on my dress. The conversation that followed was just as basic—he asked if I'd speed-dated before, what I did for work, and what I did for fun. While Keith droned on about his love for fly-fishing, I couldn't help but feel like I was wasting my time; I'd much rather be on my couch watching a Netflix show that put me in my feels.

I glanced over at Amber's table, where her head was thrown back in laughter at something the guy across from her was saying.

Think of this as an opportunity to gain clarity on what you do or don't want in a partner.

With my new frame of mind, I studied Keith. I liked the fact that he was super passionate about his hobby. I *didn't* like that he barely let me get a word in. When the timer buzzed, we said our goodbyes. I jotted down my thoughts in the designated spot on the feedback form, then circled "No" in the *Would you like a second date?* column.

I looked up just as a bald man with a well-maintained handlebar mustache sat down. Our interaction bored me just as much as the first, but the mustache distracted me the entire time.

No handlebar mustaches—scratch that—no mustaches at all. And I don't want someone who looks like they spend more time in the bathroom getting ready than I do.

And on and on it went. Man after man, tall and short, all races, sat down and asked me the same questions over and over. I continued to add to my mental list of preferences in a partner. Men who were close with their family. Men with a compatible sense of humor. No one who had already been married twice or more. Every so often, I looked over at Amber and found her animatedly engaged in conversation. As far as I could tell, none of her companions seemed to have a problem with speed-dating a pregnant woman.

"Hello, there." A man roughly the size and shape of a sturdy oak tree with gelled, dark blond hair eased his large frame onto the chair across from me. Besides the dark gray three-piece suit complete with decorative pocket square, he looked normal enough.

I glanced at his name tag. "Hi, John. I'm Zara."

He grinned. "Ah, good; you're literate. Something we both have in common."

Taken aback, I blinked at him. "Excuse me?"

"I said, we have something in common already—we're both literate." John rested against the back of his chair confidently.

"Have you met a lot of illiterate women tonight?" I couldn't resist asking.

He ran his tongue over his front teeth, then shook his head. "Shall we get to it?"

There's no point, my guy. There's a one hundred percent chance I have zero interest in conversing with you, let alone dating you.

On the other side of the room, Amber caught my eye, flashed me a sunny smile, and gave me a thumbs-up. Sighing, I returned my attention to John. "Hit me."

"Okay." He produced a laminated card from somewhere in his jacket and scanned it.

How can five minutes feel so long? Surely, we've only got, like, two minutes left. Fuck that—how many more of these "dates" do I have left?

I glanced down at the feedback sheet and gratefully found only one more name after John's. Thank God—this was a level of hell I'd never imagined.

"What's your favorite dinosaur?" John asked suddenly.

My favorite dinosaur? What were we—eight years old?

"Triceratops," I said, pulling a name out of thin air. "Yours?"

"The mighty Tyrannosaurus rex."

Having had the cheek to ask a question like that—especially after the illiterate comment—I would have at least expected a more creative answer, but as I took in his suit and pocket square again, it wasn't all that surprising.

"*Rex* comes from the Latin word for 'king.'" John smiled at me benevolently, as if he thought I was a complete idiot.

"And in Spanish, it's *rey*. In French, *roi*. And in Italian, *re*." I folded my arms over my chest and twisted my lips as I waited for his response.

John's mouth formed an "O." Once he regained his composure, he cleared his throat and looked at his laminated card again. "Okay, next question. What would you do with one hundred grand?"

I resisted the urge to roll my eyes. *You only have a couple of minutes left, Zara. You can do this.*

"I would pay off my student loans, do some renovations around my house, and use whatever's left for a vacation." I didn't really care what his answer to the question was, but asked to be polite. "And you?"

"I'd eat it, then recycle the wrapper." John grinned. "You know there's a candy bar called One Hundred Grand?"

Just as I was about to stand up and flip the fucking table, the timer buzzed, signaling one final switch. I didn't know if I could withstand another five minutes of this. I caught Amber's eye and motioned toward the entrance of the restaurant. She frowned and shook her head, mouthing, *We're almost done.*

Well, I was done *now*. I stood up, prepared to leave without her.

"Leaving so soon?" a deep male voice asked.

My head snapped in the speaker's direction. A gorgeous, clean-shaven Black man with a small mohawk stood next to the chair Socially Inept John had just vacated. I immediately found myself at ease, basking in the gentle glow of his inviting smile.

I've made it this far…I can last another five minutes.

"Maybe not," I said, sitting down.

"I'm Tyson," the man said, reaching across the table for a handshake.

"My name is Zara. I'm a teaching assistant, and no, I don't want to be a lead teacher. I also haven't done this before, and in my free time I like to disassociate by watching hours of reality

TV and thinking about how at least my life isn't so much of a shitshow that I'd choose to broadcast my dirty laundry in front of millions of people." I blew out a breath.

Tyson observed me, a smile playing on his lips. "Long night?"

Inwardly, I winced. My flippancy probably made me sound like an entitled bitch. "Sorry. I never realized how long ninety minutes could be. It feels more like ninety days."

Even as he shrugged, the amusement never left Tyson's face. "Maybe they saved the best for last."

Something about his easy-going, self-assured demeanor reminded me of Caleb. Wait—why was I thinking of *him*?

"Do you have anything to back that claim up?" I teased, forcing the sexy, stripping music teacher out of my head.

"I mean, I was talking about you, but I have no problems giving you *my* highlight reel. And for the record, besides your name, I wasn't going to ask you any of those questions." Tyson turned up the wattage on his smile, which made me melt. "I'm a morning person. There's a special place in my heart for country music. And I actually enjoy doing housework; it gives my brain a chance to chill." He ticked each point off on his fingers.

"Country music aside, with those amazing attributes, it's surprising you don't have women falling all over you. Tell me something about you that would make me pause."

"A beige flag? I can't use chopsticks to save my life, but I refuse to eat sushi with a knife and fork, so I ask the waiter to assemble them with a rubber band and wrapper like they do for little kids," Tyson said, deadpan.

I burst out laughing, and he did too.

"Did I pass the vibe check?" he asked, eyes twinkling.

Oh, you definitely *pass the vibe check,* I thought, losing myself in his impish gaze. Before I could answer, the timer buzzed.

Dammit. Surely, that wasn't five whole minutes.

Tyson stood up and held out his palm. When I slipped my

hand into his, he bent and brushed his lips across my knuckles. I sucked in a breath as my insides turned to goo.

"I hope I get to see you again," he said.

"Me too," I murmured, taking my hand back and cradling it to my chest.

With one last smoldering look, Tyson moved away. Grinning to myself, I circled my only *YES* on the feedback form, and turned it in, still bubbling with excitement as I met up with Amber.

She nudged me with her elbow. "I saw you and the last guy; it looked like you two really hit it off. He's *cah-yoot*."

"He was alright." I laced my arm through hers as we left the restaurant.

"So, any fun plans for Monday since there's no school?" she asked nonchalantly.

"Nothing but sleeping in and eating my feelings," I answered. "Why?"

Amber shrugged. "Just curious."

"Just curious" sounded a lot like she was hiding something else up her sleeve to spring on me. As I approached my car, an alarm went off further down the row. I looked up to see Tyson sheepishly disarming it. He shot me another easygoing smile.

Then again, maybe being ambushed wasn't so bad.

fourteen

"Thanks for the day off, MLK." On the couch, I burrowed deeper under my fleece blanket and picked up a book that had been on my TBR pile for years, grateful for another day all to myself.

Not much had happened on Sunday—which was more than okay after all the excitement in my life over the last couple of weeks—at least, not until the evening. I received an email from the speed-dating organizer saying Tyson and I had matched with one another, and it provided his phone number and email address. That meant Tyson had also gotten an email with *my* info—and had yet to use it.

It hasn't even been a full day, Zara! Give the man a break.

Just as I considered texting him first—and decided against it —the sound of the doorbell chimed throughout the living room. My shoulders tensed. Geoff?

He said he wouldn't show up again unannounced, but I didn't believe that for a minute. After all, he knew what he was doing when he sent the flowers to school...but who else could it be? Everyone knew that women of a certain age wouldn't bother answering the door, given our obsession with the true crime podcasts and documentaries we consumed regularly.

The bell rang once more, and again, I ignored it. My phone buzzed beside me on the couch cushion.

JULES

Open the door. We know you're in there.

Ah, Jules. I breathed a sigh of relief, but it was short-lived as another thought occurred to me. *We? Oh God, please don't tell me she brought Mom.*

I hadn't yet told my mom about the breakup and didn't know when I would. We hadn't spoken in a couple of weeks, but with the way the news had been spreading around town thanks to my friends, she'd know soon enough. I loved her dearly, but often it seemed as though we weren't merely on two different pages of a book, but two entirely different planets. Her obsession with the spiritual realm and a never-ending quest for enlightenment kept her head in the clouds, while my feet remained firmly rooted on the ground.

My phone vibrated with another text.

JULES

Bitch, IT IS COLD.

Curiosity getting the better of me, I threw the blanket off my legs and padded to the door.

"Well, *bitch,* you could have texted before—" I broke off mid-sentence as the door swung open to reveal my sister, the rest of our friends, one small child, and a car seat on my tiny porch. "Yikes, sorry! I didn't realize Rosario brought the kids. Hi, Mikey."

When I waved at the curly-haired toddler, whose mouth was encrusted with a pale pink substance, he gave me a bashful grin and stepped behind his mom's leg.

Ro shrugged. "They've heard way worse. Now, can we come in? This car seat is *heavy*."

"Uh, sure—"

"Thanks." Ro shouldered past me, Mikey hot on her trail.

I raised my eyebrow at the four remaining women, who all had their arms full of various bags and items. "So, why exactly are y'all here?"

"To help you rid the townhouse of the asshole." Jules held up two paint cans, then marched inside.

Ridding the townhouse of Geoff? Paint cans? I wasn't sure I liked where this was headed.

Max followed with another can in one hand and several full plastic bags—I made out boxes of garbage bags and paint brushes—in the other. "Hey, chickie."

"Um, hi?"

Amber carried a large white bag bearing Bojangles's iconic red-and-yellow logo, the aroma of the seasoned potatoes and flaky biscuits within making my stomach howl with hunger. She paused to peck me on the cheek before continuing inside. "Good morning!"

"Good morning to you, too."

Stevie brought up the rear, holding a small container filled with water. "Hi, Za-za!" She dropped her voice to a whisper. "This was all Jules's idea."

Can't say I'm surprised, I thought as I closed the door behind her. "Is that a fish?"

"It's a good starter pet." She raised the plastic container so that we were eye-level with a scarlet betta fish whose graceful fins flowed around it in the small space. "After reading lots of articles online and talking with the pet store employees, I've compiled some information and care instructions for you. Here."

Stevie ceremoniously handed over the fish, rummaged in the canvas tote on her shoulder, and produced a vinyl folder filled with a tabbed sheath of papers. "I also made a preliminary list of names you might like to go through. Sticky note on the first page."

I accepted the folder and opened it.

Finley
Finnegan
Neptune
Blaze
Sushi

I looked up at her. "Sushi? That just feels wrong."
Stevie heaved a sigh. "Max's suggestion."
"She's nothing if not on-brand."
"What are you two doing out there?" someone called from the kitchen. "Food's getting cold."
"Thanks for this," I said, lifting the fish.
"No problem." She patted her bag. "I've also got a small aquarium and some fish food to start you off."
We followed our friends' voices to the kitchen, where Amber was removing wrapped biscuits and cartons of Bo-rounds and cajun fries from the Bojangles bag and organizing them on the counter. Rosario bounced Mateo on her hip and tried to wipe Mikey's mouth with a damp paper towel while he jumped up

and down like he was riding a pogo stick. Max and Jules had set down their paint cans and whatever else they brought by the door and were chatting.

Despite my reservations, I took a moment to watch my friends before I joined the fray. My heart was so full, it felt like it might burst. The girls could irritate the hell out of me with their antics, but their hearts were in the right place. I wouldn't trade them for the world.

Max looked at me in the doorway. "What are you doing all the way over there? You look like you're about to cry or something."

"I was just thinking about how I have the best friends in the world." I set the fish—Finley? It didn't feel like a Finley—on the counter, walked over to Stevie, and looped my arms around her waist. I rested my chin on her shoulder.

She reached up and patted my head. "Compliments will get you everywhere."

I released her to accept the paper plate with a sausage, egg, and cheese biscuit and generous heaping of seasoned fries that Amber held out to me.

"To the living room!" Jules said, leading the way as if it was *her* house.

I quickly moved my lazy day stuff aside so everyone could fit on the couch. Back in his car seat, Mateo's eyelids grew heavy as he drifted off to sleep, and Mikey seemed content on the floor at Rosario's feet. When we were all settled, I voiced the questions that had knocked around my head since Jules announced the reason for their visit.

"I have to know—how did this come about? And just what does all of this"—I gestured to the bags and paint sitting back in the kitchen—"entail?"

"It came about because you said you wanted to wipe all traces of Geoff from the townhouse," Jules said matter-of-factly. "You don't need his energy funking the place up anymore."

"And we didn't want you to burn your house down," Ro said. "So here we are."

"'Here we are,'" Mikey repeated with a high-pitched giggle.

Ro let out a weary sigh. "He's in his parrot stage."

At this, Mikey crossed his arms over his chest and thrust out his lower lip in an exaggerated pout that looked eerily reminiscent of his mother's pouting face. "Mommy, I not parrot."

Amber leaned forward and tickled his pudgy tummy with an indulgent smile. "But if you were, you'd be the cutest parrot ever."

Max laced her hands behind her head and leaned against the back of the sofa. "We're gonna bag Geoff with a G's shit in trash bags and stick it in the garage."

"Then we'll move the furniture, tape some baseboards, throw some plastic down, and paint," Jules said.

"Ro, Mikey, Mateo, and I are leaving before the painting part, though. Too many fumes," Amber cut in. "But we're happy to help pack things up and do some painting prep."

Rosario tilted her head and made a face. "Speak for yourself. I only came for moral support and to fill you guys in about this weekend's girls' trip. Mikey, get your finger out of your nose."

I set my mostly eaten plate on the ottoman and made a "time out" sign with my hands. "Hold up—let's go back to the part about painting my house. Y'all just chose some random color and hoped for the best?"

Jules scoffed. "Hardly. In what universe do you think Stevie would ever let us do that? When I brought back that pink cashmere sweater I borrowed, I peeked in the hall closet where you keep a file of all the house stuff."

I narrowed my eyes. I knew it would have been smarter to give Amber or Stevie the spare key over my what's-yours-is-mine little sister. "When did you borrow my cashmere sweater?"

She made a bashful face. "Oops."

"Anyway," Max said, still looking like she was ready to take a nap, "we've got three cans of 'Serene Sage,' enough trash bags to fill all the dumps on the East Coast, painter's tape, and plenty of tarps."

"And *my* favorite part: matching coveralls," Stevie added.

I felt a lump in my throat as another wave of emotion washed over me. My girls had really thought of everything.

Max yawned, then got to her feet. "Alright, ladies, let's get this show on the road. I've got a hot date tonight with a super flexible Pilates instructor, and mama needs a beauty nap beforehand."

"Speaking of dates, we need to hear all about speed-dating." Rosario rocked Mateo's car seat with the toe of her shoe.

"Vroom vroom." Mikey held his hands out in front of him and jerked them around like he was driving a race car.

I reflected on my speed-dating adventure a couple nights earlier. My frustration with the parade of unoriginal men and Socially Inept John. An image of something about Tyson's smile as he stood beside my table filled my mind's eye.

"Oooh, from that moony grin on your face, it looks like it was a success," Jules said, leaning forward.

I exchanged a conspiratorial smile with Amber. "It may have been."

Standing next to the supplies she'd brought, Max clapped her hands. "And you can tell us all about it while we get to work." She bent and grabbed a couple of bags, then made her way to the stairs.

Stevie gave me a look and stood up. "We better follow her unless you want 'Geoff with a G is a dickhead' painted on your bedroom wall."

"You guys go ahead and get started. Ro and I will clean this up." Amber rose from the couch and gathered our discarded plates.

Rosario groaned. "Seriously? With these two, I clean enough at home."

Amber swatted her leg, which prompted Mikey to do the same with the monster truck in his hand, but a lot harder.

"Ow!" Ro yelped.

Hiding my grin, I followed Stevie and Jules's lead, grabbing a bag filled with painting coveralls and a box of trash bags.

"What are you going to do with Geoff with a G's office?" Stevie asked. "A home gym or cozy library would be nice."

"That's kind of cliché," Jules said. "You know what *isn't* cliché? A well-decorated guest bedroom for your little sister to crash in when she's between gigs."

If Jules and I tried to cohabitate, one of us wouldn't make it out alive. I needed routine and stability—I liked knowing something would be where I left it a week or a month later. Hurricane Jules would turn this place upside down.

"I'll think about it."

Max appeared at the top of the stairs, her hands on her hips. "Even better would be a sex room. You could put mirrors on the ceiling...install some lights to set the mood...ooh—a swing!" She pinched her fingers together and brought them to her lips, imitating a satisfied chef.

Jules stopped next to her, looking thoughtful. "I'm not mad at it. Especially if I can use it from time-to-time."

Stevie made a disgusted face. "Sharing a sex room with your sister is gross."

Jules rolled her eyes. "It's not like we'd be using it at the same time."

Well, I wasn't having any sex at all, so, if I did put a sex room in the house, at least *someone* would make use of it. Tyson grinning in the parking lot popped into my head.

When *was* the last time I had sex? Geoff had been gone a lot, and when he *was* in town, he made excuses about being tired or not feeling well. I swallowed the warning tickle in my throat.

"Um, I'll take all your suggestions into consideration, but I don't think it needs to be decided today."

"If I were you I'd make a decision quick, babe," Max said, tossing me a roll of blue painter's tape. "Use it or lose it."

fifteen

I didn't make the first move.

But neither did Tyson.

My friends' jokes and hard work at transforming Geoff's office into a gym/library/bedroom/sex room distracted me through late Monday afternoon. My preoccupation with scrubbing every ounce of my ex from my home continued even after they'd gone. I put the trash bags to good use, stuffing them with items I'd missed in my haste the night I dumped his belongings in the yard, and ended up with eight large black bags cinched tight in the garage. After setting up Blaze's aquarium—the temporary name felt better but still not quite right—and taking a shower, I was too exhausted to think at all.

By the time I returned to school on Tuesday, I'd given up on the idea of Tyson reaching out, or us seeing one another again, but that didn't stop me from replaying our quick date over and over.

As I sat in a rickety chair attached to a desk and ate lunch in my secret hidey spot, a small, forgotten storage room that probably hadn't been in use since *my* time as a student at the school,

I couldn't help but wonder if I'd done too much during our five-minute conversation. Too little? Had I been too abrasive? Clearly not, if we matched. So what was taking him so long?

The door to the storage room opened with a creak, startling me so that I nearly fell off my seat.

For the last couple of years, I'd been sneaking away to have lunch here on days I didn't want to chat with my colleagues. Enid Cartwright told me about it at her retirement party, and not once had I ever encountered anyone else.

Until today, apparently.

The intruder slipped inside the room, unaware it was already occupied since my little desk and chair were in a hidden corner out of view from the door. Holding my breath, I leaned around a dusty shelving unit and caught sight of a familiar, svelte figure cautiously closing the door behind him.

"Caleb?"

He jumped and whirled around, eyes wide. "Hey!"

"Hey," I answered, making no move to rise from my seat or invite him in. Enid had bequeathed this hidey spot to me, and besides, he had a whole empty music classroom where he could eat in peace.

"I come in here when I want a change of scenery," he said, reading my thoughts.

"I come in here when I don't want to talk to my coworkers," I said matter-of-factly.

Caleb's forehead wrinkled as he pursed his lips. "I'll leave you to it, then." He reached for the doorknob.

"No—wait." In all of our previous interactions, I'd acted like a basket case or been in some state of flight—not the best impression. Maybe if we had lunch together, I could show him I was a normal human being and not a walking neurotic mess. What would it hurt to share the space with him? "There's room for one more." I angled my head at the dusty, empty desk next to me.

"Thanks."

Caleb approached tentatively, as if I were a guard dog poised to snap. I didn't blame him. I kept eating my ham and Swiss croissant, but found my gaze irresistibly drawn to the lean thigh muscles rippling beneath forest-green corduroys as he settled into his chair and opened the rumpled, brown paper bag he'd brought. Slowly, he unpacked a Tupperware container of pasta salad, a napkin-wrapped fork, and a pack of Oreos.

He opened the cookies first and held the pack out to me. "A peace offering for disturbing your peace."

"I'll allow it." I plucked one of the chocolate sandwich cookies from the foil package.

Caleb took a cookie for himself. "So, it seems we have another elephant in the room—and I don't mean one of your students."

Unsure of what he was talking about and having just taken another bite of croissant, I raised my eyebrows in question.

"That night at Bella Cucina?"

A piece of flaky pastry lodged in my throat, launching me into a coughing fit. I grabbed the day's emergency Dr. Pepper to wash it down. "I'd rather not," I said when I was able to breathe properly again.

Caleb shrugged and pulled the top off his pasta salad. "Okay."

I stuffed the Oreo in my mouth and chewed, before relenting. "Did I make a huge fool of myself?"

"Define 'huge.'"

I groaned. "My friend suggested I take myself on a solo date, so I did, but then I got in my head about it. It's my favorite restaurant and now I can't show my face there ever again."

Another nonchalant shrug. "Screw what everyone else thinks. Good on you for going out alone—a lot of people wouldn't even dare. I've been going on a lot of solo dates myself lately."

Involuntarily, my eyes went to his left hand, devoid of any rings whatsoever, before traveling to his handsome face. I knew so little about Caleb McMahon beyond the fact that he was an engaging music teacher who moonlighted as a stripper and had a stacked ass. I supposed being married wouldn't be good for business.

Colleague, Zara. He's a colleague.

"Why? Don't you have, like, twenty stripper-brothers you could hang with?"

He wrinkled his nose. "'Stripper-brothers'? Seriously? And there are only twelve of us, thank you very much."

"*Fine.*" I rolled my eyes. "Why can't you go hang with one of your eleven stripper-brothers?"

"I *could*—I'm pretty sure you saw me with one at Bella Cucina—I just don't *want* to. I actually like doing things on my own. I'm an introvert."

I gave him a dubious look. "Get out of here."

"I am," he insisted. "I know what you're thinking, but I'm an *extroverted* introvert. Yeah, I'll shake my ass and give a lap dance with the best of them"—the temperature rose in the storage room as his words invoked a memory of him sitting in my lap on the night of the breakup party—"but I need a lot of alone time to recharge afterwards. I also think it's a holdover from being the oldest—and only boy—of five siblings."

"You have *five* siblings? And I thought it was rough having just the *one* younger sister," I muttered. Keeping an eye on Jules had been more than enough—I couldn't imagine doing that four times over.

Caleb held out the Oreos again, and I took another. "Nia, Josie, Vanessa, and Claire. Add in my parents, Angie and Felix, and it was a full house growing up."

"Well, that explains why you've got the magic touch when it comes to working with the students," I said.

"Maybe. My parents were really good about making sure I got to be a kid, and spent time with each of us, but of course, I ended up helping out with the younger ones more often than not. They wanted to try one more time for another boy to 'give me some backup,' but I begged them to stop." He paused and ate some pasta before continuing. "I love talking music with people of all ages and helping them learn to play instruments, but working with kids is the best. They haven't become disillusioned with the world just yet; they're just a bunch of tiny weirdos who won't hesitate to tell you your breath stinks or your shirt looks dumb." He glanced at his short-sleeved button-down covered with pink frosted donuts and frowned. "They said that today. I thought it looked cool."

I laughed. "Donuts *are* cool. I like it."

Caleb looked up, his face relaxing into a smile as he met my eyes. "I'm glad someone does."

A taut thread of tension thrummed between us, like a guitar string waiting to be strummed. It was nice to see this side of Caleb—the man behind the ass-less chaps, as it was. Learning that he was the oldest child in a big family shifted more puzzle pieces into place and gave me a better sense of who he was. Even so, there was definitely more to discover about Caleb McMahon, and oddly enough, I felt compelled to dive deeper.

Buzz. Buzz.

A vibrating phone broke the spell keeping us in suspension. Caleb inclined his head at where it peeked out of my lunchbox, which rested on an overturned bucket. "I think it's yours."

Flustered, I blinked rapidly, trying to get my bearings after... *whatever* that was. "Hold on—it might be Susie."

Oh. My. God.

My body felt warm and jittery like I'd downed three espressos, but sweet relief coursed through me as well. I'd *finally* heard from Tyson. Not only had I heard from him, he'd admitted he couldn't stop thinking about me. And he didn't *ask* if he could see me again—he said *when*. An attractive man with good banter, who knew what he wanted, and what he wanted was me? Yes, please!

"What?" Caleb's melodic voice sliced through my thoughts. "Walker get another pencil tip stuck in his ear? Duncan bring in his mom's menstrual cup?"

Cheeks warming, I shook my head and put my phone away even though I desperately wanted to send a reply to Tyson ASAP.

"It's nothing," I said. "So, tell me about your amazing musician skills. Don't you play a bunch of instruments?"

Caleb studied me for a moment longer, and I squirmed under the scrutiny. "A few. Guitar, bass, piano, and drums. I love to sing..." His words faded into the background as my mind strayed to Tyson's texts.

When can I see you again?

Expeditiously, Zara 2.0 declared. *How does tonight sound?*

Gosh, this all felt so weird. Breakup party notwithstanding, this was the first time I'd felt giddy about a man other than Geoff in fourteen whole years. Weirder still—and just a tad embarrassing—was to be in my mid-thirties with a crush on someone.

A *crush.*

"You should come sometime…you know, if you're interested," Caleb was saying when I tuned back in.

Uh-oh. I had no idea what he'd invited me to, but I'd learned my lesson after our last faculty meeting. "Thanks for the invite, but I've got a lot going on at the moment."

Caleb nodded, his brows knitting together. "Yeah. Sure. I get it."

I felt a pang of guilt, but it was past time for me to stop putting men's feelings ahead of my own. Zara 2.0 was determined to put her needs first.

When my phone vibrated again, I readily scooped it up, expecting a follow-up text from Tyson. What I found was the complete opposite.

SUSIE

U around? Hate to bother u on break but Buttercup broke free again & Rory just threw up in trash

"Crap!" I exclaimed, getting to my feet. I crammed my trash into my lunchbox.

"More nothing?" Caleb asked.

"Escaped hamster and a sick kid. Never a dull moment. Bye!" I hurried toward the door, then pulled up short, remembering my intention to break the pattern of running away from Caleb every time I saw him. Looking over my shoulder, I said, "Thanks for the Oreos."

"Thanks for sharing your secret spot." One corner of his mouth tugged up in a half-smile.

I ignored the flipping sensation in my stomach, no doubt an aftershock from the surge of adrenaline I got from reading Ty and Susie's texts, and smiled back. It said a lot that my students adored Caleb; kids could spot a shitty person from miles away.

"Maybe I'll see you here again sometime? But the entrance fee is *lemon* Oreos. Those are my favorite," I said.

The other side of Caleb's mouth lifted, joining the first, as he let out a full-bodied laugh. "Deal."

sixteen

Seated at a high-top table at Arcade Alley, a bar and pizzeria filled with tons of retro arcade games in Fallen Oaks' Old Warehouse District, I rolled my eyes at the screen. In my excitement about finally hearing from Tyson, I'd told the girls about our date…and instantly regretted it once the clichéd advice started rolling in.

Clichéd advice that hadn't let up in forty-eight hours. You'd think that I was going to a dinner party at the White House instead of going on my first first date in fourteen years.

My first first date in fourteen years. Jesus take the wheel.

After leaving the storage room two days before, I'd quickly sent Ty a message, letting him know I was available on Thursday, while trying not to appear too eager. When I arrived back at the classroom, the scene was a masterclass in chaos. Boxes and buckets containing Buttercup's favorite treats were turned on their sides, strategically positioned around the room. The kids were standing on chairs, pointing and shrieking every time they saw a flash of golden brown scamper by, and Susie kept diving on the floor like a WWE performer trying to take out her opponent. It took twenty more minutes, but we finally recaptured Buttercup, returned him to his cage, and placed a heavy dictionary on top.

Why the hell am I thinking about the class pets at a time like this?

"That color looks great on you."

Instinctively, I looked down at my oversized houndstooth coat, white turtleneck, and faux leather miniskirt before looking at the owner of the smooth voice who'd given me the compliment. It wasn't Tyson, but a man just as handsome, tall with a clean fade, cleft chin, and a cross dangling from one ear. *Well, hello.*

"Here by yourself?"

"Um, I'm actually waiting for someone," I said, tugging at the neck of my shirt.

He nodded slowly, then gave me a defeated grin. "Of course, you are. Have a great evening."

"Thanks."

When the guy walked off, I smiled to myself and replayed the interaction in my head. Over the last couple of weeks, it seemed like I'd been receiving a lot more attention from men. Had that been the case all along and I didn't realize it because I was so focused on building my dream life with Geoff? Honestly, I enjoyed the admiration, especially considering how long it had been since I genuinely felt desired.

"I'm feeling some serious déjà vu," a familiar, honeyed voice said behind me.

I turned around at the sound, warmth spreading through my chest. Tyson—whose last name I still didn't know—greeted me with a broad smile, his athletic frame clothed in a navy crewneck sweater and jeans. I got up and gave him a hug, registering the spicy, woodsy scent that enveloped him.

"You look wonderful," Ty said when we broke apart. "And I'm so happy to see you—it's been a *day*."

"You can say that again."

Beyond the initial texts planning our date, we hadn't exchanged many messages. I did know that Tyson worked in real estate and spent a good deal of his free time playing golf.

"How was school?" he asked.

"On a scale from a papercut to being chased by raging wild boars, a solid stubbing your pinky toe on a chair leg. I'm ready to blow off some steam."

Ty laughed. "You and me, both. Lucky for us, I think we're in the right place for that. Have you been here before?"

I glanced around the lively barcade. "I haven't. I feel like I've been missing out."

"No time like the present. What do you say we get a beer, some game tokens, and try to win one of those groovy lava lamps?" Ty inclined his head at the prize booth filled with electronics and stuffed animals.

Anytime I'd gone to a fair with Geoff and pointed out a cool prize or that the carnival games looked fun, he'd launch into a rant about everything being a money grab. *It's a scam, Zee. We could go get the same thing at the Dollar Store for what it's really worth.*

"I'm in."

It turned out Ty and I both had a competitive streak, which made for intense but fun gameplay. We competed in three rounds of air hockey—ultimately, I won, but I was fairly certain he'd let me—and a couple games of skeeball. We also went head-to-head shooting basketballs into hoops. I'm pretty sure Ty tried to let me beat him, but I was so bad that he couldn't *not* win.

"Should we claim our winnings?" He snatched the green tickets spitting out from the machine and added them to the bunch in his other hand. "I bet we have enough for something great."

"You think?" I asked skeptically.

"Guess we'll see."

We took our bounty to the prize booth, where an acne-prone high schooler sighed, took his time placing a bookmark between the pages of the thick book he'd been reading, and wearily rose from his stool. Ty and I exchanged a glance when he handed over the ropes of tickets and he began feeding them into the counting machine.

"What do you want, Zara?" Ty asked. "The lava lamp?" He pointed to where the toy sat high on the wall. "Or what about a foam dartboard?"

"That all-knowing eight ball looks pretty fun."

"You can't afford any of those," the booth worker said flatly.

Ty's brow furrowed. "Excuse me?"

"You can't afford any of those items. You only have 577 tickets. You could get a whoopee cushion. Or a miniature llama keychain." The employee tapped on the glass counter.

"A whoopee cushion?!" Ty repeated, sounding mildly offended. "Well, can I buy a stuffed rose?"

The teen shook his head firmly and pointed at a plastic sign on the wall behind him. *Prizes are earned. No purchases allowed.*

Ty dropped his voice. "Look, bruh, I'll give you..." He opened his wallet and peered inside. "Twenty bucks for the rose."

"Sir, I am not for sale." Frowning, the teen crossed his arms over his chest.

I choked back my laughter and put a hand on Ty's arm. "A llama keychain sounds great."

Ty looked down at me skeptically. "You sure?"

"Positive."

After the worker handed Ty the toy, he pointedly returned to his stool and reopened his book. Shaking his head, Ty cradled the llama keychain in his hands like it was a priceless piece of jewelry. "Zara...Zara...wait—I don't think I got your last name?"

"Whitmore." I giggled. "I don't think I got yours either."

"Haynes." He cleared his throat and held out his palms, an earnest look on his face. "Zara Whitmore, will you accept this llama as a token of my affection, even though I *smoked* you in hoops?"

"Tyson Haynes, you shouldn't have. I graciously accept."

As our fingertips brushed, a jolt of excitement zinged through me. I sucked in a breath and looked up at his face to see if he'd felt something, too, but his expression hadn't changed at all.

"You hungry?" he asked.

"Yeah," I said, masking my disappointment.

"They have great pizza, but we can go somewhere else if you want."

"Pizza's fine."

Once we put in an order at the bar and grabbed more beers, we sat at a high-top table near a Jaws-themed pinball machine. I put my new llama friend in the center of the table next to the napkins.

"I can't believe you insisted we get pineapple on the pizza," Ty said in disbelief.

"I didn't insist—you asked my preference, and I told you." I lifted my chin in the air, a smile tugging my lips up. "Besides, you can't talk. You ordered a side of ranch."

He scoffed. "Pepperoni pizza and ranch is a classic combo. Like fries in a milkshake, or ketchup on mac and cheese."

"Ketchup on mac and cheese?" I wrinkled my nose.

"Don't knock it 'til you've tried it."

"I think I'll just take your word for it." We lapsed into silence, which gave me the time to muster my courage to ask the question that had been on my mind since Tyson sat down across from me on Saturday night. "Why were you at speed-dating? I'm sure you can go anywhere and pick up women with no problem. Some of the other guys I met on the other hand…"

Ty shrugged. "My friend convinced me to do it. Because I put so much of myself into my work, I don't have a lot of time to date. And I keep striking out on the apps."

Oh no, Geoff vibes. When he *was* home, he would beg off from doing the things I'd been looking forward to because he "needed downtime" after work. Though Tyson's answer gave me the ick, I gave him the benefit of the doubt.

"What about you?" he asked.

How much did I tell him? *I discovered my boyfriend of fourteen years was cheating on me and my friends think the fastest way to move on is to find somebody new? After being in a dead-end long-term relationship, I don't know how the hell to put myself out there, so it was either speed-dating or die alone as a spinster, which I still might?*

"I'm newly single and figured it was a good way to ease back into the dating pool."

"Makes sense. I'm just glad you were there."

"I'm glad I was there, too."

We smiled at each other.

"So, Zara Whitmore, what would life look like with you?"

The question caught me off guard…but in a good way. Like how Amber suggested I use speed-dating to identify the qualities I wanted in a partner.

Life with Geoff had been static and kind of dull, which I didn't realize until after we were through. I prioritized his wants and interests over my own to keep the peace, and I now realized, to keep *him*. We'd gotten to a point where we didn't feel like a couple in love—just two people who'd invested so much time into a relationship that it made sense to keep patching it with duct tape and pretend everything would magically turn out great in the end.

I never wanted to experience that again.

"Ideally, life would be full of fun. Dance parties in the kitchen. The occasional date night. Discussing our favorite songs and movies for hours but it only feels like minutes. I know relationships aren't exactly fifty-fifty, but I want *both* of our needs and wants to be met." I tugged at the neck of my shirt again. "I guess I'm just…looking for a best friend…with whom I have great sex."

Ty nodded slowly, his eyes appraising me. "That all sounds amazing."

I gave a self-effacing shrug. "I thought it was pretty good. Now, it's your turn."

"Well, I've always wanted to be part of a power couple. My life is half black-tie galas and half hanging with my boys at the gym or on the golf course. My ideal woman would be just as comfortable in both places."

While I could envision myself in a floor-length gown holding on to Ty's tuxedoed arm, working out had never been my thing. Maybe that's why Geoff had found someone else whose it was.

"And I really value my independence. I need my space and time alone to recharge, so she should be fine on her own."

The alarm bells that tinkled in my head earlier were now full-on blaring. *She should be fine on her own. I need my space.* Was he basically telling me upfront to expect him to cheat? Was Tyson Haynes my ex in another form?

Is that why I was attracted to him? Because I'm apparently attracted to emotionally unavailable men who want a trophy wife? Universe, is this a test?

When a server brought our pizza over, I was relieved. Tonight was supposed to be about having fun and getting to know Tyson—*not* dredging up my past and reliving it.

We journeyed into more neutral territory while we ate, talking about our families, favorite travel destinations, and favorite foods. I even dipped the tiniest corner of a pizza slice into Tyson's ranch and didn't vomit.

After finishing his fourth slice, Ty wiped greasy fingers on a napkin and yawned. "I think I'm going to have to call it a night. I've got circuit training first thing in the morning."

"Oh."

I was surprised to find myself feeling disappointed. Our conversation over dinner had been so engaging that I questioned if I'd overreacted before. Tyson wasn't someone I saw myself with long-term, but maybe he could be a stepping stone. Without warning, my brain replayed the memory of Jules declaring I should have a one-night stand, closely followed by Max's suggestion that I turn what was formerly known as Geoff's office into a sex room. I pictured Tyson's wrists tied to bedposts with black silk ties, another tie acting as a blindfold while I tickled him with a long feather.

I swiped my hand across my forehead where beads of perspiration had gathered, wondering when the temperature in the arcade bar increased. My imagination already on overdrive, a tiny Max, Rosario, and Jules, dressed as sexy devils, appeared on my left shoulder in a puff of smoke. On my right, Stevie materialized wearing a white robe and halo. And Amber settled herself on the crown of my head, riding the middle of the fence per usual.

"Babe, you know the best way to get over someone is to get under someone else," Max said with a wicked grin.

Rosario kicked her feet back and forth. "Or at the very least, ask him, 'What dat mouth do?'"

"Ask if he has a brother!" Jules piped up.

"He's probably a serial killer." Stevie adjusted her halo. "The FBI says there are between twenty-five and fifty active serial killers in the United States at any given time. Don't get murdered, girl."

"This is more entertaining than any ratchet 90s talk show," Amber said.

I agreed with Imaginary Amber. If the group chat was pure chaos, this was five times that—and cause for making an appointment with a psychiatrist to boot.

I'm just going to do it, I told the figments of my imagination. *I'm going to be bold, step out of my comfort zone, and have my first one-night stand!*

The three little devils on my shoulder jumped up and down in glee, then broke into the cabbage patch, while Angel Stevie facepalmed and poofed away. When I shook my head, the other figures disappeared.

"Uh, Zara, you okay?" Tyson asked, a concerned look on his face. "You looked like you were in a trance or something."

"Oh, I'm just fine," I said quickly. I took a deep breath and tilted my head, giving him what I hoped was a coy, enticing look. "I was just thinking that the night's still young. We could, I don't know, maybe continue the evening elsewhere?"

Ty's eyes widened in surprise before his face settled into a reserved smile. "Okay. Sure."

We left the barcade, me with my prized llama keychain safely held in my left hand, and a pizza box with the remaining slices tucked under Ty's right arm. His other arm looped around my waist, where the weight of it felt alien.

It's because he's the first man to touch you like this since Geoff. That's all. It would be weird with anyone.

I shoved my discomfort down as Ty stopped in front of a flashy red Camaro. He set the pizza box on the car's hood and turned toward me, running his hands up my arms. I shivered as goosebumps erupted along my skin, even though I still wore my winter coat.

He grinned and rubbed his hands together before gently taking my face between them. My eyes grew large as his face neared, his full lips parting in anticipation.

Relax, Zara. Just go with it. You are a bad-ass—of course, Tyson wants you, Zara 2.0 whispered.

I am a bad-ass. Of course he wants me, I silently chanted as I closed my eyes. *I am a bad-ass. Of course he wants me.*

Ty's mouth met mine with the confidence of someone who had done this many times before. Meanwhile, I felt as awkward as a teenager on prom night who'd never been kissed. Where did I put my hands? Should I slide my tongue into his mouth or wait for him to do it first? Why didn't I sneak a Lactaid pill when he wasn't looking?

Fuck, Zara. Stop thinking!

I tried to block everything else out and give myself over to the moment—the way one of his hands slipped beneath my coat and crept toward my breasts, the taste of marinara and beer—but Tyson's words from before about valuing independence wouldn't stop echoing in my head. Things only got worse when Geoff's face superimposed itself over Ty's.

I ripped my lips from his and pushed him away, feeling like I was about to throw up.

"Tyson, I'm sorry—I...I can't." I took a step back, shaking my head. "I changed my mind."

His brows furrowed in confusion as he blew out a breath. He scrubbed a hand over his face. "No worries."

"It's just—"

"Zara, you don't owe me any kind of explanation. It's fine."

I searched his eyes for any hint of irritation or frustration, but only found kindness.

"Thanks." Even though I appreciated his chill response, my

stomach still rolled and tumbled like a clothes dryer. I wanted to get out of there as quickly as possible. "I did have fun tonight."

"Me too. Maybe we can do it again sometime?"

"Yeah," I said half-heartedly, inching away from the Camaro. "Have a good night."

He took a step forward. "I'll walk you to your car—"

"No, no, I'm good," I said. "I'm just right over there. And I've got Lawrence to watch over me." I held up the stuffed llama and awkwardly wiggled it.

Ty bit his lip, then nodded. "Okay, well…safe travels."

"You too." I waved, then booked it for my car.

I barely got in, locked the doors, and fastened the seatbelt before dialing Jules.

"Hi, Za-za. Date over so soon?" Jules hummed, and I heard a high-speed mixer in the background. "I'm guessing there were no sparks?"

"I tried. I really did." Sighing, I rested my chin on the steering wheel. "I thought I was making progress, but he kept giving me Geoff vibes."

"Ew." I pictured Jules wrinkling her nose. "We don't want Geoff vibes. We don't even want to *think* about Geoff."

"Exactly." I let out a groan. "Is it me? Something I do to attract these guys who just want a woman they can pull out and trot around to make themselves look more desirable?"

"Whoa, whoa, whoa—pump the brakes. You're only *just* getting back out there," Jules said. "This is your first date with someone new in over a decade, right?"

"Yeah, but—"

"No buts. Your problem is that you dig your heels in and stay in the same place for so long that you get stuck."

"I do not," I said, indignant.

"Geoff with a G, Zara. *Fourteen years.*"

"Okay, okay."

"So, the first guy you date after that asshole isn't the one you're gonna marry—fine. Pat yourself on the back for putting yourself out there, and then do it again for recognizing he's not what you're looking for. You'll forget all about him during our girls' trip this weekend. Even though it's *my* birthday, I'll make sure of it."

Jules was right; going on a date—and even the failed kiss—*was* progress. Three weeks ago, I hadn't even been able to look at Geoff's side of the bed without bursting into tears.

"Just think about it this way: when it comes to dating, you are a baby giraffe taking its first steps. You're gonna look awkward as fuck and fall on your face a few dozen times, but I'll be there to help you back up every single time," Jules said. "And eventually, you won't need me anymore."

"I'll always need you." Feeling a smidge better after a quintessentially Jules pep talk, I started the ignition and sat back. "Who else is going to cheer me on and humble me in equal measures?"

seventeen

When I woke up the next morning, a *Good Morning* text, courtesy of Tyson, awaited me. I couldn't help but breathe a sigh of relief to know he wasn't holding the way I'd abruptly ended our kiss against me. In response, I sent a text thanking him for a fun time and telling him I'd be busy celebrating my sister's birthday with friends all weekend, and he said he looked forward to catching up next week.

Now, back home after a half-day at school with Bubbles the betta fish—nope, not a Bubbles—squared away with a time-release feeding block, and my weekend bag haphazardly packed and stuffed into the trunk of Stevie's gray Subaru, I looked across my driveway. Max and Jules leaned against the side of the car, the string of a helium-filled balloon with *Happy Birthday* printed on it tied around Jules's wrist. When we all got to college, the two of them—Rosario, too, before she made things official with Edgar—became notorious serial daters with a steady stream of hookups. Even now, Max had a dating roster full of men and women, even though she'd only been in town for a couple of months, and Jules hopped from situationship to situationship as frequently as she changed her underwear.

Were certain people built for one-night stands? Was a one-night stand even what I wanted? Sure, I'd been with Geoff for a long time, but even during my short experience dating other people in college, the idea of having sex with a stranger and never seeing them again hadn't appealed to me.

Jules walked over with the birthday balloon bobbing behind her in the air. "How are ya, sis?"

"Ask me when I'm not in the middle of an existential crisis."

She nodded knowingly. "Been there. If you want, we can back out of the trip—"

"And ruin your birthday? Absolutely not." I resolved to stop wallowing and get out of my head for my little sister's sake. At least out of town, I didn't stand the chance of running into Tyson, Geoff, or anyone else I might know besides my friends. "How does it feel to be thirty-three?"

Jules stared up at her balloon, an unimpressed look on her face. "I want a refund."

I let out a genuine laugh.

"Anyone have an ETA for Amber and Ro?" Stevie asked. She glanced at her watch before joining us on the porch steps. "The whole reason we decided to leave at one was to avoid rush hour traffic."

"We still will—it's only a two-and-a-half hour drive to Wayside Beach," Max said. "Amber texted me right before she got to Ro's house, so they should be close."

"They better be," Stevie muttered.

"Look!" Jules pointed to where Amber's blue Honda Pilot cruised down the street.

Amber pulled her beast of a vehicle behind Stevie's and hopped out as soon as she cut it off. Rosario took a more leisurely approach. "Sorry, sorry, sorry! It's all Ro's fault."

"Of course it was," Jules said.

Rosario stuck her tongue out. "You try walking out the door with a kid wrapped around each leg like an ankle weight. My mom had to bribe them off with ice cream sundaes."

"Happy birthday, beautiful," Amber told Jules, giving her a huge hug. To me, she asked, "Mind if I use your bathroom?"

I dangled my keyring from my fingertips. "You know where it is."

"*Seriously?*" Stevie tossed her hands in the air. "At this rate, we won't get to Wayside until the Fourth of July."

"And *that* is precisely why I'm driving—well, besides being the designated driver by default," Amber said over her shoulder as she unlocked my front door. "This baby is sitting on my bladder, and I don't want to hear Stevie's mouth when I need to stop for a pee break."

Stevie opened her mouth as if to disagree, then snapped it shut.

"This would have been the perfect occasion for a party bus," Jules said.

"*Any* occasion's the perfect occasion for a party bus," Max declared. She slid on a pair of tortoiseshell cat-eye sunglasses.

Scowling, Rosario put her hands on her hips. "I get the party bus, you complain. I don't get the party bus, you complain."

"It's better to have two cars, anyway," I quickly cut in, stepping into the role of peacekeeper in Amber's absence. "That way we can splinter off and do different things if we want."

"And I'm more than happy to drive, but I'm taking *either* Rosario *or* Max," Stevie added. "I can't handle both of them in the same car for two and a half hours."

"I don't think even Jesus has the patience for that," I said.

"We're right here, you know!" Max exclaimed indignantly.

"How about this," I continued. "Me and Max in Stevie's car, and Jules and Ro in Amber's?"

Jules blew out a breath. "Crisis averted."

Amber exited the house and locked it after her. "What did I miss?"

Rosario rolled her eyes. "Apparently if Max and I ride down together, it'll summon the Antichrist."

"Sounds about right."

"Well, fuck all of you." Rosario flipped us off with both hands. After a beat she added, "Did you girls bring what I requested?"

"You mean the fugliest onesie ever?" Jules asked.

"Pretty sure my instruction was 'bring the most ridiculous one-size-fits-all onesie you can find,' but if that's how you chose to interpret it, okay."

From anyone else, the request would have raised eyebrows, but after knowing Rosario for more than twenty years, it was pretty tame. Unsure whether she intended for us to wear "the most ridiculous onesie" out in public, I'd opted for one that looked like a kangaroo, with a removable baby joey in its pouch.

When everyone nodded, Ro steepled her fingers like a diabolical villain. "Excellent."

"Uh, are you going to tell us *why* we had to buy these?" Stevie asked.

"They're for Jules's birthday slumber party." Rosario sighed. "We may as well do this now. Go ahead and get them."

Amber, Stevie, and I exchanged a look as if to say, *Do what now?*, but did what she asked.

"Do you know what's going on?" I whispered to Jules while grabbing the shopping bag holding my onesie from the passenger seat of Stevie's car.

"Not a clue."

Once we returned to the center of the driveway, Rosario instructed us to hold up what we'd purchased at her count of three. Jules held a white chicken number with yellow buttons up the front and a drooping red comb on the hood. Max and Stevie had shied away from animals—Max with a red-capped mushroom that looked more like a giant pale penis, and Stevie with a fleecy, hot pink jumpsuit covered with donuts. It conjured up a memory of Caleb sitting beside me in the storage room, complaining about the kids making fun of his shirt.

Amber's flying squirrel was actually pretty cute—the webbing under the arms almost looked like a cape. "It's got pockets," she said proudly.

"Well, mine has pockets *and* you can hold things in the diaper." Rosario wiggled the plastic hanger in her hand, sending the neon green suit swinging as she enthusiastically showed off the front. A silver spaceship was embroidered on one side of the onesie's chest, and the top of the hood revealed giant, black bug eyes and neon green antennae. But what made absolutely no sense was the white, fabric diaper. Had the onesie come with it? Or did Ro buy it separately and attach it? No matter how the diaper got there, it was completely absurd.

And undeniably Ro.

"Surprise!" she exclaimed. "We're doing a onesie swap!" She pushed her hanger into Amber's hand and held up a zipped plastic baggie with scraps of paper inside. "Since it's Jules's birthday, she gets first pick. The rest of us will choose our order from here." She shook the bag.

From the twist of Stevie's lips, I knew she wasn't a fan of the idea. I could understand where she was coming from—I'd bought something I, myself, wouldn't mind wearing, just in case —but none of them were *that* bad. All of us minus Jules selected a scrap from the bag.

"Jules?" Rosario prompted.

"I want the flying squirrel." She stepped forward to take the onesie from Amber.

"I've got number one," Max said, waving her number high over her head. She took her time walking around the circle, carefully studying each onesie like she was inspecting final looks before a dress rehearsal. In the end, she snatched Stevie's donut onesie. With her massive sweet tooth, I saw it coming a mile away.

Amber was next, predictably selecting the mama kangaroo, followed by Rosario, who chose the mushroom Max had brought.

That left just the chicken and diaper alien—neither of which would have been my first choice. But, if for some reason, we ended up going out in public in these, I'd rather be seen in the chicken suit.

Which left Stevie with the alien.

She folded her arms over her chest. "Nope. I'm not doing it. I refuse to be seen in a *diaper*."

"Oh, come on, Stevie. Everyone else is playing fair," Amber said.

Jules thrust out her lower lip and made it quiver. "Pwease? It's muh birfday."

"Yeah, Stevie," Max said. "It's her birfday."

"Then *you* wear it." Stevie raised a pointed eyebrow.

Max clutched a hand to her chest and backed away as if Stevie might snatch the onesie back. "But...donuts."

I glanced around the street, wondering if Mr. Cornelius or any of my neighbors happened to be watching through their blinds. Between the hot pink party bus rolling up in the middle of the night and fighting over silly, oversized pajamas, I wouldn't be surprised if a letter from my HOA showed up in my mailbox shortly.

"It's just us," Ro insisted. "No one else will see."

Stevie gave her head a firm shake.

Frustrated by her stubbornness, I held in a sigh. If we pushed her, Stevie would be crankier than usual. Not only would it make for a miserable drive down to the beach, but it was bound to cloud the whole weekend, which was, yes, about helping me embrace my inner twenty-something, but also about celebrating Jules.

"I'll switch," I said, holding out the chicken outfit, which Stevie grudgingly took from me.

"You're too nice for your own good, Zee," Jules muttered.

The story of my damn life…and the perfect title for my autobiography.

"I think being the chicken suits Stevie better, actually," Ro said sweetly.

Stevie narrowed her eyes, but before she could deliver a comeback, Amber opened her car door. "Time to get this show on the road before I have to pee again."

I held up the alien onesie. "You suuure you don't want this one? It's got a diaper."

Amber, Max, and Jules giggled, while Stevie just shook her head. As the tension dissipated, so did the weight on my shoulders. With each of us so absorbed in our own lives, who knew if we'd have another opportunity to gather like this again? If this was the last time, I wasn't about to let anything spoil it.

eighteen

osario had outdone herself.

After a pleasant enough two-and-a-half-hour car ride, during which Max regaled Stevie and me with celebrity gossip and stories from her time on set, we arrived at Rosario's family's house in Wayside Beach where an abundant spread awaited us. Trays of oysters on the half shell, crab cakes, and individual shrimp cocktails in martini glasses made me arch a brow. Fresh caprese salad, chicken skewers, and grilled veggies were also on offer—and that was just what I could see from the doorway. Two caterers in red aprons continued to pile food on the kitchen island counter.

While Ro, Stevie, Amber, and I grabbed plates, Jules and Max raced through the nautical-themed house in search of the best room. After a brief tussle over the master bedroom, which apparently featured a king-size bed and a giant picture window that overlooked the beach, it was decided that Jules and I would share it. Amber and Ro would share one of the rooms with two double beds, and Stevie and Max would share the other.

It was only once we stuffed ourselves and retrieved our bags from the cars—both Rosario and Max had brought enough luggage for a month away—that Ro revealed another surprise up her sleeve: she'd hired a team of massage therapists and aestheticians to come to the house. As I eagerly embraced Ro's generosity by indulging in a Swedish massage, detox facial, and manicure, all of my stressors from home melted away.

"How much do plastic surgeons make again?" Max asked under her breath. She removed the cucumbers from her eyes and sat up from where she'd been stretched out on the couch. "I think I need to ask Ro if Edgar has any available friends."

"Me too," I said. Call me a gold digger, but if marrying rich meant relieving the chronic tension in my shoulders and always feeling this relaxed, I'd consider marrying a man three times my age in a heartbeat.

Then again, Geoff made good money—though, not plastic surgeon money—and he hadn't spoiled me a fraction of the way Edgar spoiled Ro. Not that I begrudged Ro for it; she absolutely deserved it. But I would love someone in my life who regularly showered me with affection and little treats.

"Za-za?" Max's concerned voice brought me back to the present.

Blinking, I pasted on a fake grin. "Sorry. That massage was just too good."

Max studied me a moment longer before laying back down with a skeptical, "Uh-huh."

I glanced away, feigning interest in the massage therapists and aestheticians packing up their belongings. My relationship with Max was all light and laughter; we never ventured very deep like I did with Amber and Jules. Max was the friend I could always depend on to bring me out of a funk, and I wanted to keep it that way.

"So," Stevie began, turning to Ro with a raised eyebrow after the last aesthetician walked out. "What's next?"

Jules, who had mysteriously disappeared sometime while I was getting my facial, descended the stairs, bundled up like she was about to go hunt elk in the Arctic. She and Rosario exchanged a look. "I thought we could check out the beach."

Check out the beach? I looked out one of the expansive living room windows that faced the Atlantic Ocean, but given that it was nighttime, there was nothing but darkness. *What's there to see on the beach in January?*

Stevie wrinkled her nose. "It's wintertime. I thought we were just going to stay inside and enjoy the view while drinking cocktails."

Rosario put her hands on her hips. "If the birthday girl wants to go to the beach, we're going to the beach. Put on a jacket."

Stevie heaved a sigh. "If we must."

"Oh, we must." Jules's face broke into a wide smile. "I'll meet you guys down there. I've gotta do something really quick."

"What could you possibly have to do down here?" I asked, perplexed.

"You'll see." She wiggled her fingers in the air. "See you ladies in a bit."

Summoned by the birthday girl, the rest of us zipped up jackets and coats over the comfy clothes we'd changed into for the pampering. As soon as I opened the door, chilly, salt-tinged air stung my cheeks, but the cold was quickly forgotten as I took in the natural beauty ahead of me. With minimal light pollution, the sky dazzled with more stars than back home, scattered across the heavens where they twinkled like small celestial gems. The sky and ocean bled into one another seamlessly, but the ocean made its presence known with the relentless crash of choppy waves attacking the shoreline. The vast mysteriousness of it all left me feeling equal parts impressed and nervous— much like when I tried to imagine what lay ahead for me.

Not far from the end of the boardwalk, a fire blazed, a large driftwood log parked next to it. A small figure struggled with a second log across the sand.

"Is that Jules?" I asked.

"Yep," Amber said.

"That's one helluva fire," Max said. "How'd she do that? I thought she got kicked out of Girl Scouts after that one girl called her a coconut and she decked her."

A worried crease formed between Stevie's brows. "Is that even allowed?"

"What? Calling someone a coconut? I mean, it's not illegal, but it's pretty fucked up."

"I meant the fire! I know there are regulations about these things."

"Relax, Stevie," Rosario said, pressing forward to the front of the group and turning on her phone's flashlight. "I've been coming here for years; the neighbors are cool."

Stevie harrumphed, but kept close as we walked across the wooden planks of the boardwalk and onto the sand.

Standing right next to the fire, it was even more impressive. Or maybe it was just the sum of everything in the moment—the vibrant red and orange flames dancing high, blowing kisses of smoke up to the velvety night sky while the ocean roared in the background.

"Are we not concerned about fire safety?" Amber asked. "Like, what happens if the wind blows an ember into the grass?"

Jules brandished a bright red extinguisher. "I've got it covered."

"I'm not even going to ask where you got that or if you actually know how to use it." I pulled the neck of my coat tighter around me. "This is cool and all, but what are we doing down here?"

Jules set the extinguisher down and beamed at us. "Welcome to our ceremonial release ritual!"

"Our what?" Stevie said.

"Yeah, our what?" I repeated.

"Ladies, we are here tonight to let go of the shit that no

longer serves us," Jules announced. "Obviously, I had Zara in mind when I planned this little gathering, but all of us could use an energetic clear-out for sure."

Max shook her head in disappointment. "You missed a prime opportunity in calling this an 'energetic enema.'"

"'Energetic enema.'" Rosario snickered.

Ignoring the two goofballs, I leveled my gaze at Jules and narrowed my eyes. "This has Mom's fingerprints all over it."

Jules shrugged. "Well, I mean, that makes sense. I got the idea from her."

"Wait—you told Mom?"

I felt the muscles at the base of my skull tighten, the relaxed feeling from my massage flowing out with the receding waves. I wanted to tell my mother about Geoff in my own time, after I'd processed my feelings. I couldn't deal with the woo-woo bullshit that Yvonne Reed—who now went by the moniker "Infinity Love" and taught classes at a holistic arts and healing center—was bound to try and spring on me on top of everything else I was dealing with.

"*No, I did not tell Mom*—well, not about you, anyway. I told her Stevie was trying to get over a fling with a controlling, self-centered, pretentious freak."

"What the hell, Jules?" Stevie said. "Now your mom is going to think *I'm* the one dating narcissistic asshats, when it's *your* sister."

"Hey!" I exclaimed in indignation.

"Hey!" Amber held her palms up for peace. "Jules, I think this is a great idea. And you're right—we could *all* stand to offload some baggage."

She eased herself down next to me on the log. Following the pregnant woman's lead, one by one, the rest of us sat. Jules walked along the logs, handing out strips of blank paper, pens, and mini clipboards from a tote bag. How long had she been planning this?

"I don't have a big speech or any shit like that. I just thought we could take some time to write down whatever we want to release," Jules said. "A fear, worry, regret—anything you feel that's holding you back. Write it down." She dropped her tote bag and sat at the end of my log, her own small clipboard and sheet of paper in her lap. "You can start with something like 'I release...' or 'I let go of...' if that helps."

"I'm about to release this fart I've been holding in for ten minutes," Max joked.

"There's more room on the outside than in," Amber said.

"Yeah, and maybe Stevie can release that stick up her ass." Rosario laughed.

"What the hell did I do?" Stevie asked.

Jules frowned with an uncharacteristic solemnity. "This is serious, guys. If you're not up for it, you can go back to the house—but I hope you stay."

Max swallowed and nodded, a chastened look on her face. Rosario ducked her head guiltily.

We fell silent as we retreated into our thoughts, the crackle of the fire and thundering surf filling the air. The radiating heat chased away the cold wind that whipped my hair around my face. I stared down at the far too small blank strip of paper on my clipboard. Was it even possible to come up with just one or two sentences that encompassed everything I wanted to let go of?

My gaze lifted to the fire's core, entranced by the shapes moving in a graceful, fluid dance. It was in a constant state of motion and would continue to blaze bright and strong, so long as someone tended to it and kept the heart of it alive.

And then it hit me.

When we'd first started dating, Geoff stoked my fire by doting on me and promising to give me the future I'd always dreamed of—the big, fancy wedding, three kids, and way-too-expensive family vacations that we'd talk about decades later while holding hands in the nursing home. But it had been years since he'd made me feel like a priority, or even appreciated. And yet, the fault didn't just lay with Geoff; *I* was responsible for dimming my own light—neglecting my heart as I tended to his, allowing his fire to glow brighter at the expense of mine.

It was a sobering realization, and so completely obvious that I didn't know how I'd missed it until now.

Surreptitiously, I glanced out the corner of my eye at the girls on either side of me, wondering if they were experiencing their own epiphanies. On my left, Ro's chin rested in her hand as she stared out at the waves. On my other side, Jules furiously scribbled on her paper.

As I returned my gaze to the fire, my thoughts stayed with the women around me. Almost three weeks earlier, I'd been a smoldering pile of ash, but in the time since, they'd fed my soul with their daily check-ins, offbeat jokes, and solidarity. They'd built me back up with their unwavering support and encouragement. I almost felt like my old self—no, *better* than my old self. Like one of those pieces of broken Japanese pottery repaired with gold. There wasn't enough gratitude in the world for me to show them my appreciation, but now I needed to free Jules, Stevie, Amber, Rosario, and Max so that they could return to their own hearths and pour back into themselves.

I pulled back the sleeve of my coat and ran my fingertips over the scabbed tattoo on my wrist. It was time for me to embrace my strength, buck up, and fan my own flames.

"You guys almost done?" Jules asked softly.

Shit. I glanced down at my empty paper. "Just a sec."

"No rush."

I uncapped my pen and tapped it half-heartedly against my chin, waiting for the universe to synthesize my sprawling thoughts into one neatly wrapped package.

And then, the words flowed from my pen with a mind of their own.

I release all the thoughts and memories of Geoff that are keeping me from moving forward. I embrace my self-worth and let go of my need for external validation.

Taking a deep breath, I reread what I'd written. The universe had delivered the sentences to me, but committing them to paper was scary. It made my intentions real.

But maybe that was what I needed.

"Is everyone finished?" Jules asked again.

Heads bobbed up and down the logs.

"I was thinking we could share…that is, if anyone wants to? You don't have to."

We looked around at one another, daring someone to break the seal. Sure, we'd been friends for ages and supported each other through difficult times like the death of Rosario's abuelo and when Jules dropped out of college, but this was some *deep* inner work. At least, it was for me.

"I'll go. I, uh…I release wishing I was normal." Max cleared her throat and kept her eyes in her lap, a far cry from the larger-than-life jokester who wouldn't be caught dead in the same outfit twice. "I'm tired of comparing myself to others and feeling like I don't measure up."

Maxine Noelle Baldwin, who wore no less than three sparkly accessories at any given time and turned heads when she walked across a room, wanted to be *normal?* And who the hell was she comparing herself to? Max was in a league of her own. She'd always stood out—and not just because of her funky outfits. Max carried herself with confidence as she marched to the beat of her own drum, emitting an infectious energy that made others feel safe enough to embrace their own authentic selves. The fact that she looked damned good doing it was just icing on the cake. It was hard to believe that something I saw as a superpower was the very thing Max apparently wanted to get rid of.

Jules smiled. "Normal is fucking overrated."

"Preach." Ro raised her hands in the air and shook them like a tambourine player at a tent revival.

"I want to release feeling like I have to overcompensate," Amber said suddenly, folding and unfolding the paper in her hands. "I don't know if it was the same for you guys, but my parents drilled it into my head as a kid that because I was one of two Indian kids at school, I had to be three times as good at things."

Everyone nodded vigorously; oh, we *knew*. My grandmother had practically said the same every morning before dropping Jules and me off. *If you want to get anywhere, you have to be stronger, smarter, and work ten times harder.*

As a ten-year-old kid, none of that sounded particularly fun. And as a thirty-four year-old woman, I could attest that Grandma had a point, it *definitely* wasn't fun, and it wasn't fucking fair.

"I'm *tired*," Amber continued. "And I don't want my daughter to feel like she's not good enough as-is."

"Hear hear," Stevie said.

Rosario shared next, declaring that she wanted to release feeling like a bad mother because she sometimes missed her life before kids, and worried that she was "screwing them up for life."

The atmosphere around the fire, laden with confessions, was weighty, and Jules, Stevie, and I hadn't even said anything yet.

"I want..." The words seemed to catch in Stevie's throat, resulting in a pained look on her face as she wound the end of her French braid around her finger. "I want to open myself up to support from you guys...others...people." She let out a big exhale and looked at each of us in turn. "I'm with Amber; I'm tired of being the strong, independent woman who can do it all on her own. It'd be nice to have some help."

"Aww, Stevie." Amber dropped her head onto Stevie's shoulder.

"Yeah, okay, alright. Enough of that." She turned her face away and swiped at her eyes.

I was proud of her; allowing us to see a crack in her perfect facade was a huge step—not just for Stevie, but the group as a whole.

"Um, okay, I guess I'll go," Jules said. "I release the fear that I'm missing out on stuff and thinking the grass is always greener somewhere else." She gave a resolute nod. "I'm just gonna trust that I'm exactly where I need to be."

"You are," I said, patting her knee. Even if *I* understood that Jules would never find the peace and perfect life she was chasing outside herself it was something she had to figure out on her own.

The girls turned to me with expectant expressions. Swallowing, I looked down at my slip of paper, then up at my friends. "I think I'm going to keep it to myself."

Jules smiled. "That's alright."

When everyone else nodded in agreement. Jules stood up and faced us, her back to the flames. "Now, we're going to throw these into the fire, and while we do it, I want us to imagine all the icky, negative feelings associated with them transforming into ash and being carried away."

Amber, Stevie, Max, Rosario, and I stood and inched closer to the fire. Snapping my eyes shut, I squeezed my paper as tight as I could, then hurled it into the fire. On my right side, Jules took my hand in hers. On my left, Ro did the same. When I opened my eyes and looked around, we were all united.

It was a beautiful, poignant moment of connection—or it was, until Ro frowned and said, "Godammit, Max. Did you fart?"

"I told you I had to let one rip. It must have been that salad."

Before anyone could respond, the crunch of tires over seashells and wet sand accompanied by a bleating siren and the flash of red and blue lights startled the hell out of us. Shrieking, we let our hands fall and turned around to see two police offi-cers emerging from a UTV.

This is not *good,* my brain screamed. *Six women of color holding hands around a fire on the beach in fucking January? We'll be lucky if they* only *think we're witches.*

"Evening, ladies," said the first officer, a short, stocky man with a bulbous nose and pink cheeks. He swung the large flash-light in his hand around the circle. Rosario shielded her eyes while Stevie went pale and Jules just stood there wide-eyed. "Got a permit for this bonfire?"

"'Bonfire?'" Max crossed her arms over her chest. "This is just a tiny, little campfire."

Amber tried to catch Max's gaze and subtly shook her head.

Rosario stepped forward with her hands clasped demurely in front of her, a contrite expression on her face. "Gosh, officers, I didn't know we needed one. When I asked my Uncle Danny—that's Danny Briones, mayor of Wayside Beach—about it, he said we'd be fine."

"Mayor Briones is your uncle?" the second officer asked, shooting a look at his partner.

"Sure is!" Rosario exclaimed. "It's kinda late, but I can get him on the phone if you want."

The officers exchanged another coded look, uttering a whole conversation without a single word.

"Alright, here's the deal," the second one said. "Put out the fire, clean up the mess, and make sure you get a permit next time."

"Sir, yes, sir." Ro brought her hand to her forehead in salute.

The first officer's mouth twitched. "Have a good night, ladies. Don't get into too much trouble."

"Us? Never, officer!" Ro said. To avoid laughing, I turned my head.

The short officer looked around once more, then nodded at

the vehicle, and he and his partner left. We stood frozen, watching until they drove away.

And then we erupted into laughter. Well, everyone but Stevie. The poor thing was breathing hard, both hands resting over her heart.

"I told you so!" she gasped.

"'Sir, yes, sir?'" Max said. "Really?"

Rosario shrugged. "I was thinking on my feet."

"Guys, I asked for one thing." I held up a single finger. "One freaking thing."

Jules held out her wrists. "I don't see any cuffs."

"I'm glad they let us off easy," Amber said. "I thought I was going to have to pee myself and pretend my water broke."

This time when we burst into hysterics, Stevie joined in. I laughed so hard, tears formed in the corners of my eyes.

"But seriously, guys, I really do have to pee." Amber grimaced in distress. "A bitch is about to release her bladder right here on the beach."

nineteen

Aside from Max standing spread eagle in the doorway of her and Stevie's room to prevent Stevie from packing up all her stuff and driving home, the rest of the night after the fire was pretty chill. After changing into our onesies—I had to admit that being a diapered alien was more comfortable than I anticipated—we watched a couple of movies we'd adored as teens that hadn't aged well. I didn't know if it was truly because of Jules's ceremony, or simply because I was away from Fallen Oaks with the people who made me happiest in the world, but I felt as though the storm cloud that had recently been following me around had finally dissipated. If it *was* because of the fire release ritual, the real challenge would come once I was back home facing the triggers in my daily life.

Saturday morning, we cooked breakfast together while belting out 90s R&B hits we grew up with, using kitchen utensils for microphones and plowing through the case of Prosecco that Rosario brought. That afternoon, at Jules's request, we shed our onesies to go play mini-golf, where she, Ro, and Max passed a joint back and forth. I'm sure the other golfers got a kick out of seeing Max in her cherry-print swing dress and layers of crinoline, squatting down as she sized up the hole in a giant clown's mouth, only to stand up and repeat the process three more times in her pot-induced haze. Our golfing excursion came to a close not long after when Jules's wild swing nearly took out a toddler. Back at the house, we watched *Never Been Kissed*, another childhood fave...which also hadn't aged well.

"Did all of us collectively have terrible judgment and/or bad taste?" I asked after turning the movie off. "Maybe that's why we click so well."

"It was a different time," Rosario replied.

"Pretty sure student-teacher relationships have always been looked down on," Amber said.

Evening rolled around and we ate leftovers from the night before. I was content to return to rotting my brain with TV, but Ro couldn't stop talking about Sandbar Landing, a shopping and entertainment complex with lots of options for nightlife. When Jules and Max jumped at the idea, Amber, Stevie, and I figured we should go to keep them out of trouble.

Which is how I ended up sitting on the closed lid of a toilet, wearing the Bad Decisions Dress while Max glued fake lashes on me.

"There!" she said, stepping back to admire her handiwork. She'd traded her mini-golf outfit for another form-fitting wiggle dress and enhanced her makeup with small crystals around her eyes. "Beautiful! Not that I can really take credit for it—your bone structure is to die for."

"Thanks." I stood up and studied myself in the mirror mounted over the sink. With expert hands, Max had spent an inordinate amount of time painting my face for the night out. Even her worst effort would be better than anything I could do if left to my own devices.

Her reflection appeared behind me and she sighed. "I can't help but be a little jealous of you, Zee."

"What?" I turned around and stared at her in disbelief. What on Earth could make Maxine Baldwin jealous of *me*?

"You got your world rocked by this Geoff situation three weeks ago and you've already bounced back. Cecilia's heart attack was three *months* ago, and I'm still shaken up." She shuddered.

"That's totally understandable, Max," I said gently. "Cecilia's your favorite person in the world. You thought you were going to lose her. It took me losing Geoff, albeit, in a different way, to realize he hasn't been that person for me in a long time."

Max shook her head. "But you've also got Jules in your corner. If someone even blinks at you the wrong way, she'll pick up a baseball bat and beat their ass. I've got...*Nico*." Max's nose wrinkled at the mention of her older sister, who was her complete opposite.

"And Jules would do the same for you, too. But the difference is you don't need her—you're Maxine fucking Baldwin, chaos goblin and costume designer to the stars." I grinned. "I envy *you*. Your courage to leave everything you knew to chase your dreams in New York. The way you're just so effortlessly glamorous and sure of yourself. Meanwhile, I'm seriously the least interesting woman in our group."

"Oh, don't you fucking dare." Max draped her arms over my shoulders and met my eyes in the mirror. "Zara, you are the heartbeat of this group. It was *you* who inspired me to apply to Tisch and helped me with my application. It was *you* who drove to Wake Forest at four in the morning and held Rosario's hand when she went to the emergency room for her appendix."

I shrugged. "She only called me because Amber was out of town."

"So fucking what? You were there for her and it still counts. What I'm saying is, if you weren't here, we wouldn't be us. So shut your trap."

I smiled and gave one of her arms a squeeze. It seemed that

the release ritual didn't have the immediate magical effect that Jules thought it would. It did, however, force us to bring our shadows into the light and name them so we could begin the process of letting them go.

"Uber's here!" Jules burst into the bathroom in a tiered maxi dress. "Carlos in a black Ford Expedition."

We followed her down to the living room where Rosario perched on a barstool in a skintight leopard print dress, holding her phone at arm's length in front of her.

"Mommy misses you both so much," she cooed. "Mikey, *Mikey*, be nice to your brother. And be good for Daddy." She waved at the screen animatedly. "Okay, press the red button. Top of the screen." The waving grew less enthusiastic. "The red button, Mikey. Right there—good job! No…no…you had it—"

She dropped her arm as the call ended abruptly, leaned back against the counter, and addressed us. "You bitches ready to go ham?"

"Uh, *duh*," Jules said. "*I'm* the one who told everyone the Uber was here."

"Ooh, Zee's wearing the Bad Decisions Dress again. We love to see it," Amber said, slipping her purse strap over her shoulder. "Get our money's worth, girl."

"I told you, I'm happy to share the wealth." I spun around, making the jewel-toned fabric ripple along my body.

Amber patted her round stomach. "Maybe once the bub decides to evacuate the premises."

"Can we continue this conversation outside?" Jules asked, firmly propelling us toward the front door.

"Just a heads up—I'm feeling a little tired so I'll probably come back earlier," Amber said.

"Me too," Stevie added.

Ro pulled a face as she climbed into the idling car. "Party poopers!"

In the driver seat, a young guy wearing a bunch of silver

chains and pearl necklace, looked up as Jules sat in the passenger seat and the rest of us filed into the back after Ro.

"Y'all look nice," the driver said.

Jules preened. "Thanks, Carlos!"

Max leaned forward between the driver and passenger seats. "It's Jules's birthday, and Zara here"—she jerked her head in my direction—"is super single."

Carlos slowed at a red light and twisted in his seat to face Jules. "Happy Birthday!"

"Thanks," she said again, batting her lashes.

Carlos's eyes found mine in the rearview mirror. "How is *super* single different from *regular* single?"

Max turned around, her eyebrows raised, seemingly forgetting that she was the one who'd bestowed my current status upon me.

"Well, um, right now I'm focusing on being my best self and catching up on lost time with my girlfriends. I'm not looking for a relationship."

Carlos jerked his chin up. "Cool."

"So, Carlos, where should we go?" Rosario cut in, thankfully steering the conversation in a different direction.

"Well, I mean, it's only nine; it's pretty early," Carlos said. "I'm not even sure what's going on now since me and my boys don't head out 'til eleven."

"Well, we're old," Amber said simply.

"Will you stop saying that?" Stevie hissed.

"Humor us, Carlos," Rosario said.

As he drove through the small city of Wayside Beach, the driver gave us a brief rundown of a few different clubs only a couple minutes' walk from our drop-off point.

"You seem very knowledgeable," Stevie said.

"I grew up here." He pulled to a stop in the busy parking lot and handed Jules a black business card. "This is my number. Call when you're ready to go back and I can take you."

Max clutched her hands to her chest. "Our hero."

We got out of the car, and I waited until Carlos drove off to snatch the card still dangling from Jules's fingers. "I wonder how many women he's given this too."

Jules snatched it back and stuffed it into her crossbody purse. "It's his job, Zee."

"First stop: the daiquiri bar!" Ro exclaimed, speed-walking in her heels. "Last one there buys!"

"How is it that she's faster than me and I'm in flats?" Jules complained as we hurried after her.

"Don't forget she did track," Amber said. "Maybe we should take it easy tonight—some of you have been drinking a lot today."

"Okay, Mom." Max rolled her eyes. "We can hold our liquor. We'll be fine."

Amber harrumphed but didn't say anything else as we walked into Beachy Keen Daiquiri Bar. Though I didn't say anything aloud, I agreed with her. We'd been lucky so far, but usually when these girls drank for an extended period of time, shit went sideways. One time, Jules threw a drink in Max's face, and another time, Stevie—responsible, cautious *Stevie*—bounced off a bush and somehow rolled into a patch of poison ivy.

In the brightly lit bar adorned with tropical decorations and fake palm trees, we sampled all sixteen flavors of frozen alcoholic slush, forgetting what some of them tasted like and trying them again. Poor Amber didn't have much of a choice—for non-alcoholic options, it was only Strawberry Sipper or Tangerine Tease—but she was a good sport through it all.

She raised her frosty cup in the air. "To decades of friendship behind us, countless more adventures ahead, and a bond that only gets stronger with time. Love you girls to the moon and back."

"Chin chin," Rosario said heartily.

"Love you, too, Amb."

We all clunked our plastic cups against one another, then sipped slowly to avoid a brain freeze. The bar contained giant Jenga and giant Connect Four, so we battled one another before joining—and failing miserably—a limbo contest.

"I'm bored," Ro whined after a while. "I didn't put on *this*"—she gestured at her dress—"to play Jenga. We could do that back at the house."

I hid a yawn behind my hand. "Not gonna lie, the house sounds pretty good right about now."

Ro wound her arm around mine. "No, no, no. We haven't even gone dancing yet. You wanted to go dancing, right, Jules?"

Jules nodded, her eyes bloodshot as she slurped the daiquiri remnants in the bottom of her cup.

"See?" Ro wheedled. "Can't let the birthday girl down!"

Stevie glanced over at Amber, who shrugged in response. She turned back to Rosario. "One club. *One.*"

"One's all we need, babe," Ro slurred.

After bidding *adieu* to the bartenders who'd good-naturedly provided us a ridiculous amount of samples and shouted encouragement during the limbo contest, we ventured to Quicksilver, one of the clubs Carlos had described. The interior was sleek and modern, filled with metallic decor and reflective surfaces that bounced vibrant neon light all over the place. We grabbed drinks and made our way to a dance floor made of clear cubes, the club thumping with deep, pulsating beats.

Despite the blaring music and flashing lights, my yawns increased in frequency and I felt heavy on my feet. When I looked around, I saw I wasn't the only one. Stevie's face was pinched like she was in pain, and Rosario was swaying back and forth in place even though this had been her idea. Jules and Max held hands as they danced, though it seemed more like they were using each other for balance rather than enjoying themselves. Amber was seated on a bar stool, her head propped in her hand, eyes drifting shut. We made a sad bunch.

"Hi, laaadies," cried a server balancing a tray of cloudy, pale yellow shots. They nodded at a table of preppy white guys who looked like they belonged on a golf course somewhere. The men promptly waved. "Those guys said you looked like you needed a pick-me-up."

Max let out an offended gasp.

Rosario shrugged and stepped toward the server, her hand extended to take a drink. "I'm not gonna turn down a free shot."

Before her fingertips could graze the glass, Stevie reached out and slapped her hand.

"Ow!" Ro jerked the hand back, scowling. "What's your problem?"

Instead of answering, Stevie made a shooing motion at the server. "We don't know those men from Ted Bundy. Accepting those drinks is how we end up the stars of a Lifetime movie or a true crime podcast. Not on my watch."

Fully alert now, Rosario glared at her. "God, Stevie, give it a rest. It's okay to let loose and have fun sometimes."

Stevie's head reared back as if she'd been hit. "Excuse me? You've been loose all day. *I'm* the one trying to keep us safe."

"Um, I'm going to just…" The server carefully raised the tray and made a hasty exit in the direction of the men who'd apparently sent it.

"Bye bye, shots," Max said sadly.

"No one elected you Captain Save-a-Ho, *Stephanie.*" Ro planted her hands on her hips. "We all made it this far, no worse for wear."

"That's because of me, and I *never* get any thanks for it." Stevie's voice grew louder. "You're just mad because it's not so easy to boss us around anymore. You took charge when we were kids, but things have changed. You think we haven't peeped why you're throwing money around?"

"Fuck. Should we step in?" I whispered. I glanced to my left to find Max dancing in her own little world as if a bomb wasn't detonating right in front of us. "This is the Corn Dog Incident all over again."

Max threw her hands over head and continued to flail around to a rhythm that apparently only she could hear, because she was *not* on beat with the song. "I'm not stepping in *shit*."

"Seriously?" I asked louder. I turned to my right, where Amber watched Stevie and Rosario with a worried expression. Jules's brows were furrowed. "Are we just going to let this happen?"

"I'm going to the bathroom." Rosario spun on her heel and nearly fell over.

"Thank God," I breathed. Both women needed a time-out.

"Go ahead and do coke in the bathroom, then." Stevie tossed her hair over her shoulder. "But don't come crying to me when you get tossed behind bars."

"This isn't *Brokedown Palace*. We're not in fucking Thailand, Stevie," Ro snapped.

"She couldn't think of a more recent reference?" I whispered. "And what the hell are they even arguing about *now*?"

"I'll go after her." Amber slid off her stool and took off after Rosario, once again no match for her fast pace.

I watched Max bop over to Stevie and try to get her to dance with her. Stevie shook her head, hands fluttering in front of her as she gestured angrily. I couldn't make out what she was saying, but it couldn't be anything good.

Jules threw her hands up in the air. "Jesus Humperdink Christ on a biscuit. I just wanted to dance. Maybe it's time to call it a night."

"Good idea," I said.

"I'll text Carlos." Jules fished her phone out of her purse, tapped out a message, then paused. "He says he'll be here in fifteen."

"Can we keep things on ice for that long?"

"Yeah. We'll just keep them apart. I've got Stevie; you take

Ro. Fuck, I'm too drunk for this." She ran a hand through her hair.

"You're surprisingly coherent."

"Why, thank you. Uh-oh, they're coming back."

I looked in the direction Jules indicated to see Rosario and Amber returning from the bathroom. In accordance with our plan, Jules drifted toward Stevie and Max. I met the other two girls halfway.

"Jules texted Carlos. He's on the way."

Thank goodness, Amber mouthed. I expected pushback from Ro, but she shrugged with slumped shoulders.

"Fine," she said wearily, plopping down on a vacant stool.

"Amber, you want to sit?" I gestured at the stool next to Ro's.

She shook her head. "I could use some fresh air. I'm going to see if the other girls want to wait outside too." She met my eyes with a meaningful look.

Once they all exited through the front door of the club, Ro scrubbed her hands over her face. "I just wanted to have fun this weekend, Zara. Do you know when the last time I had a full twenty-four hours to myself was? Because *I* don't. And Edgar and I need space; we can't stop arguing and it's gotten to the point where we can't hide it from the kids."

Aha! I knew that blow-up was about more than the unsolicited shots. Leave it to Jules to break the group with her woo-woo. But that fire didn't exacerbate anything that wasn't already there.

Before I could open my mouth to reply, Rosario barreled on. "I barely recognize myself anymore. We've been talking about you 'embracing your inner-twenty-something' and doing all these fun things, and all I can think about is how *my* life has done a complete one-eighty."

"You're still your sexy, life-of-the-party self, Ro, and we love you for it."

"Do you?" Ro asked earnestly. "Never repeat this to anyone,

but Stevie really hit a nerve. *I* used to be the one to organize things and bring us together, but now the kids take up all of my time, and you're doing things without me. I don't want you to forget about me." A tear slipped down her cheek and she swiped at it, as if embarrassed.

And now her throwing money around—this trip—made sense.

I placed a hand on her knee. "We could never forget you, Ro—you're the one who brought us all together way back when. But life is just one change after another; the only constant is yourself. What are you doing to stoke your fire?"

Rosario looked at me with a puzzled expression. "Huh?"

"What are you doing to practice self-care? Nights out where you get white girl wasted won't do much in the long run. You need steady, nourishing stuff like short walks outside...or journaling for a few minutes each day. Maybe finding a hobby."

She sniffled. "I haven't heard anyone say 'white girl wasted' in ages."

I grinned. "That should tell you just how long it's been since I've partied my face off."

"I love Edgar, Mikey, and Mateo—I really do."

I patted her knee again. "No one's ever questioned that."

"It's just hard," she said in a small voice.

"I can imagine."

The door to the club opened and the upper half of Jules's body folded around it. She waved us over.

"Looks like our ride is here," I said. "Give me a hug before we head out."

When we hopped down from our stools, I wrapped Rosario in the tightest embrace possible. "Take a deep breath," I said. It was a trick I used with my students during times of upset. Ro froze at first, then relaxed in my arms, before I felt her chest expand and contract. "That's good. Another one."

Ro breathed deeply again. "Thanks, Zara." She stepped away

and tucked a few loose strands of hair behind her ear. "You know, there's another constant in my life."

"Oh?" I asked as we walked toward the exit.

"Knowing I can count on you. It's why all of this"—she waved her hand at the club around us—"has been so important. I might not be able to come to every tattoo appointment or hang out at your house on short notice, but I want you to know you can count on me, too."

"I appreciate that, Ro. I love you."

"Love you too." She sighed. "I guess I should apologize to Stevie, huh?"

"That's a good idea…but maybe when you're sober."

"Do I look like a mess?" Though Ro's eyes were red-rimmed and puffy, her mascara was only slightly smudged. Dislodged from its sleek bun, her hair fell in disheveled strands around blotchy cheeks streaked by tears.

"No more than usual," I said with a grin. "That waterproof mascara is doing the Lord's work."

Outside, Carlos's Ford Expedition waited with the rest of the girls already seated inside. Stevie sat in the rear back corner and stared out the window, as far as she could get from the remaining seats. After Rosario got situated in the passenger seat, and I buckled in next to Jules, Carlos shook his head and pulled off. "You're lightweights—it's not even midnight."

A quick glance at the screen on the dash revealed he was right; it was only 11:15.

"Okay, Judgey McJudgerson," Max said belligerently. "You don't know our lives."

"Someday, Carlos, you will learn that once you're over thirty, you can either day drink or night drink, but you can't do both. Isn't that right, Ro?" Amber said. After a beat with no response, she tried again. "Ro?"

Within a mere two minutes into the journey home, Rosario had nodded off, her head resting peacefully against the glass.

twenty

By the time we got back to the beach house, Max, Amber, and I were the only ones still awake. After rousing everybody and saying goodbye to Carlos, we managed to get everyone upstairs and into their respective rooms without injury. In Amber's room, I unbuckled Rosario's strappy heels while Amber pulled back the covers of her bed. With teamwork—and a firm grip because she kept flopping around like a limp noodle—we tucked Ro in.

"Thanks for helping," Amber whispered as we gazed at her. "I'm going to call Dwayne and head to bed, myself. Have a good night."

"You too."

Emotionally and physically exhausted, I wandered back into the room I was sharing with Jules, ready to collapse on my side of the bed. Normally after being out, I preferred to shower before getting into bed, but tonight, I'd be lucky if I even took off my dress. But life had other plans. Apparently powered by a second wind, Max and Jules were stretched across the king bed, still in their clubbing clothes, giggling at something on Jules's phone.

"What are you two looking at?"

They jumped, and Jules clutched the phone to her chest. "Don't get mad."

Warning bells rang in my head. *Don't get mad* is exactly what Jules had said right before handing me the two halves of the glass unicorn sculpture she'd stolen from my room and broken when we were kids. It was also what she said after borrowing my favorite leather jacket and spilling nail polish on it a few months earlier.

"If you start with that, she's *definitely* gonna get mad," Max said.

I glared at them. "I repeat, what are you two doing? You both look guilty as hell, and I just want to go to sleep."

Jule's uneasy gaze slid to Max before she blurted in a rush, "I kinda, sorta, maybe created a profile for you on the WooMe dating app last weekend."

I blinked at her, the words taking time to sink into my alcohol-addled brain. But when they did, the effect was instant. My chest tightened as blood began to pound in my ears. "You did WHAT?"

Jules held up her hands. "Hear me out—you said you weren't ready to move on *then*, but I wanted things to be ready to roll when you finally decided it was time."

I took a menacing step toward the bed, ready to throttle not only her, but Max as well, just because she happened to be there and because I *knew* she was somehow involved.

Stevie showed up in the doorway in a flannel pajama set, apparently having caught her own fresh burst of energy. "Max, there you are!" She paused, taking in the vibe of the room. "Uh-oh. What did I miss?"

"Jules created a profile for Zara on WooMe without telling her," Max explained.

"Oh my God!" Stevie exclaimed. "Has she been messaging men as Zara?"

Jules frowned. "No! What do you think this is—a Netflix rom-com? Who has time for that in real life?"

I'd moved past questioning *if* I wanted to murder my younger sister to *how*.

"Wanna see your profile?" Max asked.

"*No*," I said firmly. "I do not. Delete it now."

Jules hesitated. "You sure? I think I did a pretty good job on it."

"You did," Max reassured her.

"Well, I want to see." Stevie walked past me into the room, took a seat on the bed, and crossed one leg over the other. With Rosario conked out in bed, Stevie's good humor had clearly returned.

"Seriously?" I asked.

Ignoring me, Jules handed over her phone.

"'Loyal and caring teaching assistant who loves to unwind with craptastic reality TV,'" Stevie read. "'Big fan of pop music and impromptu car dance parties. Looking for someone to sweep me off my couch.'" She looked up, impressed. "That last line is really clever."

Jules patted herself on the back. "I thought so, too."

I had to give it to her—the profile wasn't half-bad, though "craptastic" wasn't a word I'd ever use, myself. Maybe once Jules got tired of house-sitting, she could give crafting dating profiles a try.

Stevie wrinkled her nose. "She sounds like a homebody."

"It's not far from the truth," Jules said.

"Really, guys?" I asked.

Stevie scrolled through the profile again. "You chose some gorgeous photos. Wait—this is from Amber's wedding. I *know* I was in this one. Did you crop me out?"

Jules quickly snatched the phone back from Stevie. "Za-za, I just wanted to help. But I can delete the account if you really want me to." She wiggled the device in the air. "But you have some interested men. Forty-seven, to be exact."

Forty-seven interested guys? I didn't even think I knew forty-seven *people*, and that many men were interested in me?

Jules let the phone hang loosely between her thumb and forefinger. Even though I was still heated with her for setting up the profile, curiosity got the better of me. I grabbed the phone and sat down beside Stevie. After a deep breath to steel myself, I looked down at the screen.

The main profile photo had been taken at a cousin's destination wedding in Tulum two years earlier. Jules and I had been goofing around, and she told me to pose like a free-spirited magazine cover model. In response, I grabbed the trunk of a nearby palm tree and threw my head back, lifting one leg to show off a strappy sandal. My basic info was superimposed on the bottom. *Zara W. 34. Teacher.*

"Look, I'm not making any promises about keeping this, but what do I do?"

Was this how an alien visiting Earth for the first time felt as they tried to figure shit out? Dating apps hadn't been nearly as widespread before I started dating Geoff; back then, people were actually ashamed to be seen on them.

"It's easy peasy," Max said. "If you like the guy's picture, swipe right. If you don't, swipe left. It's like a catalog of men. A *true* beefcake buffet."

Stevie frowned. "Don't they have bios like hers? Shouldn't she read them?"

"No one reads bios," Jules scoffed. "But I knew if Zara made a profile, she'd have one."

"So would I," Stevie said. "And I'd read them, too. How else do you find someone with substance?"

I tuned them out and tentatively started checking out profiles, taking time to skim the bios. A lot of profiles didn't have one, or if they did, it only consisted of one or two lines and was riddled with emojis.

It took only a minute of scrolling to come to the conclusion that I was doomed.

I lost count of the number of men who had clearly visible wedding rings in their photos and proclaimed themselves "ethically non-monogamous." I was shocked at how many couples were "looking to add to their fun."

And then there were the weirdos.

So many weirdos.

Like the profile where the guy had five photos—but every single one showed his lap beneath an Audi steering wheel in a different outfit.

"Is he at least wearing gray sweatpants?" Jules asked.

Or the profile that featured a million photos of a black-and-white cat named Julius, with the accompanying bio written from the cat's point of view.

"I don't get it," Max said. "Is he just a super proud cat dad, or should we call the local humane society?"

"'Fun fact about me: I make sourdough,'" I read aloud from another profile. I paused and looked up at Stevie, Max, and Jules. "Who can't these days?"

"You!" they chorused.

I frowned. "How was I supposed to know if you seal the jar too tightly, the starter will explode? Do you know how long it took me to sanitize my kitchen?"

Still, I kept swiping. Not because I thought I'd find the great love of my life, but because I wanted to see just how weird things could get.

And boy, did I get my wish.

"Oh no." I gasped and almost dropped the phone.

The picture dominating the screen contained a familiar pair of pale green eyes sparkling with warmth and mischief as if they held a trove of secrets. Eyes I'd committed to memory as they bored into mine from a face mostly obscured by leather and fringe. In the photo, his mouth was again hidden, this time by a petite espresso cup cradled in long, elegant fingers, but the corners of it were upturned, adding another layer of impishness.

Caleb M. 33. Musician.

"What is it?" Jules crawled forward and peered at the screen. "Why does he look familiar?"

I held my breath, waiting for her to figure it out. When she didn't, I connected the dots for her. "He's the cowboy from my breakup party."

"The stripper?" Stevie screeched. "Wait—how do you know it's the same guy?"

"No way!" Jules exclaimed, cocking her head to the side and glaring at me like I was lying.

Max bolted upright and held out her hand. "Let me see."

I sighed, knowing all hell was really about to break loose. "Because he's also the music teacher at school. The one I'm helping with the spring concert."

Max's mouth dropped open.

"What's his profile say?" Jules asked.

"Oh, *now* you want to read profiles?" Stevie said.

"'Jack of all trades, master of few. I'm passionate about all things music (I teach, give private lessons, and play in a band) and consider myself a bit of a coffee snob. I might let you strum my bass if you're lucky,'" I read.

Caleb's profile read just like he came across in life—playful and enthusiastic about music with a healthy dose of confidence —but I found it interesting that there was no mention of his other adult extracurricular activities.

"Me likey," Max said. She nudged Stevie in her side. "I wonder if your pirate is on there."

Blushing, Stevie fiddled with the sleeve of her pajamas. "Are you going to swipe right?"

I bit my lip. The situation was complicated. If I'd never met him before, I'd probably be mesmerized by his photos and curious enough about him to say yes. But since we were already acquainted, the stakes were higher. Did I have any romantic feelings toward Caleb? What happened if I swiped right and he swiped left? Or vice versa?

"I don't know. We work together, and he's also a stri—male entertainer."

Max scrunched her face up. "What does being a stripper have to do with anything? It's just a paycheck."

"If this blows up, I'll still have to see him at school," I protested.

"But if it goes great, think about the *sexual tension*." Max's eyes shone. "Heated glances during faculty meetings. Your fingers straining toward each other as you pass in the hallway. Pulling each other into the breakroom for a quickie."

Damn her. The scenarios Max had dreamt up made me think about the lunch period I'd shared with Caleb in the storage room. The moment I'd felt *something* awaken between us.

"Maxine Baldwin, when did you become a romantic?" Stevie asked, sounding amused.

Without warning, Jules's hand darted out and wrapped around the phone. Before I had time to register what was happening, she rolled away, time slowing as she pressed a fingertip to the screen and dragged it to the right.

"What did you do?" I yelled, leaping across the bed and tackling her. She curled into the fetal position, clutching the phone under her tucked chin. I tried to pry her arms away from her body, then resorted to tickling the sensitive spot just below her ribcage that always got her. "Whyyyy?"

Jules rolled away again, the phone still firmly in her grasp. "It's a match!" she cried triumphantly.

I froze. "What?"

"It's a match!" She turned the phone so I could see.

Against a dark red background with pink silhouettes of chubby cupids aiming arrows, my photo and Caleb's danced in heart-shaped frames beneath the words *It's a Match!* in bold letters. A large, yellow button at the bottom of the screen read, *Start Chatting*.

The fight drained out of me as my soul left my body.

"Are you going to message him?" Stevie asked from the safety of the doorway. She'd been quick to move when I'd lunged at Jules.

"Message him…message him," Max chanted, pounding her fists on the mattress up by the headboard.

Jules chucked the phone in my direction, where it landed within arm's reach on the white duvet patterned with anchors and sailboats. Without hesitation, I picked up the phone, closed the app, and tossed it back to her. "Nope."

"But it was a match, Zara!" Jules said.

"*You* matched with him. *You* created the profile and *you* swiped on him. I had no parts in this." I crossed my arms over my chest.

"Boo, I'm bored now. And I'm ready to get out of this dress." Max slid off of the bed. "Nite nite."

"Right behind you," Stevie said. "I've had enough excitement today to last me the rest of the year."

"Night." Jules warily eyed me from the other side of our bed, as if worried I might dive across it. And with good reason. After the door shut behind Stevie and Max with a soft click, Jules inched toward the bathroom. "Well, seems like a good time for a shower."

"Hold up, Catfishing Cupid."

Jules froze, then slowly turned around.

"You can't just do shit like that, Jules. That's *my* name and picture you're putting out there. What if one of my kids' parents saw the profile?"

"Clearly they're on the app too, so what's the problem?"

"The problem is I didn't agree to it, and now I'm stuck cleaning up your mess like always."

"Okay, okay. I get it." Jules brought her shoulders up around her ears. "It won't happen again."

"It better not," I warned. There was more I wanted to say, but a more thorough scolding would have to wait until morning when we were both clear-headed. Maybe accompanied by a headlock.

"Can I go shower now?"

"Please do."

I turned away and shimmied the Bad Decisions Dress over my head. Now that I was on high alert, I could use a freaking shower to cool down. I should have made Jules pay penance by letting me use the bathroom first. Pulling out my pajamas and clean underwear did nothing to ease my irritation.

Did Jules think I couldn't find someone on my own? She'd said she signed up for the app last weekend—that was when I'd gone speed-dating, before I made plans to go out with Tyson. And why the hell was Caleb popping up everywhere all of a sudden?

On the duvet, Jules's phone chimed once, and then again a moment later. I ignored it and continued my preparations for bed. I didn't say anything when she emerged from the bathroom, which felt like fifty years later. At least, not until she picked up her phone and cast a sly grin in my direction.

"What is it?" I asked suspiciously.

"It's for you."

"Huh?"

"Cowboy"—Jules looked at the screen—"Caleb. He sent you a message in the app. Two messages, actually." She tossed the phone near me.

I stared at it with wide eyes, like it was a snake ready to strike. My mind was a jumble of racing thoughts, each too fast to grasp. "What should I do?"

"Um, pick it up. Duh. Read the message."

"'Pick it up. Read the message,'" I repeated.

"That's what I said." Jules hoisted her towel up higher around her body and started slathering lotion on her legs as if she hadn't pulled the pin from a grenade and launched it right at me.

Heart thundering, hands trembling, I opened the app.

CALEB

Fancy meeting you here. 😊

I'm a fan of craptastic reality tv and car dance parties myself.

"What'd he say?" Jules asked.

I read out what he sent, then chewed on my lower lip as I thought about my response. *I should really come clean, shouldn't I? What kind of relationship starts out with a lie? Wait—who's talking about relationships?*

Good grief. Maybe I *would* be better off having Jules pretend she was me and writing to men on my behalf.

ZARA

Haha, I didn't write that.

CALEB

Ah. So someone hijacked your phone, and instead of draining your bank account, they altered your dating profile?

ZARA

It's a long story.

CALEB

I can't sleep but can't bear to watch a fifth hour of Top Chef...I think I have time.

I grinned.

"Ladies and gents, we have a grin!" Jules exclaimed.

I glared at her, grabbed my shower stuff, and carried everything into the bathroom.

"Hey! That's my phone!" Jules's muffled voice said.

Ignoring her, I sat on the closed toilet lid for the second time that night, folded my legs under me, and started typing.

twenty-one

I didn't fall asleep until three a.m.

After I typed out the mortifying truth about Jules setting up my WooMe profile and hit SEND, I jumped in the shower, cursing my impulsivity. And I kept cursing it all the way until I got out and checked the phone to find a message from Caleb saying that it sounded like the plot of a romantic comedy.

In order to avoid seeming desperate, I didn't reply until I'd moisturized, put on my pjs, tied up my hair and climbed into bed next to Jules, who ground her teeth in her sleep in typical obnoxious younger sibling behavior.

ZARA

Right? But in Jules logic, it's not because she didn't message anyone.

CALEB

Well, I think I owe Jules a high five anyway.

ZARA

I'll be sure to tell her that tomorrow—well, later this morning.

I set Jules's phone on the nightstand and turned out the light, not expecting a response until a decent hour, but within moments, the device let out a happy chime. For the next two hours, our conversation hopped from one topic to another until it felt like we'd covered everything under the sun. Annoying younger siblings and family holiday traditions. Items on our bucket lists—after Caleb told me he was determined to complete the Snow Cone Kingdom Flavor Challenge in one summer by trying each one of their fifty-fifty flavors to win a t-shirt, I felt a little basic with my own wish to try karaoke—and embarrassing moments that would haunt us into old age. For every off-the-wall question I lobbed, Caleb batted it back, unfazed. The conversation flowed effortlessly, each response painting a richer portrait of Caleb and drawing me down a path that made me eager to learn more. I was sure that if I hadn't mentioned that I could barely keep my eyes open, we would've continued talking until sunrise.

When I woke with a throbbing head and parched mouth a few hours later, the other side of the bed was empty. On the nightstand, Jules's phone lay facedown, untouched.

The silly smiles, satisfied smirks, and stifled giggles of the early morning came flooding back to me, bringing with them cautious excitement. After I'd gotten over my initial reluctance, ending my night out with the girls by flirting with Caleb McMahon over text had made total sense. In the bright light of day, however, I wondered if I was reading too much into things. Caleb himself had said he was bored; maybe talking to me was just a diversion.

Don't overthink it, Zara. Don't overthink. Don't overthink. Don't over—

And then the phone chimed.

I scooped it from the nightstand and saw a message notification from Caleb through the WooMe app.

CALEB

Good Morning!

Two little words, but they brought yet another smile to my face. It was fascinating how the same two words from two different people could generate such contrasting reactions. Tyson's message had made me want to change my number and possibly move states. Caleb's message, on the other hand, made me feel special. I knew he'd gone to sleep with me in his thoughts, but this text suggested I was on his mind as soon as he woke.

Just as he was in mine.

So much for overthinking.

ZARA

Morning, yourself. Get any sleep at all?

CALEB

Nope. You were running through my dreams all night.

I sent an eye roll emoji in response to the corny line. I wonder if he really did dream about me, or if he was just pulling my leg.

Either way, it added a pep to my step even though my body screamed for water and ibuprofen.

I was still grinning when I walked into the kitchen a few minutes later. A fully dressed Amber flipped pancakes on a griddle while Max, clad in her donut onesie, held out a plate and danced around. I'd never understood how the woman managed to bounce back so easily after a night out. While I felt like I'd been run over by a garbage truck at least a few times, Max looked like she'd just been gifted an all-expenses paid trip to Disney World.

At the island counter, Stevie, still in her pjs and slightly less put-together than usual, sipped from a ceramic mug. Beside her, Jules—at least, I assumed it was Jules based on the flying squirrel hood pulled over her head—leaned on the counter with her arms crossed, her head resting on top of them.

Maybe I wasn't as bad off as I thought.

Humming, I grabbed a mug of my own and poured some coffee into it.

"Someone's in a good mood," Amber said, sounding amused. "What's got you so chipper?"

I gave her a mysterious shrug and grabbed a piece of bacon from beside the griddle.

Jules lifted her head from the counter, half of her face covered by large white sunglasses. "It's probably because she was up half the night talking to the cowboy."

I froze. How the hell did she know? When I came back from my shower and got into bed, I'd been sure she was conked out.

"The cowboy?" Amber turned, a crease forming between her brows. "Who the hell is 'the cowboy'?"

"You remember the stripper from the breakup party?" Stevie asked. "The one who gave her a lap dance?"

"That was more than a lap dance." Jules pushed the sunglasses up into her hair. "That man gave her a pelvic exam with his face."

My cheeks grew warm. That night felt like a lifetime ago, yet the memory was as vivid as if it happened only yesterday.

Amber's mouth dropped open as she looked at each of us. "How the hell did I miss this? When did Zara get his number?"

As Max filled Amber in—just like she'd done the night before with Stevie—a spark of irritation ignited in my belly. They were talking about me and my life in third person like I wasn't even there. Like some sort of C-list reality star with a last-ditch storyline.

"Speaking of which," Jules cut in. "I downloaded WooMe on *your* phone while you were sleeping so you can give me mine back."

I froze, my mug hovering in mid-air, as frustration flared alongside my annoyance. "You know my passcode?"

Jules shrugged. "Of course. It's the last four digits of Nana and PopPop's old landline from when we were kids. You're kinda predictable that way. I don't even see why you bother to have one." She jerked her chin. "Can you pass me some bacon?"

The patience I prided myself on snapped like a brittle rubber band and I slammed my mug on the counter. "That is *it*. We need to have a Come to Jesus meeting. Now."

Max paused in the middle of pouring a gallon of syrup over her stack of pancakes. "You and Jules, or...?"

"All of you!"

"Uh-oh," Amber murmured.

Rosario chose that moment to enter the living area, still sporting last night's leopard print, her hair sticking out in every direction. Wordlessly, Stevie grabbed her mug and phone and slipped off her stool.

"What's going on?" Ro rubbed her eyes. "Zara seems pissed."

"I *am* pissed." I snatched the spatula from Amber and pointed it at Stevie. "Sit your ass down." I turned it on Ro. "You too."

Eyes wide, Stevie reclaimed her place on the stool, and Ro gingerly sat in an armchair.

"You gonna be cool if I eat my pancakes?" Max asked tentatively. "It's just, they're still warm…"

"God, Max. Eat the damn pancakes." Releasing the spatula, I put my palms on the counter and closed my eyes, willing myself to take deep, even breaths. When I opened them, the girls were staring at me in various degrees of disbelief and apprehension. "I love all of you, so, I say the following with love: I need you to stop fucking meddling in my life."

"Who's meddling?" Max asked, her mouth full.

I gave her a pointed look. "Well, how about we start with the way y'all have been springing shit on me out of nowhere. The wine bar? Male entertainers? Speed-dating?"

Amber had the decency to look sheepish, while Rosario frowned and Jules made a face like she sniffed milk two weeks past its expiration date.

"But—" Jules started.

I held up my hand and finished my thought. "I know you're excited and you think you're helping, but I need you to respect my autonomy. Sometimes I feel like I'm not even in control of my own life—like you're puppeteers pulling me by the strings or I'm a sim in a pool and you're about to remove the ladder. Even a minute ago, you were talking about me like I wasn't standing right here."

Max and Stevie exchanged a guilty glance.

"That brings me to another point," I said, warming to my topic. The words tumbled out as if they'd been waiting for the perfect chance. "I want to be able to tell y'all stuff in confidence and not have to worry that Hilary at the boutique or JimBob at the gas station will know my whole life story."

Out of the corner of my eye, I spied Stevie's hand creeping toward her phone.

"Stevie, leave the Notes app alone," I snapped.

Chastened, she pulled back her hand and put it in her lap.

Turning ever so slightly, I fixed my sights on my little sister. "And finally, Jules…*stop taking my shit!*"

"Sharing is caring," she muttered.

My body trembled as I caught my breath. Having gotten everything that I wanted off my chest, I felt depleted. I hadn't fully grasped how much I kept bottled inside to avoid rocking the boat. But part of stoking my own fire meant standing up for myself and putting my foot down.

Amber looked at the other girls, then cleared her throat. "I think I can speak for all of us when I say we're really sorry, Zara. Each of us has been wrapped up in our own shit for so long… you gave us an opportunity to escape."

Stevie nodded, her face solemn. "We were just really excited—"

"And we did the most," Max interrupted. "Maybe too much."

A wave of relief washed over me that they seemed to understand and were receiving my words with grace. At least, most of them. My narrowed gaze traveled to Jules.

"I'll ask *before* I borrow things. You might want to change your Netflix password, though—I shared it with my hair braider," she said. "But from this point on…" She made a stern face and smashed her fist into her palm.

"We promise we'll do better at respecting your boundaries." Stevie looked around the group. "All of us."

"And if you feel like we're doing too much, tell us," Ro said.

"We love you more than donuts," Max added, tugging at her onesie. "And you know how much I love donuts."

"We just want to see you win," Amber said.

"Thanks, everybody. I really appreciate it."

There was no doubt they were going to slip up; I just had to remind myself that everything they did came from a place of love. And there was no doubt that *I* was going to backslide, but all that mattered was for me to keep showing up for myself.

I picked up a piece of bacon and flung it at Jules. She opened her mouth wide to catch it, but it bounced off her nose. "And for the record, I'm already winning. I've got you dorks."

"Group hug." Amber wrapped an arm around me and gestured for Rosario to join the group with the other. She slid between Max and Amber, giving Stevie a wide berth. Jules squeezed in on my other side and we tightened our huddle.

"Go team!" Max exclaimed.

"We're still not a functional team at the moment." I shot pointed looks at Ro and Stevie.

Ro sighed and tried to run a hand through her tangled hair, but it got caught in the snarls. "Stevie, can I talk to you for a sec?"

Stevie lifted her nose in the air. "I suppose so."

Amber, Max, Jules, and I watched them go to the far side of the living room. I crossed my fingers, hoping they'd resolve their issues and move on so we could all leave the beach with a fresh start.

"Maybe we should give them some privacy," Amber suggested.

"They're in a communal space," Max said, but turned her back to them and speared the remaining bite of pancake on her plate. "So, Zara, are you still going to finish the list of mistakes?"

"Well…I've come this far. May as well."

"What's left?" Jules asked.

"A one-night stand." I cringed as I remembered diving beneath the table at Bella Cucina. "And the solo date could probably use a redo."

"Well, don't feel like you have to sleep with a rando on our account," Jules said.

"Trust me, if I want to sleep with a rando, it's going to be because *I* want to."

"Good boundary setting." Amber raised her hand for a high five.

I slapped her palm with mine. "I'm a work in progress but I'll get there."

twenty-two

"Duncan, why does that Bluey band-aid look awfully familiar?" I frowned at the striped band-aid flagging from the little boy's elbow as I led the class down the breezeway to the music room.

He shrugged. "I have an ouchie."

"Duncan likes Bluey, so I gave him my band-aid 'cause I didn't need it anymore," Walker proudly said from my other side. He stopped walking, lifted his leg, and pointed at the red, exposed skin on his knee. Hadleigh plowed into him from behind. "See? Ow!"

It took everything in me to keep from throwing up in my mouth. During recess earlier that morning, Walker had skinned his knee on the blacktop during a rough game of soccer. I'd cleaned up the little bit of blood, and after he spent an inordinate amount of time poring over the selections in the band-aid box, I slapped one on.

The one currently half-attached to Duncan's body.

"Walker, Duncan, you can't share band-aids because we don't want to share germs."

"So, we're brothers now? Since we shared our germs?" Duncan asked hopefully.

I breathed deeply as I massaged my temples. "That's not quite how it works; brothers share DNA—not germs. Nobody's sharing DNA here."

"We do sometimes," Hadleigh said. "Girls need boys' DNA to make babies. Walker, can I have your DNA?"

I came to a full stop just outside the building. "Hadleigh, we *do not* ask anyone for their DNA. *Ever*."

"But—"

"Here we are!" I opened the door and waved the kids ahead.

Eager to have some alone time and a bed all to myself, I'd been glad to get back to Fallen Oaks after a girls' weekend that was fun, exasperating, and everything in between. But this band-aid situation and accompanying conversation had me ready to cut my workday short and drive the two and a half hours back to Wayside Beach.

Except then I wouldn't be able to see Caleb.

True to her word, Jules had installed the WooMe app on my phone, and as soon as it was back in my possession, I promptly changed the password and then the passcode for the phone itself. I spent the ride home from the beach exchanging favorite songs and memes with Caleb, half-heartedly listening to Max and Stevie chatter about Stevie making up with Ro, until Caleb said he had to go and that he'd see me at school. Now, we were finally coming face-to-face for the first time since I'd shared so much of myself over text, and while excited, I wasn't sure if I'd revealed too much.

But that didn't stop me from taking special care when I dressed for work that morning. It was all in vain though, because during snack time, I helped Carissa open her carton of mixed berry yogurt, only to have it explode all over my lap.

As my rambunctious students formed a haphazard line along one wall, Marjorie, a third-grade TA, nodded at me in acknowledgement before returning to scrolling on her phone next to the music room's closed door. When the noise inside the classroom quieted, I ran my hands down the front of my blouse and turned to the door, holding my breath in anticipation. It opened slowly, but instead of Caleb's lean frame filling the doorway, it was Ms. Tandy, a gruff older lady who'd been subbing at Fallen Oaks Prep since I attended myself. I tried to conceal my disappointment as Marjorie's class exited the classroom and mine went in.

"Where's Mr. McMahon?" I asked nonchalantly.

Ms. Tandy shrugged. "They don't tell, I don't ask, honey. I'm just here to supplement my social security."

And with that, she pulled the door closed after my last student.

I stood there, staring in confusion at the blond wood for a solid minute. Was Caleb avoiding me? Had I read too much into our texts?

With a sigh, I headed to the break room to grab the coffee I'd earlier passed on because I was jittery enough on my own. As I waited for the Keurig to finish doing its thing, my brain continued its ruminations. Did I overshare and now Caleb had to take the whole day off to figure out how to let me down easy?

"Fuck it, Zara. Put yourself out of misery, and just message the guy," I muttered as I poured hazelnut-flavored creamer into my mug. Before I could think twice, I pulled out my phone.

ZARA

Just checking to see if you're still alive.

CALEB

You missed me. Cute.

ZARA

False. I don't want the kids to run off another sub. It's hard enough to find one as it is.

CALEB

Suuuure.

But if it eases your mind, I've been dealing with a bad migraine.

The tension melted from my body as relief washed over me, knowing Caleb's absence wasn't my fault.

ZARA

That sucks. Hope you feel better.

CALEB

You're only worried that if I don't come back, we'll start losing subs left and right.

ZARA

Maybe.

CALEB

I should be back tomorrow. Want to have a working lunch about the program?

ZARA

I can't do lunch, but I'm open after school.

CALEB

Works for me.

ZARA

I paused, my thumbs hovering over the screen, then took the plunge.

ZARA

Want to send me your number so we can talk outside this stupid app?

Just in case I have a musical emergency or something.

Three gray dots bounced up and down while Caleb typed out a reply.

CALEB

Sure. But fair warning…I charge extra for musical emergencies after work hours.

I smiled to myself and took a sip of coffee as his number popped up on the screen. *Gold star for you, Zara.*

* * *

While the kids didn't run off the substitute music teacher, they'd been close. When I picked them up, Ms. Tandy looked like she was weighing just how much she could stretch her social security check.

Try spending seven hours with them five days a week, I wanted to tell her. Luckily, we made it through the rest of the day without issue.

At home that evening, I stood in front of my open fridge and sighed. I hadn't been grocery shopping in a couple of weeks, and while I needed to restock, I knew if I went shopping tonight, there was a zero percent chance of me actually cooking anything I'd buy.

My eyes lit on the Koi Sushi Garden menu affixed to the front of the freezer with a mushroom-shaped magnet reading "I Don't Give a Shiitake." Take-out was always a good idea.

Or you could have a solo date redo.

The disastrous last time I'd tried going out alone sprang to mind. I already couldn't show my face at one of my favorite restaurants in town—what if I choked again? Given my lack of cooking skill or enthusiasm, I couldn't risk embarrassing myself at another one of my usual spots.

Aren't you supposed to be releasing your need for external validation?

My stomach let out warning grumble that hanger was quickly approaching.

Fuck it. I was doing it.

But this time I was going in prepared.

After making sure my phone had a full charge, I grabbed another dusty book from my TBR pile, and looked down at my yogurt-crusted jeans. I still hadn't unpacked the bag that held the Bad Decisions Dress, but it was just as well. The garment could use a break after this weekend.

To Koi Sushi Garden I went.

"Hi. Just one?" asked a hostess stationed by the door.

Clearing my throat, I lifted my chin in the air. "Yep. Just me. One person. *Uno.*"

Too much, Zara. Pull back. Pull back!

"Party of one. Got it." The corners of her mouth tipped up with amusement. "Table or bar?"

I scanned the fairly empty restaurant. Two men sat in front of the sushi counter with its case filled with ice and fresh fish, an empty seat separating them.

My people.

"Bar, please."

"Okie dokie. Feel free to seat yourself."

Self-conscious, but not as much as before, I walked toward the sleek bar only a few feet away from the entrance. When I slid out a chair on the far end, one of the men glanced up from his bowl of edamame and nodded ever so slightly. I nodded back and sat down.

A handsome sushi chef in a neat, black uniform smiled at me from the other side of the case. "Welcome. Let me know when you're ready."

"Thanks."

See? This isn't so bad.

After looking over the menu, I marked my order on the little paper, placed it on top of the case, and pulled out my book. It felt weird at first, like I was playing at reading, because who reads at a sushi restaurant? And I kept getting distracted watching the chef prepare rolls so I'd have to read the same paragraph three times. Eventually though, the awkward, performative feeling went away, and I became so absorbed in the story that the buzzing of my phone on the bar scared the hell out of me.

Once my heart returned to its normal rhythm, hope rose in my chest at the idea of Caleb texting me. I'd sent him a quick *Hey! This is Zara,* after receiving his number, and he responded that he got it and was going to lay down. I hadn't heard from him since. Eagerly, I picked up the phone.

TYSON

Hey there. How was the girls' weekend?

The lightness in my chest gave way to a sudden tightness that took me by nearly as much surprise as the ringing phone.

I didn't want to hear from Tyson. I wanted Caleb.

Oh, hell.

Being a people pleaser and sensitive to rejection, myself, I'd always cowered at the idea of having to disappoint someone. But in the life of Zara Harmony Whitmore, whose feelings were more important—mine or his?

ZARA

Hi Tyson. Girls' weekend was really fun. It almost felt like we were kids again. Thanks for asking.

Also, thank you again for such a fun night. I've had some time to think and I don't feel our lifestyles are compatible at the moment. Wishing you all the best, and good luck out there!

I held my breath as typing bubbles danced on the screen, disappeared, then materialized again.

TYSON

Thanks for being straight up. Good luck with everything.

ZARA

You too.

I exited the message, set the phone facedown on the bar, and spread my palms on the cool surface as my heart thumped in my chest.

I did it! I told him I wasn't interested, and I didn't die.

It was a baby giraffe step that would make Jules proud. Actually, screw Jules—I was proud of my own damn self.

When the sushi chef leaned over the case to hand me my plate, I took it and ate my meal without incident. By the time I paid the bill and left Koi Sushi Garden, I was bursting with confidence. Still flying high when I pulled into my garage, my eyes landed on the cluster of black garbage bags containing my ex's stuff.

It's time to let go once and for all, Zara.

I pulled out my phone, navigated to my list of Blocked Contacts, and found Geoff's name.

<h1 style="text-align:center">twenty-three</h1>

Of course, when I finally came face to face with Caleb after four days of semi-flirtatious texting, it happened to be the Ellis Elephants' first pajama day of the new year. A beloved tradition in our classroom, Susie, our students, and I wore pajamas and brought our favorite stuffed animals to school. We kicked off the morning with a Pajama Parade, incorporated the theme into all of our lessons, and even had parents come in to serve breakfast for lunch.

For five brief seconds, I'd entertained the idea of wearing the freshly laundered diaper alien onesie. But after remembering how badly Caleb had been roasted for his donut shirt, I decided against it. Yes, I was learning to ignore how other people viewed my actions, but sharp-tongued first graders were on another level. I also thought about bringing another outfit to change into, but I didn't want Caleb to get the impression that I thought this meeting was anything special.

Which is why I was in the same kid-size bathroom in which I'd hidden after hearing about Geoff's infidelity, applying lipstick in a cozy, pink matching pajama set after dismissal.

I'd just finished fluffing my hair when the bathroom door

opened, accompanied by a small grunt. The Bathroom Talker skipped inside, then pulled up short when she saw me at the sink and scowled.

"You had pajama day? That's not fair! We didn't get pajama day."

"Well, you'll have to—"

"Sometimes my grandma doesn't wear pajamas. She says it's too hot. When it's hot, I like to go to the pool." Seraphina skipped to the bank of stalls and locked herself in. "Do you like to go swimming?"

"I like—"

"The pool is nice because there are no sharks there. My brother likes the beach, but I'm scared of sharks."

I shook my head as I zipped up my makeup case. How did Blair and Mrs. Robinson put up with this all day? Although, I'm sure the same was often said about my and Susie's class.

"Won't they be looking for you in aftercare?" I asked.

The toilet flushed and Seraphina emerged from the stall with a grin. "Nah." She bounded to the sink next to mine, turned on the tap, and pumped the soap dispenser a good four or five times. "It's raining outside so we're watching a movie in the commons."

"Oh. Well, that sounds fun." I retrieved my bookbag where I left it next to the door. "Have a good afternoon, Seraphina."

"Hey, Miss Whitmore?"

Heaving a fatigued sigh, I turned around, one hand on the handle. "Yes, Seraphina?"

"You look really pretty."

Warmth spread through my chest at the compliment, and I smiled at the pint-size motormouth. "Thank you."

"But Mrs. Robinson looks prettier. I liked her dress today. It was purple and that's my favorite color."

"Get back to aftercare, Seraphina."

Leaving Seraphina to grab enough paper towels to soak up

an oil leak, I slung my bag over my shoulder and made my way to the music room, letting my thoughts wander. Things were bound to be different between Caleb and I now. Since he always addressed things head-on, would he bring up our flirtation as soon as I walked in the door? Or would he sit back and follow my lead?

When I entered the building, the door to the music room was open. I took a deep breath and stepped inside, looking around for Caleb, but the room was empty and silent. Like the first time we'd met to discuss the program, two white folding chairs faced each other in the center.

"Knock, knock. Anybody home?"

Caleb's head appeared around the door leading to his office. A faint, fluttery sensation took flight in my belly as he looked me over with a smirk. "Nice pajamas. I might have to tell Mrs. Foster that you're slacking on the job."

Damn it. I knew I should have packed a change of clothes.

"I'd counter that pajama day is even more work than a regular school day."

"I don't doubt it."

When the rest of Caleb's body materialized, I noticed he'd traded his usual loud, short-sleeve button-up for a thick, hunter green fisherman sweater that added a depth and richness to the green in his eyes. He held up a bright yellow plastic package.

"Are those lemon Oreos?" I asked in disbelief.

"Yup." Walking to a chair, Caleb opened the pack of cookies, then held it out to me.

Tingling in my fingertips joined the butterflies in my belly. I dropped my stuff next to the other chair, sat down, and helped myself to a couple of cookies.

"You know, I was only kidding about charging you an entry fee," I said.

"I thought we could use some brain food for brainstorming. It's also an I'm-sorry-I-wasn't-here-yesterday olive branch. I know you were devastated." He grinned as he made himself comfy in his chair.

"Well, I appreciate it. How's the migraine?"

"Much better. So much better, in fact, that I've been thinking a lot about what you said—"

Ah. Here it is. We're getting it out in the open first thing.

"—and I'm right there with you—"

My heart beat faster.

"We need some *real* music, and I think I've found a happy medium. How do you feel about the theme, *Motown Mania?*" He moved his hands in the air like a movie director selling his vision to a roomful of producers.

Huh? We were seriously just going to sit here and talk about the music program like we hadn't been sending each other memes with terrible pick-up lines that not-so-secretly revealed our feelings for one another for the last four days?

Caleb studied my face, incorrectly interpreting my perplexed expression as disapproval for the theme. "Hear me out. Who doesn't love Motown? It's upbeat and engaging. The kids will love it, it'll have the parents clapping, and the grandparents toe-tapping. We can have a lot of fun with the costuming, and most importantly, it's an opportunity to educate the students about diversity and incorporate some history."

Focus, Zara.

"Motown sounds good. And less likely to make me want to slam my head against the wall after listening to them practice the songs a thousand times."

"Because *that's* the most important thing," Caleb said wryly. "Any songs I should stay away from?"

"Uh, let me think about it?"

Was there something wrong with me for being so fixated on the fact that we connected through a dating app while Caleb was the poster child for professionalism? No, there wasn't. Caleb had already demonstrated his exemplary compartmentalization skills when he talked about how he kept his role as Colton the Cowboy separate from his daily life. Clearly, I could use a lesson or two.

Or maybe it was just like I first thought—I was a momentary diversion. With his good looks and secondary line of work, I doubted he lacked for attention.

Whatever. This was better for all parties involved, anyway. So, why did my heart ache just a little?

"Sure," Caleb said. "But we've gotta get a move on with nailing things down so we can sort out costumes and the kids can start practicing."

"Roger that." *Roger that? Kill me now.* "I've got your number, so…I'll let you know."

Was I purposely giving him an opening to see how he ran with it? You bet.

Like a boxer light on his feet, he sidestepped my comment and started talking about the program order.

After another half-hour of hashing out logistics, Caleb was satisfied with our progress. Meanwhile, *I* was anything but. Would we walk out these doors, things going back to how they'd been over the weekend with us being goofy over text? Or had this meeting closed the door on whatever this was?

I kept my disgruntled thoughts to myself as we gathered our stuff and exited the building to a cold downpour.

"Damn it," Caleb groaned. "I rode my bike today." He pointed out a dark blue bike chained to a rack at one end of the parking lot. He'd told me his ride to school was twenty minutes. I looked out at falling sheets of miserable rain.

"You can't bike home in this."

"What choice do I have? It's my fault, though. I should've checked the forecast."

"I'll take you," I blurted out. As Caleb assessed me, his face unreadable, I hurried to add, "Consider it my good deed for the day."

"Well…if you don't mind."

I shook my head. "Of course not. We can't have you getting sick and missing school again—I seriously think if Ms. Tandy has to sub for my class one more time, she's done."

A grin brightened Caleb's face. "Okay. I'll leave my bike overnight and drive tomorrow. How are we gonna do this?"

"We make a run for it." I hoisted the straps of my bag higher on my shoulders. "On the count of three. One…two…three!"

We ran down the sidewalk like our lives depended on it, the rain pelting us relentlessly the whole way. Teeth chattering, I unlocked the car and we clambered inside. Immediately, I started the ignition to get the heat going, only for a sultry, raspy voice singing about touching herself to blare through the speakers.

Curse my urge to listen to my *Ready for Romance* playlist during my morning commute.

I thought I'd experienced mortification before, but nothing in all of my thirty-four years on the planet even came close to this. I switched the stereo off, facing forward, before risking a sideways glance at Caleb out of the corner of my eye. His lips were pressed tightly together, cheeks puffed out and chin quivering. Unable to hold it in any longer, he let out a guffaw, and a moment later I joined in with a few giggles.

"What would you say if I told you I listened to the very same thing in my AirPods this morning?"

"I'd say you were lying to try and make me feel better."

"You'd be right. But it *is* a great karaoke song."

We didn't talk much for the rest of the drive beyond Caleb directing me to his apartment just outside downtown Fallen Oaks. He really did live close to the school, but with everyone driving slowly in the rain, it probably took just as long by car as it would by bike. At least this way, he wouldn't catch pneumonia.

"Right there," Caleb said, pointing to a multi-story red brick building with brightly lit retail stores and cafés on the ground level.

I slowed just in front of it and put the car in park. "Door-to-door service."

"I really appreciate the ride." He went to open the passenger door, then paused.

A mix of emotions flickered across his face, giving the impression that he was warring with himself about something. "Look, I really enjoyed chatting with you…"

Oh no. Rejection incoming. Brace yourself. I squeezed my steering wheel in a death grip and held my breath.

"Would you be interested in going out sometime?"

"'Going out sometime'?" I repeated slowly as if I was new to learning the English language.

Caleb nodded. "Yeah. I think we have similar senses of humor and what I've discovered about you intrigues me. I feel like we kind of…get each other."

"Yes!" I blurted. I cleared my throat and tried to reclaim at least a smidge of dignity. "I mean, I agree, and I'd love to. But, um, why didn't you say anything earlier?"

"I don't know how to play this with us being coworkers. I didn't want to say anything at school and make you feel uncomfortable and it turn into…*a thing.*" He ran a hand over his hair. "Honestly, I'm not even sure if I should be saying anything right now, but I'd regret not asking."

"I'm really glad you did," I admitted. The butterflies were back in my stomach. "I've been over here sweating through my pajamas all day, wondering if this was one-sided."

"Definitely not one-sided. Sorry I set your nervous system on fire." A smile stretched across his face. "Is Friday good for you?"

I nodded enthusiastically, my nervous system still smoldering. "Friday's great. I don't have any plans, and there's no school on Saturday."

Stop talking, Captain Obvious.

"It's a date," Caleb said.

"It's a date."

It. Is. A. Date.

"Talk to you later!" Caleb opened the door and splashed up the sidewalk with impressive speed. Under the protection of a balcony, he turned and waved, then let himself into the building. When the door shut behind him, I cranked up the stereo and got my dance on.

twenty-four

Two days after dropping Caleb off at his apartment, I found myself getting ready for our date. Once I'd finished my celebratory dance party, I'd driven home and stared at Geoff's contact information in my phone. Even though I'd unblocked his number a couple days before, I hadn't texted. With adrenaline still surging through my body, I messaged him that if he wanted his stuff, he had to come get it before the weekend. Anything that couldn't be given away was going straight to the dump.

It just happened to be a coincidence that the only time our schedules aligned was right before my date with Caleb. I looked damn good—thanks to the Bad-Decisions-slash-Revenge Dress and a FaceTimed makeup walkthrough with Max—and felt even better.

ROSARIO

It's a power move is what it is. We love to see it.

JULES

I'm still mad you wouldn't let me come over for backup.

ZARA

Jules, he's a salesguy with the gift of gab. I don't need a bodyguard. Thanks tho.

JULES

Well, I'm only a text away if you need me.

Through the open bathroom door, I heard a faint chime ring out through the house.

ZARA

He's here. Gotta go!

STEVIE

Tell us how everything goes.

I flicked off the bathroom light and padded downstairs to the front door. I paused before it, breathing deeply to ground myself.

My feelings matter most. Mine.

After another deep inhale, I pushed my shoulders back, lifted my head and opened the door.

Geoff stood staring down at the "Good Vibes Only" welcome mat Jules had gifted me, a frown on his face. When he looked up, he did a double take, his mouth dropping open and eyes growing comically large as they raked over me from head to toe. One side of my mouth lifted in a smug smirk. Revenge Dress for the win.

Regaining his composure, Geoff snapped his mouth shut and gave me a tight smile. "It feels weird ringing the bell."

"Then it's a good thing you don't have to get used to it." I left the door and walked into the living room without bothering to see if he followed.

"Uh, you look good," he said, hurrying behind me. "Is that a new dress?"

"Yup." I added a little wiggle to my walk that would make Rosario proud.

"What's the occasion?"

I stopped and turned around so abruptly he almost crashed into me. "I'm going on a date."

Geoff's face did that comical shock thing again. "Seriously? It hasn't even been a month."

I raised an eyebrow. "Do you really think *you* should be the one to talk about how fast I've moved on when you had a side piece *during* our relationship?"

Geoff's Adam's apple bobbed as he swallowed.

"Anyway, I need you to get a move on so I can finish getting ready."

"Yeah. Okay."

As we continued through the house, I tried to view the changes I'd made through his eyes. The way I rearranged the furniture in the living room. How I'd replaced all of the framed photos of Geoff and I with some of Stevie's beautiful mountain landscapes and photos of the Sensational Six throughout the years. I wondered what he'd think if he knew I'd repainted the upstairs and started turning his beloved office into a guest room.

"You got a fish?" Geoff asked in disbelief, as if I'd acquired a pet tiger.

"Yup."

"Does it have a name?"

I opened my mouth to tell him I hadn't decided on one yet, when the name I'd been searching for all along rolled off my tongue with a quickness.

"Phoenix."

"Phoenix?" Geoff stared at me with a baffled look.

The beta fish had come into my life when I was picking myself up from the ashes and trying to find my new normal. It felt right.

The corner of my mouth quirked up. "Yeah. Phoenix."

Geoff nodded. "Okay, then." He jerked his chin at the stairs. "So, where's my stuff?"

A real smile bloomed on my face. Full of glee, I strolled to the garage door and opened it. "In here."

"You put it in the garage?" he asked, his tone exasperated. "If that's the case, why didn't you just raise the door and let me in that way instead of parading me through the house?"

"Yes, I *could* have piled all your shit on the porch, or let you in through the garage, but then you wouldn't see how I upgraded the place."

The muscle in Geoff's jaw tensed as he clenched his teeth. Slowly, he shook his head. "What's gotten into you, Zara? You're not the person you used to be."

"Thank God for that. That Zara put other people's needs before her own and let them walk all over her." I slammed the button on the wall to raise the garage door, then pointed at the black trash bags in the corner. "You can see yourself out."

I closed the door to the house, not bothering to stick around and watch Geoff move his belongings. I didn't know nor care where he was staying these days—I was just glad it wasn't with me.

After I buckled my feet into my heels, I peeked back into the garage and saw both the garbage bags and Tesla were gone.

Good riddance.

Shrugging on my trench coat, I sprinkled some fish food into Phoenix's bowl on my way out. "Wish me luck, little fishie."

The vibrant fish opened its mouth and released a single bubble that floated to the water's surface.

In an even better mood than before—I filed the look of shock on Geoff's face away for safekeeping—I drove myself to a dive bar in downtown's Historic Tobacco District to meet Caleb, my music turned all the way up. He'd offered to pick me up, but I didn't want to chance him and Geoff crossing paths. I also wanted to be able to leave on my own terms. I appreciated that he'd taken on the onus of planning the date himself—attending 90s karaoke night at the bar where his band often played—and that he'd given me the option to veto his choice.

I almost did.

But I wanted to free myself from seeking others' approval. To feel confident and secure in myself. Karaoke seemed like a trial by fire.

If I worked up the courage.

When I pulled into the crowded parking lot, I spied Caleb already waiting outside the entrance. Instead of the gentle fluttering of wings, fireworks filled my stomach, each burst hot and exhilarating.

"Hi," I greeted him.

"Hey."

An awkward pause ensued. Did we go in for a hug? A kiss on the cheek? A handshake? Caleb looked just as unsure as I did.

This is silly.

I stepped forward and hugged him, noting the scent of sandalwood that floated around him.

"You look absolutely incredible. I'm feeling just a tad inadequate standing next to you," Caleb's velvet voice reverberated through my body.

"Am I overdressed?" I asked, pulling back in alarm. Even though he'd already seen me in the Bad Decisions Dress, I'd worn it again because it gave my confidence a much-needed boost. Caleb looked stylishly casual in a navy blue crewneck sweater, gold chain, belted jeans, and boots.

"There's no such thing," he said. "You ready?"

Still doubtful, I made a face. "As I'm gonna be."

Inside the dimly lit bar, karaoke was in full swing. On the small, raised stage, a stooped man with a shock of white hair passionately belted out "I Don't Want to Miss a Thing" by Aerosmith.

I jumped at the feel of Caleb's hand landing on the small of my back to guide me through the room crowded with mismatched chairs and tables, then relaxed against it.

"You want to get some water? Maybe a shot of liquid courage before you hit the stage?" he asked, after pulling out my chair at a table covered in scratches in the rear of the room.

I snorted. "I said I would come…I didn't say anything about getting up on stage. That's *your* thing."

Caleb slowly lowered his eyelids in a sultry gaze that sent my pulse racing. "It could be *our* thing."

I cleared my throat and shifted on the chair. "I'll take a rum and coke."

"Be right back."

While Caleb sourced drinks—and I gathered my wits about me—I scanned the room, his comment about this being "our thing" bouncing around my brain. I didn't know what I expected out of the evening. I liked talking and joking around with Caleb, but he was right about things potentially getting messy with us working together.

"That was fast," I said when he reappeared a few minutes later.

"I've got connections." He set the two glasses on the table, along with two strips of paper and a small golf pencil that reminded me of Jules's fire ritual. "Just in case you change your mind."

I pulled my sweating glass close. "Pretty sure it's gonna take an act of God for that to happen. You're asking me to voluntarily make a fool of myself in front of a room full of people."

"Everyone's here for the same reason." Caleb pointed at the stage where a man in a polo shirt, crisp khakis, and boat shoes enthusiastically humped the air as he sang along to Bloodhound Gang's "Bad Touch." "See that guy? He doesn't give a shit what anybody else thinks."

"I'll think about it," I said, my voice promising the opposite.

He put a hand on his chest. "That's all I ask."

"What are *you* going to sing?"

Caleb slid a paper strip across the table, picked up the pencil, and used his other hand to shield what he was writing. "It's a surprise. You'll just have to wait and see with everyone else."

"Not even a little hint?"

He shook his head. "Nope."

After he finished writing, he took his selection up to the DJ who'd set up shop beside the stage, then reclaimed his seat.

A trio of obviously drunk women slurred their way through "No Scrubs," and a pair of older gay men in coordinated tracksuits crooned "A Whole New World" as they gazed lovingly into each other's eyes before Caleb's name was announced over the speakers. He got to his feet, and tugged on the hem of his sweater.

"Knock 'em dead."

He flashed me a grin, then strode to the center of the stage and took the microphone from its stand, oozing confidence. A tattoo of funky drums started, and Caleb immediately burst into the running man, setting the crowd on fire before even singing a note. My amusement reached a new level when I recognized the song as "Poison" by Bell Biv Devoe.

His charm flew off the charts as he sang about never trusting big butts and smiles. Showman that he was, Caleb made use of the whole stage, doing the cabbage patch, Roger Rabbit, and other dance moves I hadn't seen in decades. I saw glimpses of Colton the Cowboy in his bold strut and the way he engaged with the audience, doling out small bites of personalized attention, and found myself just as mesmerized as I'd been on the night of my breakup party. Around me, people got to their feet, dancing and clapping along as his infectious energy filled every corner of the room.

A woman at the next table leaned over. "Hon, you're one lucky lady."

I fixed my mouth to correct her, then looked back at Caleb, warmth spreading through my body. "I am, aren't I?"

Caleb finished the song to resounding applause and cheers. He replaced the mic, hopped off the stage and started toward the table, slapping outstretched palms and giving gracious nods like a celebrity. When he made it back to the table, I couldn't help myself, I leapt out of my seat and wrapped my arms around him.

"You were amazing!"

"Thanks. It's almost as if I do this for a living." He grinned and used a napkin to mop the sweat from his forehead. "Did I convince you to go up?"

"And follow that performance? Ha!"

Caleb downed his drink. "I have an idea. What about a duet?"

"Me and you?"

He gestured around, another amused grin pulling his lips upward. "Unless there's someone else you'd rather sing with?"

The idea of getting up on stage was still terrifying, but less so if Caleb was by my side. The crowd loved him—at the very least they wouldn't be chucking tomatoes at us.

"What song?"

Caleb took a few laminated sheets from another table and dropped them in front of me. "I leave the decision in your very capable hands. I'm good with whatever."

Yeah, you are.

He picked up his empty glass and wiggled it. "Refill. Need anything?"

I shook my head. When he left, it was just me and the song list. I eyed the pages strewn on the table with distrust before finally giving in. I lifted one and scanned it, nervousness scrabbling in my stomach. A glance in the direction Caleb had gone revealed him leaning on the bar, chatting it up with the bartender. At that moment, they both looked over, Caleb's face breaking into a wide smile and wink.

Ducking my head as my cheeks suffused with heat, I picked up the pencil and wrote down my song choice. When Caleb returned shortly to the table with a fresh drink and two bottles of water, I waved the paper in the air. He snatched it, looked at the title, and gave me a thumbs-up. "Excellent choice. Let me go turn this in to the DJ, but fair warning—it's a full house tonight. It might take a minute."

Great. Plenty of time for me to freak out and talk myself out of it.

As more people went up and down from the stage, my palms grew clammier by the second.

I regret everything. Agreeing to go up there. Coming here at all.

"Zara? Zara! We're up," Caleb's voice broke through my spiral of hysteria.

Still, I remained frozen in place.

"Zara and Caleb! Za-Za-Zara and Caleb!" the DJ sing-songed. "Going once...going twice..."

A dry hand with calloused fingers took hold of mine where it rested on top of the table and squeezed. I met Caleb's probing stare. It was time to put up or shut up.

I gave one firm nod.

"We're here!" Caleb shouted, jumping up from the table and pulling me with him. "We're here!"

"About time," the DJ muttered. Remembering he was mic'd up, he again adopted his exuberant announcer voice. "Please welcome to the stage, Zara and Caleb!"

My hand still in Caleb's, we walked to the front of the room. With every step, it became harder to breathe. Somehow, I found myself on the stage, blinking and squinting at an eager audience. Caleb took one microphone and handed me another.

"Keep your eyes on the monitor," he whispered. "And no matter what happens, just keep singing."

A strangled sound came from the back of my throat as the keyboard intro of Real McCoy's "Another Night" joined the blood pounding in my ears. White lines of text appeared on the small TV screen at the front of the stage as the song's thumping bass and background vocals kicked in.

Clinging to the microphone tightly, my voice was barely above a whisper as the first chorus started. Out of the corner of my eye, I saw Caleb doing the robot on the other side of the stage with the same dynamic energy as his earlier performance. I could do this. I'd just pretend I was alone in my car and rocking out like I was on my way to school. My movements began to loosen and grow bigger as Caleb launched into the spoken-sung verse. The way he sang it made him sound like a creepy vampire in an old movie, and I laughed out loud. As the song continued, we danced around each other, exchanging playful nudges and teasing glances. The audience ate it up.

As the final chorus faded out, Caleb spun me around and we

ended face to face, breathing hard, our mouths separated by mere inches. Caleb's face loomed large as he moved even closer, and my lips parted in expectation. At the last moment, he pulled away and faced the crowd before folding into a cheeky bow.

What the fuck?

Plastering a smile on my face, I did the same and followed him off the stage. The lack of kiss was disappointing, but as the adrenaline continued to course through my veins, I couldn't help but be proud of myself. My performance may not have been anything to write home about, but I'd faced my fear and did it anyway.

Once we got back to the table, Caleb cracked open a bottle of water and gulped it down. "See? Wasn't that bad, right?"

I shrugged and didn't say anything.

"Uh-oh." Caleb's eyebrows knitted together. "Maybe it was."

"It's not that." I hesitated. "I don't want to sound...*forward*... but I thought you were going to kiss me."

"I thought about it," he said matter-of-factly.

I nearly spit out the sip of water I'd taken. *And you didn't because...?*

"I didn't want our first kiss to be in front of an audience. I mean, we basically got to second base at the revue a couple of weeks ago. We should keep some of the mystery alive, right?"

"Right," I said, my cheeks hot. "Wouldn't want to be known as the neighborhood exhibitionists, haha."

Those cool, assessing eyes swept over my face. "Don't worry, when I get you alone, I'll more than make up for it."

Oh.

The entire lower half of my body tingled with anticipation. After shooting me a saucy wink, Caleb returned his attention to the current performer, leaving me free to study him unobserved. I noticed that some part of his body always moved in time with the music, whether it was his fingers drumming on the table, or bouncing his knee. It made me want to see him in action with his band, so I could have the full Caleb McMahon experience.

As if he could feel my gaze boring into his profile, he turned to me with a smile. "Mind if I go again?"

I gestured at the stage. "Have at it."

By the time Caleb took the stage again, my desire and libido were working overtime. It didn't help that the song he'd chosen for this number was "I Wanna Sex You Up" by Color Me Badd. The moment his eyes locked on mine, he did a little shimmy and followed it with a slow body roll, making it clear he'd chosen the song just for me.

Heaven help me.

I alternated chugging down water and fanning myself with a stack of napkins. Sure, I had sexual urges, but none on this level in a long time. A *really* long time.

I thought about the night of the breakup party, specifically the ride home during which the Sensational Six and I came up with the plan to reclaim my twenties. With the completion of a successful solo date at Koi the other night, I'd crossed off every item on the list…except for one.

Before leaving the beach, Jules told me not to sleep with a random guy simply because my friends thought I should. But Caleb wasn't just a random guy; we'd built a rapport over time, and clearly, there was a mutual attraction there. If I was going to have a one-night stand with anyone, a guy like him would be the ideal candidate. Handsome, funny, *and* the little circle move he did with his hips? Yes, please.

You're not that girl, my brain whispered.

But I could be.

I had grown beyond being the pushover who allowed others to overstep her boundaries in the name of keeping the peace. And I'd already done one thing I never thought I'd do tonight— why not make it two?

Stevie's disapproving face popped into my head, but I shooed her away. This decision was all mine.

When Caleb finished his song to much fanfare and returned to the table, I greeted him with another hug, holding him a little tighter and a little longer. "You obviously don't need me to tell you that you killed it. Nice song choice, by the way."

He gave me a devilish smile. "I was hoping you'd appreciate it."

"Oh, I definitely did." We stared at each other, still in close proximity. Close enough for me to smell the beer on his breath. Close enough to wonder if those full lips would taste as good as they looked if I leaned forward just an inch more.

My mouth made my decision for me.

"I believe you promised to make up for earlier?" I asked, surprised by the husky tone in my voice. I hadn't heard it in years.

Hunger gleamed in Caleb's gaze. "Actually, I'm pretty sure I said I'd *more than* make up for it."

My tongue lazily traced my bottom lip, savoring the way his eyes followed its path. "So, what are we waiting for?"

twenty-five

We couldn't get to Caleb's apartment fast enough.

We chose his place because it was closest to the bar, and as a bonus for me, I wouldn't have to upset the peace I'd only just established at the townhouse. When we stepped over the threshold, Caleb flipped a light switch, and a floor lamp in the corner of the room turned on, emitting a warm, amber glow that chased away only some of the room's shadow.

"You'll have to forgive me—I didn't think I'd be having anyone over."

Trust me—this isn't how I thought the night would go either.

I stepped deeper into the apartment as Caleb crossed the living room and pulled the cord on a table lamp next to a low, brown leather couch, giving me my first glimpse at the place he called home. The walls were painted a sultry, dark green, adorned with album covers and moody abstract art. On one wall, a vintage storage cabinet housed a huge vinyl collection and accompanying turntable, and on another, a tall bookcase was crammed with hardcovers, paperbacks with cracked spines, and framed photos of young girls who had his same expressive green eyes and mischievous smile. With surprise, I noticed amethyst and rose quartz towers sitting atop a boxed tarot deck.

"Those are from my little sister, Nia," Caleb said. "I think the purple one's for protection and calmness, or something like that. The pink one..."

"Is for love." I cleared my throat. "Romantic and self."

Caleb's brow furrowed in pleasant surprise. "Yeah. How'd you know?"

"My sister and mom are into the witchy woo, too."

"But not you?"

I shook my head. "That's their thing; not mine."

"Interesting," Caleb murmured. "Nia told me I should charge them, but it's not like I can stick them in an outlet."

"Leave them on the windowsill under the moon or the sun," I said with a laugh, drifting toward the corner where his instruments lived. A keyboard, small drum kit, two guitars...and a trumpet? "You never mentioned a trumpet...only the others."

"Ah." An endearing grin lit up his features. "I'm just learning; my buddy, Rodney, is teaching me. As of now, I can only play 'Taps.'"

"Well, I can't play anything, so you're already ahead of me," I joked.

"So"—he gestured around the living room—"is it what you expected?"

"No expectations," I said, my mouth going dry. "I'm just going with the flow here."

"In that case..." Caleb stepped forward and cradled my face in his hands, pressing his mouth to mine with unexpected tenderness. A sigh escaped me. I couldn't remember when I'd last been touched with such care.

But now wasn't a time for reminiscing or thinking about anyone else.

I deepened the kiss, bordering on aggressive as I entwined

my tongue with Caleb's. Gentleness was all well and good, but it had a time and place.

Right now wasn't it.

Lips still locked on mine, he propelled us backward. When I finally pulled away, gasping for air, we were in a dimly lit bedroom, the only light coming from an industrial-style table lamp with an exposed bulb on the end table next to his bed. Caleb's hand remained on my hip.

"Wow," I said, my hand going to my swollen lips.

Caleb let out a small chuckle. "Same." He hooked a finger beneath one strap of the Bad Decisions Dress, the gentle contact eliciting goosebumps along my skin. The fabric molded itself around my body in response, warming ever so slightly. "I really do love this dress, but I think it'd look even better on my floor."

I sucked in a breath as his hands traveled down my arms and over my hips before gathering fistfuls of wine red satin and tugging it upward in a single graceful motion. The Bad Decisions Dress went over my head, leaving me topless and clad only in a pair of lacy leopard-print panties Rosario coerced me to buy ages ago but I'd never worn, and my heels.

Self-conscious, I crossed my arms over my breasts while Caleb's piercing eyes drank me in. This moment was the reversal of the breakup party, where it was his body that had been on display. But clearly he spent hours at the gym to keep himself in tip-top shape. I did not.

Gently, he peeled my hands away and laced his fingers with mine, planting another kiss on my lips. When he let go to rest those agile hands on my hips, I fumbled with the buckle of his belt, yanking the leather through the loops of his jeans and wrestling with his zipper. He didn't even break the kiss as he stepped out of his pants, instead, moving us as a unit until the back of my knees bumped the mattress. We tumbled onto the bed, dissolving into laughter as Caleb fell on top of me. He rolled off so that we were both laying on our backs and gazing at one another.

My chuckles subsided as I searched his face, where earnestness and a tentative vulnerability stared back at me. I reached out and caressed his cheekbone with the pad of my thumb. He smiled, and I felt his jaw muscles tighten and move beneath my finger.

"One sec," Caleb whispered. He slid off the bed in his sweater and black boxer briefs, and landed at my feet.

"What are you doing?" I laughed and sat up to see.

He lifted his head and waggled his eyebrows while taking my right ankle in his hand. Deftly, he unbuckled the gold heel and tossed it aside, before doing the same with the other.

"Um, where have you been all my life?" I joked.

Instead of answering, Caleb jumped up, pulling his sweater and undershirt over his head to reveal his lean body, with which I was already very well-acquainted. "Wait right here."

Clad only in boxer briefs and black crew socks, he disappeared through a connecting door that I could only assume was the bathroom.

And then I was alone with my thoughts, sprawled on a strange man's bed, basically naked.

What the hell was I doing? I was no Max, or even Jules. What if being with Geoff ruined all other experiences for me?

Caleb reappeared holding a box of condoms, but froze when he caught sight of my face. "Uh-oh." He sat down on the edge of the mattress and set the box on the floor. "We don't have to do anything tonight. We can just hang."

"No!" I said quickly. "No—I want to. It's just…" I pulled myself into a sitting position and grabbed one of the throw pillows leaning against the green velvet headboard, hugging it to my chest in a charade of modesty. "I know it's taboo to talk about your ex on a date, but…I thought he was the man I was going to marry and spend the rest of my life with." I shuddered at the thought. "It's weird to think about being with somebody new. Doing…*things* with somebody new. Geoff and I…we had a routine. Clothes off, a few minutes of kissing, missionary, clean up, go to sleep."

Good grief. It sounded like I was reciting a pound cake recipe.

Caleb considered me, his expression neutral. "That doesn't sound very fun."

I shrugged. "It is what it is. I just figured that's what sex was like after you've been together for so long. If it ain't broke, don't fix it."

"Well, I have good news for you."

"Oh?"

"Your ex isn't here right now. I don't know the details of your breakup, but what I *will* say is that he fumbled big time. Lucky for me, his loss is my gain. Thanks, ex!" He pressed two fingers to his lips, then raised them to the sky, making me laugh. "*And* I have even better news."

I arched an eyebrow.

"Sex doesn't have to be a chore just because you've been with the same person for a long time. You just have to find ways to keep things interesting."

"I suppose you're about to give me some tips?"

He shook his head slowly, one corner of his mouth lifting in a smirk. "I'm about to ask you what turns you on."

Oh. Well, that was unexpected.

I hugged the pillow tighter to my chest, my mind going blank. No one had ever asked what *I* liked in bed. Once Geoff and I had found something that worked well enough, we kept doing it. There was a whole world of things out there that I'd never experienced, and probably even more that I *didn't know* I didn't know. I blurted out the first thing that popped into my head.

"Maybe you could, um, nibble my ear?"

Without a word, Caleb wrestled the pillow from my arms and placed it back against the headboard. I bit my lip, crossing my hands over my chest again as he inched closer and used the back of his hand to push the loose strands of hair from my face. In the next instant, he leaned forward, his tongue darting out to swipe my lobe before sucking it into his mouth.

"Oh—oh! That's good." My eyes fluttered shut as a gentle heat radiated throughout my body.

"That can't be all you like," Caleb murmured around my ear.

I let out a contented sigh. "No, but it's a damn good start."

"What's next?" Caleb's mouth hovered just above my neck, his breath hot on my skin.

"You could…touch me?"

While Caleb's lips branded me with a flurry of kisses, his hands took the opposite approach, feather-light on my breasts. In time, his soft caresses morphed into firm squeezes and playful pinches as he rolled my nipples between the pads of his fingers. My entire being felt tipsy—looser—much like when we performed our duet.

I let out a mew of disappointment as he released me.

"Shh. I'm not done with you yet," he whispered, hands skimming down my stomach to give my thighs the same treatment.

I moaned as he massaged and kneaded the large muscles, his fingertips teasing me every time they grazed the embarrassingly damp fabric between my legs. I wished I could just let go and lose myself in the moment, but Caleb had done so much for me already; I felt like I should be doing something for him.

I trailed a hand down the center of his bare chest, smiling at the shudder that ran through him when I hit a ticklish spot on his ribs. He froze when I found the waistband of his boxer briefs, reaching between us and capturing my hand with his.

"I can wait, Zara." Moving backward on the bed, he sat on his heels, and pulled me away from the headboard by my ankles. "I want you to get what you need first." He ran his palms up my legs again, this time taking hold of my panties and easing them down. "Just relax."

When he got the fabric to my feet, he flashed me a wicked smile, then took the panties between his teeth and tugged them the rest of the way off.

Sweet Baby Jesus.

Nudging my legs further apart, Caleb's hands scaled my body, his fingers climbing higher than before. Pausing at the juncture of my thighs, he met my gaze with lust-filled eyes, waiting for the go-ahead.

Holding my breath, I gave a single nod.

His thumb glided through my slick folds in one long, leisurely stroke that wrenched a low moan from my throat. When he reached my clit, the circle he traced was so agonizingly slow I was ready to command he strum me like his bass. Hell, I'd take his remedial trumpet skills. Anything to take me over the edge.

As if he'd read my mind, Caleb slid two fingers inside me while continuing his work on my clit. Involuntarily, my body bucked against his hand. He chuckled and reclaimed his fingers, but before I could protest, his head dipped down, and those full lips feathered kisses along my inner thigh. I squirmed against the bed, gasping when he planted a quick kiss where I needed it most. He let out a pleased hum, giving me an impish smile that lulled me into a false sense of security.

And then he launched his attack.

Caleb's tongue slid and swirled over my heated flesh until I thought I couldn't take anymore. His fingers dug into my hips, holding me in place as he worshiped me with his mouth. My hands gripped the comforter, toes curling as pleasure built and built, swelling like a cresting wave. Mouth full, Caleb looked up and locked eyes with me.

That was all it took.

I came apart, my orgasm a powerful wave crashing on the

beach. Bliss rippled throughout my body, making me feel happy and free and *alive*. I was flooded with warm fuzzies that filled my head with a drowsy fog and made my limbs heavy.

I glanced down at the man who'd made it happen. Kissing the inside of my knee, he moved to the other side of the bed and raised himself up on one elbow, watching me with a satisfied expression.

"Are you sure you're good?" I asked, unable to stifle a yawn. "I don't mind—"

"Zara, I'm fine," Caleb said firmly. "Besides, you can barely stay awake. How are you feeling? Can I do anything else?"

I hesitated, wondering if my next request—what I *really* wanted after going days and weeks without—would be too much.

"Can you hold me?"

A slow, sweet smile spread across his face. "Of course."

Together, we pulled back the black comforter and sheets and slid under them. Caleb scooted across the mattress, closing the gap between us as I rolled onto my side. I released a blissful sigh as the hard planes of his body pressed into my back. The way we fit together was perfect, like the final piece of a jigsaw puzzle clicking into place. His arms, comforting and strong, held me just under my ribcage, locking us into place. I drifted off to sleep without another thought.

twenty-six

I woke up the next morning, tangled in a mess of sheets, feeling well-rested for the first time in ages. Sunlight streamed through the sliver of space left open by blackout curtains. I was stretching my arms over my head and smiling at the memory of the previous night, when a panicked thought took hold.

What the hell was the protocol for leaving after a one-night stand?

Should I say "Hey, thanks for the good tongue-down but I gotta go?" Or maybe, "Sorry to run out on you, but I have to feed my fish?" I rolled over to look at the other side of the bed. And where the hell was Caleb?

I slid from beneath the covers and hastily grabbed the discarded Bad Decisions Dress from the floor, feeling like a complete hussy. My last walk of shame had been almost a decade ago when Geoff was still sharing a bachelor pad with two other guys. Even though we'd already been in a solid, committed relationship for a long while by then, it was still humiliating to scamper out the back door in the previous night's clothes.

And again—*where the hell was Caleb?*

I glanced at the slightly ajar bathroom door, but there was no light shining through the crack or noise coming from beyond. Had I run him out of his own home?

As if in answer to my question, the door to the bedroom opened without warning, and the man in question walked in wearing last night's sweater and jeans. In his hands he balanced a tray of food, a mason jar with daisies in water, and two steaming coffee mugs, all while humming softly. When our eyes met, he stopped humming and froze in place. We stared at each other for a beat before he raised his eyebrows.

"Leaving so soon?"

"I-I didn't want to cramp your style." I clutched the slippery satin to my body. "I need to feed my fish?" I cleared my throat and repeated more confidently, "Yes. I need to feed my fish."

"Ah." Caleb nodded slowly. "Wouldn't want a hungry fish. And to that point, I don't want a hungry Zara, so you can't leave before breakfast. Not when I got dressed, went all the way downstairs out into the cold, and begged Louisa to make her famous brioche French toast with mixed-berry compote," he teased. "Do you know what I had to do to get this lemon curd?"

My stomach growled. Damn, did that sound good. "I suppose the fish can hold on a little longer."

"Good." Grinning, Caleb nodded at the dress I'd yet to pull over my head. "I've got something that's probably more comfortable to wear, if you'd like."

Heat blazing across my cheeks, I gripped the dress tighter as if I could draw strength from it. "I don't want to impose—"

"It's no problem." He placed the breakfast tray at the foot of the bed and went to the black chest of drawers against the wall. He rummaged around for a few moments, then turned and held out a threadbare *Purple Rain* t-shirt showing Prince astride a motorcycle, and well-worn, black sweatpants.

"These won't break away, will they?" I joked.

He chuckled. "Unlikely." Clearing his throat, he spun around and stuffed his hands in his jeans pockets. It was pointless, seeing as he'd already seen me completely naked, but it further endeared him to me. I pulled the super soft shirt over my head, which smelled like he'd just plucked it from the dryer, and tied the drawstring of the sweats tight.

"Done."

Caleb turned and gestured at the decadent French toast. "Breakfast in bed for the lady?"

"Yes, please!" I tugged the comforter up and sat on top while Caleb did the same on the other side of the bed. Was this normal one-night stand behavior? It couldn't be, because if it was, I was ready to kick myself. I never got breakfast in bed during any of my fourteen years with Geoff—not even once.

"I wasn't sure how you take your coffee, so I brought sugar and a little half-and-half just in case." He pushed the bowl of sugar in my direction.

I felt a rush of affection as I spooned some into my mug. "Thank you." I poured in a splash of creamer and watched Caleb saw through a slice of toast.

Don't do it. Don't do it. Don't—

"So, about last night," I said brightly.

Caleb looked at me with raised eyebrows, but continued to cut the piece of toast and swirl it through the syrupy liquid on his plate.

"That was nice," I continued.

"It was."

"And, um, like I said last night, this is new for me…" I trailed off, trying to appear nonchalant as I chose my next words carefully. "Would you, um, consider this a one-time thing?"

Caleb's forehead wrinkled in confusion until clarity set in and turned his expression stony. He took his time finishing the bite of food in his mouth before offering a cool reply. "You mean, is this a one-night stand?"

Wincing at his tone, I nodded.

"Is that what you want?" He wiped his hands on a folded paper napkin and stared at me, his face now unreadable.

Clearly, I'd offended him, which wasn't my intention at all. "I—I don't know what I want, Caleb." I hesitated. "Full transparency, I'm kind of a mess right now. I *just* got out of a long-ass relationship, and I'm working on myself. I don't want to dump all my baggage at your feet."

The corner of his mouth quirked up, but the half-smile lacked its usual warmth. "I hate to break it to you, but you already have."

Well, fuck.

I covered my face with my hands. "I'm sorry."

Caleb sighed. "I guess I should be used to it by now. It comes with the territory."

I risked a peek between my fingers. "What do you mean?"

"Usually, when women find out I'm an entertainer, their whole mindset shifts. Either they drop me because they don't want to be with someone who gets paid to take off their clothes—fair—or they get really into it and hypersexualize me. But I'm not some manwhore or playboy; I have feelings."

Guiltily, I remembered my line of thought during his karaoke performance.

"And honestly, I'd like to think I'm a bit of a romantic," he continued. "I *want* to commit. Preferably to someone who understands that stripping is just one part of my life and it doesn't define me. Someone who knows that I'm loyal, faithful, and all about open communication. I would *never* cross any line." He shook his head. "But sometimes it feels like that's too much to ask for."

Feeling like a complete shithead, I rested my hand on his arm. "It's not. And I'm sorry, Caleb, I didn't mean to make you feel like a piece of meat."

"Thank you, I appreciate the apology. Besides, it's not like I plan to be cracking a whip onstage and ripping my pants off five years from now."

"Is that so?" I gave him a tentative grin. "Gonna learn a few magic tricks instead?"

A ghost of a smile finally returned to his face. "Not quite. By that time, I'll have saved up enough money to open a music store that plays a huge role in the community. Group classes, private lessons, open mic nights, jam sessions…"

"Still performing with the band?"

"You know it. And my lady will be right there, cheering me on at every show…or most of them."

I pictured myself proudly watching Caleb perform karaoke the evening before. "So, you've definitely settled down with someone by then?"

"Yup. And we'll have an equally strong physical and emotional connection. She knows I can be intense at times and doesn't resent me for it. She accepts all parts of me—even the messy bits." He cut his eyes at me playfully.

"She sounds lovely. I hope you find her." Was that ache in my chest from imagining some other woman who wasn't me cheering on Caleb while he played with his band? From picturing someone else being the recipient of mind-blowing oral sex and glorious French toast in bed?

"Eh. I think I'm going to let her find me when she's ready. I never want to force anything." He shrugged. "How about you?"

"I never want to force anything either," I joked.

Caleb rolled his eyes. "I mean, what are you going to be doing five years from now?"

"Well…I hope to God Susie's retired by then. And I don't want to work with anyone else, so…"

Even though I knew it was bound to happen eventually, I hadn't really let myself sit and imagine life after the Ellis Elephants. Geoff and I had always talked about me being a stay-at-home-mom and homeschooling our future children, but now that there was no more Geoff, it was something I had to consider.

"I don't have everything quite mapped out like you do—I used to, but not anymore. Maybe...get my Master's? Or look at an administrative role?"

"You don't have to have everything all figured out. You've got ideas, and that's a great start."

"What I do know is that I'll still be getting into shenanigans with my best friends." Who knew where life would take the Sensational Six five years from now. More kids? More marriages? What I could say for certain was that Jules, Rosario, Max, Stevie, Amber, and I would all still be in each other's lives.

"Does that include attending all-male revues at Dusty Spurs?" Caleb teased.

"Ehhh. I heard my favorite entertainer won't be there anymore." I leaned over and bumped his shoulder with mine.

He gave me a full-fledged grin, and another wave of affection washed over me. While I might not be watching Caleb's bare butt cheeks wiggle and jiggle as he gave lap dances to the horny women of Fallen Oaks five years from now, I could see myself sharing lemon Oreos and learning K-pop choreography with him before meeting up with the girls at an open mic session.

"You know, I think the messiest times are the most fun," he said. "And it doesn't matter whether you think you have your shit together or not—the right person will enter your life when it's time."

"You make some great points."

"Why thank you." He pretended to dust off his shoulder. "In sophomore year, I took a rhetoric class for three whole weeks."

"Well, look at you!" The grin we shared sent my heart cartwheeling in my chest. "Caleb...I would actually be cool if this was more than a one-time thing—like...a multiple-time thing."

"'A multiple-time thing,' huh? When you put it that way, how can I resist? But I would like that very much." Leaning in, he pressed a sweet kiss to my forehead. "Now eat up—your French toast is getting cold."

twenty-seven

y head remained in the clouds as I drove home in Caleb's clothes, barefoot, singing along with the radio at the top of my lungs. The Bad Decisions Dress and my heels took a rest in an old shopping bag on the passenger seat.

I wouldn't mind starting more mornings like this one—delectable food, delightful company, and divine kisses. Having established that what we had was officially *not* a one-night stand, I found myself reluctant to leave, and Caleb was even more reluctant to let me go. But he had a private lesson soon, followed by an Alphas show later that night, and I didn't want to get in the way of his preparations...despite my unease at the thought of him dancing on and tossing other women around. That left me with the rest of the day to do as I pleased, and antsy as I was, I didn't want to stay at home.

Maybe I'd call Jules, buy a bunch of snacks at Dollar Tree, and smuggle them into the movies. Or I could take myself on a solo date to Kittens & Cream, the new cat café that had recently popped up downtown. I'd been dying to go ever since I saw videos of cats sprawled on plush cushions, chasing feather wands, and winding around people's ankles.

But all my illustrious plans for the day went up in smoke when I turned onto my street and saw my mother's red Mini Cooper parked in the middle of my driveway. An involuntary groan slipped from my lips, morphing into a horrified "Oh no" when I spied Mom standing outside her car, chatting with the neighborhood busybody, Mr. Cornelius. God only knew what they were talking about.

Hurriedly, I parked on the street and scrambled out of the car with my bagged dress in one hand and shoes in the other.

"Four o'clock in the morning!" Mr. Cornelius was grumping when I approached. "That pink bus kept me awake half the night. You know who's out getting up to no good at those hours? Troublemakers, that's who! Drug dealers and pimps, the lot of 'em!"

Great. Now Mr. C thought I was pushing cocaine or sex workers.

I pasted on a contrite, saccharine smile. "Sorry, Mr. Cornelius. It won't happen again."

"Better not," he muttered. "I don't want to have to get the HOA involved. I already have to draft a letter about 308's Christmas lights still being up. It's almost February."

"You have my word, Mr. Cornelius."

He sniffed as if it didn't count for much, and without so much as a 'goodbye,' shuffled down my driveway. Once he made it across the street, I turned to my mother, who looked every bit of her 'Infinity Love' persona with a lacy shawl atop a flowy, loose-fitting dress and large evil eye pendant. The honey brown locs she'd cultivated since I was a child were tucked on top of her head in a silk turban, and a rhinestone bindi over her third eye twinkled in the sunlight despite the numerous conversations I'd had with her about cultural appropriation. Her trusty tapestry bag, as old as I was and containing her spiritual supplies, hung from her forearm.

"Morning, Mom." I gave her an awkward side hug.

"Good morning, Sunshine." She adjusted her shawl. "I've been waiting here for a while."

"Well, that's what happens when you don't call in advance." I started toward the front door.

Mom tutted behind me. "Did something happen to your clothes? That doesn't look like your usual style."

And how would you even know what that is?

"Where are your shoes? Do you need some grounding?"

"I'm trying something new," I said, my voice pained. I unlocked the door and stepped inside.

Please God, let this be a short visit.

While I was thankful that I didn't have such a strained relationship with my mom that it was at the point-of-no-return like Max and *her* mother, things between us were complicated. After leaving us with our grandparents, Mom flitted in and out of our lives, giving up the role of reliable, stable parent in favor of being the fun, zany friend who popped in every so often. Now that she'd found a like-minded community of woo-woo enthusiasts here in Fallen Oaks through the holistic healing center she worked at, she was trying to make up for lost time. Unfortunately for her—and my sister and I—it was a couple decades too late.

"Love what you've done with the place!" Mom chirped, close on my heels as I made my way to the kitchen.

"Thanks." I pulled a glass from the cabinet and filled it with water from the fridge pitcher. "Can I get you something?"

Mom shook her head. "No thank you. I finished my chakra-balancing tea while I waited."

"In that case, do you want to tell me why you're here?"

"I just thought I'd come say hello." She hefted her carpet bag onto the counter and started pulling out items like a metaphysical Mary Poppins. A satiny, rainbow-colored scarf. Various colored crystals and decks of cards. A bundle of dried herbs wrapped with string. She produced a lighter and lit the bundle, sending a plume of earthy smoke into the air. "Open the windows, will you, Sunshine?"

I held my hands up. "Whoa, whoa, whoa—what are you doing? You're going to set off the fire alarm!"

Ignoring me, she moved around the room, using a feather to disperse the fragrant smoke. "I'm saging, of course."

After the beach weekend, I'd had enough with the rituals. "Mom? Mom? *Mom. Stop.*"

She paused and turned to me with a surprised expression. "Zara, darling, there's no need to shout."

I took a deep breath to try and keep my cool. "Why don't we go sit in the living room?"

"But I didn't get to finish saging."

"That's okay."

When she moved to grab her crystals and cards, I gently took her by the arm, told her they'd be safe, and steered her to the couch. She sat down, pulling her legs up criss-cross applesauce, and pouted at me. "Frankly, Zara, I'm hurt."

My brow furrowed. "Because I told you to leave the crystals in the kitchen?"

"No—that I had to hear from someone else about your breakup."

Godammit, Jules. I'd told her to let me tell Mom in my own time, but did she ever listen? No.

"Exactly what did Jules say?"

Mom gasped. "You told Jules but didn't tell me?"

I frowned. "You didn't hear it from her?"

"No. I heard it from Stevie's mother, Belinda. She attends my bi-monthly women's healing circle."

I pinched the bridge of my nose. For someone so secretive

about her own private life, Stevie's lips were awfully loose when it came to anyone else's.

"Why didn't you say anything?" Mom asked.

I gestured at the kitchen. "Because I knew *that* would happen."

"*What* would happen?" She blinked, totally oblivious.

"You ranting about the patriarchy and evils of marriage, then trying to use potions and sage to fix everything."

Mom placed her hand on her chest, her face stricken. "Zara, you know I don't make *potions*. Tinctures and teas? Yes."

Of course that's what she chose to focus on.

I inhaled deeply. "All I'm saying is that what I needed in the moment was someone to tell me that despite spending fourteen years with a shithead, I shouldn't give up on love—that there's still someone out there for me."

"I would have gladly done that. The shithead part, I mean," Mom said. "I always knew that man was a rotten egg. There was something about his aura that I just couldn't put my finger on."

Sighing, I fell back against the couch and looked up at the ceiling. *Lord give me strength. I'm trying here.*

"As far as the other part, I raised you girls to be independent and strong so you'd never have to rely on a man. And look at you and Jules—you're amazing women in your own right. Anything you can do with a man by your side you can do on your own."

"That's in spite of you, not because of you," I said, my frustration reaching a boiling point. "I agree that we should be able to stand on our own feet, but like always, you took it to the extreme. You tossed me and Jules into the deep end, said 'See ya,' and high-tailed it to the nearest 'intentional community.' I had to figure out things for myself while parenting my little sister."

"I never—"

"You did," I said firmly. As I took a deep breath, a realization dawned on me. "Geoff was my act of rebellion in response to everything you shoved down my throat."

Everything from his stuffy, corporate personality to the way I deferred to him—all of it had been a big middle finger to my mother.

"After doing so much heavy lifting with Jules, I can't tell you how much of a relief it was to let someone else take control and make the decisions. To sit back and be cared for." I shook my head. "But I've learned that I can't hand everything over like that—I have to keep some of it for myself."

Mom looked down at her lap, running her hands over the patterns on her dress. "I didn't realize you felt this way."

I didn't either. The relationship with my mother had always bugged me—when I was younger, I used to wish for a "normal" mom who would do things like make cupcakes for the school bake sale and take me to the park. A mom who would show up to my dance recitals and proudly call out, "That's my baby!" But it wasn't until this very moment that I realized how very much everything—my issues with my mom, Geoff, the people-pleasing—was connected.

"I thought I was saving you from making the same mistakes that I did," Mom said quietly. She wasn't staring at me but somewhere over my right shoulder like she was lost in a memory.

"I know—believe me, I do—and I can appreciate that. But I also know that being on your own is what works for *you*. I, on the other hand, want to find love and get married and plant roots. Geoff wasn't the right one for me, but I'm confident my person is out there."

A vision of Caleb sitting in front of a wall of mounted instruments, an acoustic guitar on his knee as he played a chord for a little girl with her own guitar seated opposite him, materialized in my mind. Surely it was too soon to be thinking about a future with him…right? But I could picture it so clearly it was like it'd already happened.

Mom was quiet for a long time, then sighed. "I refuse to wear one of those frumpy mother-of-the-bride dresses at the wedding."

My lips twitched. At least I'd gotten through to her a little bit. "Play your cards right and I might even let you use your singing bowls during the ceremony."

twenty-eight

The Monday morning after my date with Caleb—and long overdue chat with Mom—Susie and I sat on the alphabet rug at the front of the classroom cutting mittens out of construction paper to prepare for the day's math lesson. With the kids off at their science class, the room was eerily quiet.

"Motown Mania, huh?" Susie said, after I shared some of the developments for the spring music program. She narrowed her eyes in concentration as her scissors followed the thick outline on the paper. "That doesn't sound half bad. If this was your influence, maybe we should have you help organize *all* the concerts."

I shook my head vehemently. "No thanks. This is a one-and-done situation."

Ring. Ring.

Oh no. An irrational thread of dread knotted in my stomach at the sound coming from my desk. Susie and I locked eyes.

"You should get that," she said.

I shrugged, feigning nonchalance. "Or I could just let the call go to voicemail."

"And let them blow up *my* phone trying to get ahold of you? I don't think so."

With a sigh, I set down my scissors and got to my feet.

"Guess who?" Kimiko sang down the line when I picked up the phone.

"Hi Kimiko," I said flatly.

"There's another delivery for you!"

"Is it flowers?"

"You'll just have to come down and see," Kimiko replied.

That was the absolute last thing I wanted to do. I set the receiver back on the cradle, grumbling under my breath.

"Another delivery?" Susie asked.

I nodded.

"Interesting. Grab some blue construction paper from the faculty room on your way back, will you, dear?"

"Sure thing."

Common sense be damned, a tiny spark of hope ignited at the idea of Caleb sending me something. There was no way he'd make a big gesture like that so soon, right?

When I stepped into the office, that same spark of hope extinguished itself quicker than a line forming at Krispy Kreme when the *Hot Now* light turned on. In the same spot on Kimiko's desk as before sat a bouquet made up of various white flowers and frou-frou greenery. It looked like something you might send after a death in the family. There was no question in my mind who they were from.

"How can you have a long face with such pretty flowers?" she asked.

Because they come from a self-absorbed, cheating asshole, that's why.

Fuck what people would say.

"Do you want these?"

Kimiko blinked. "Are you sure?"

"I've never been more sure of anything," I said firmly. "Let me just grab the card."

I stepped forward, plucked the cream envelope from among the flowers, and pocketed it. Even though I might be opening myself up to my colleagues' speculation and gossip, I didn't have to give them a smoking gun.

"Well…thanks," Kimiko said, head tilted slightly as she studied me.

"Enjoy."

I stalked straight back to the classroom, shaking with rage the whole way. What did I have to do to make Geoff realize that things between us were well and truly done? Did I need some kind of restraining order? I knew I could probably hire Jules to break his ankles, but that was an absolute last resort. Why the fuck was he so persistent now, when he could barely make an effort before?

Without a word to Susie, I let out an exasperated sigh, dropped down into my desk chair, and rested my head on the desk.

"My construction paper?" she asked.

I groaned. "Sorry, I forgot. Give me a minute and I'll go get it."

She was silent for a moment, then said, "Can I make an observation?"

"Sure. Why not?" Without lifting my head, I motioned for her to go on.

"You've come to school in a much better mood in the last few weeks—not that you were ever a Grumpy Gus. But there's a light in your eyes that wasn't there before…well, with the exception of a couple of days. And coincidentally, on both of them, you were called to the office for a delivery."

I raised my head an inch to find Susie's sharp gaze on me, her eyebrows lifted, beckoning me to unburden myself.

So, I did. I told her all about my problems with Geoff. About finding out that he'd cheated, and dumping his stuff outside. About being scared to start over.

"What a turd!" she exclaimed when I was done.

"I prefer the term 'douchecanoe'."

"He's not a douchecanoe, he's a douche*ship*." Susie scowled. "It makes me want to call him up myself and set him straight."

Her fiery indignation sent the corners of my mouth upward. "I'm glad to have you in my corner."

"Of course, dear."

"I will say Geoff's fuck-up did bring about one good thing—it helped bring my best friends and I back together. We all attended Fallen Oaks Prep in middle and high school when there were hardly any students of color, so we were super close. But then some of us got married and others moved away…you know how it goes."

Susie nodded. "Good on you for looking at the silver lining!"

"I learned from the best," I said, grinning at her.

My cell buzzed on the desk.

CALEB

I wish the kids had music today so I could see you.

"Mmhmm. Make that two good things," Susie said, her voice smug.

How did she know?

I quickly relaxed my face into a blank mask even though it was too late. I started to type a reply to Caleb, but another text notification popped up on the top of my screen.

GEOFF

> Did you get the flowers?

It was like the man had some kind of radar for any time I felt the least bit happy. Thoroughly and completely over his bullshit, I tapped the banner and sent a response.

ZARA

> YES AND I GAVE THEM AWAY. Why can't you just leave me alone? I'm THISCLOSE to siccing Jules on you.

"Uh-oh," Susie said. "Your face looks like that time Eliana put her Nutella sandwich on your chair and you sat on it."

I made a face at the memory. "It's the doucheship."

Typing bubbles appeared and disappeared. Appeared and disappeared again. I was moments away from exiting the chat and blocking him again when another message finally showed up.

GEOFF

> Zara, please. Can we meet up? Just one little dinner at Bella Cucina for closure, and I won't bother you again. I mean it.

Closure? *He* needed closure? And he wanted it at Bella Cucina—the place where I could never show my face again—no less?

Susie picked up her scissors and resumed cutting. "Don't leave us hanging, hun. What does the doucheship want?"

"To have dinner." I made a face. "For *closure*."

Susie wrinkled her nose like she smelled something foul. "You don't owe him a darn thing."

She was absolutely right, but if Geoff was being true to his word, attending this dinner might be my chance to kick him out of my life for good. And if he was out of my life for good, there'd be nothing holding me back from going all in with Caleb. Sacrificing one more hour in his company for a lifetime of peace? Not such a bad deal.

ZARA

I'll think about it.

twenty-nine

MAX

You said NO, right?

STEVIE

You can't seriously be considering it.

ZARA

He said if I met him for dinner, he'd leave me alone.

ROSARIO

You actually believe that?

JULES

I can take him out.

Just say the word. Pinecone.

STEVIE

Pinecone?

JULES

That's the word.

AMBER

Zara, you at home? I'm visiting my parents now, but I can stop by after.

Panic took hold as I glanced up at the stage on which I popped my karaoke cherry a few days earlier. Caleb's band, Flow State Rebels, were picking back up their instruments after a short break between sets. He'd invited me to come watch the gig, and eager to see him in action—and to distract myself from Geoff's stupid text, to which I still hadn't replied—I accepted. I'd considered inviting the girls, but after imagining Stevie giving him the third degree, or Jules begging him to take his shirt off or introduce her to his stripping associates, I decided to keep Caleb all to myself for just a little while longer.

ZARA

I'd love to but I'm turning in early. These kids are shaving years off my life.

Gotta go!

Quickly, I tucked my phone away and refocused my attention on the Flow State Rebels. It was odd—even though I was sitting by myself toward the front of the crowded room, watching the band perform felt like the most natural thing in the world. Not only that, but I was enjoying it; I hadn't expected them to be so good. For their first set, they'd put their own reggae-ska spin on several 2000's hits, and performed a couple of original songs apparently written by their drummer, Scott.

But even with how good they were, I couldn't stop thinking

about Geoff's request. Like I'd told the girls, my inclination was to go to dinner just to shut him up…but I wanted to discuss it with Caleb first. Though we hadn't yet defined what we were doing or spoken about being exclusive, I wanted to be completely open with him.

I just didn't know how he'd take it.

The second half of the show was even better than the first. At one point, the band led the crowd in a sing-along that had even the bartenders belting out lyrics. When the show ended and Caleb lined up with his four bandmates at the front of the stage for a bow, I leaped out of my seat, clapping and cheering wildly. He caught my eye and winked. As canned music took over the speakers and the Flow State Rebels packed their instruments away and chatted with fans, I drifted toward the stage.

"Hey, you," Caleb said, a goofy grin lighting up his face—and my heart—when he saw me. He jumped down with Cosmo, his bass, strapped securely to his back, and embraced me. "What'd you think?"

"You were terrific." When his bandmates carefully placed their instruments beside the stage and joined us, I added, "All of you. Seriously."

Beaming, Caleb gestured at me. "Everyone, this is Zara. Zara, this is Ace, Scott, Rodney, and Kat." At the sound of their name, each person waved in greeting, except for Kat, the band's guitarist. Tall and slender with bone-straight platinum hair and flamboyant eye makeup that would make Max drool, she darted forward and gave me a ferocious hug.

"We finally get to meet the mysterious, dazzling Zara," said Ace, the lead singer and keyboardist. I'd spent the entire show unable to figure out why he looked so familiar, but it didn't hit me until a woman shouted out his name on the other side of the bar, and he did a body roll in response.

He's the pirate from Alphas Unleashed! I'm definitely *glad I didn't invite Jules.*

"Caleb's never brought anyone around," Rodney said. He played trumpet or trombone depending on the song.

Caleb rolled his eyes. "There was no one *to* bring around."

The thought of Caleb talking about me to other people and being the first person he introduced to his friends filled my chest with warm fuzzies.

Ace ran a hand through his hair. "We're gonna grab a drink. You two coming?"

Caleb shook his head. "Nah, it's a school night."

Rodney shrugged. "Okay. See you next time, Zara."

"Bye." I waved as they all headed to the bar, then turned to Caleb. "You sure you don't want to stick around? If you want to hang out and have a beer with them, I don't mind."

Caleb brought his lips close to my ear. "I'd rather hang out with you."

I shivered even though the room was packed with so many bodies the windows had fogged up. As we walked toward Caleb's car—he'd insisted on picking me up and I let him—I continued to gush about his performance, stalling so I didn't have to bring up Geoff.

"If you liked that, just wait until the spring concert," Caleb said with a mischievous grin. Once he buckled Cosmo the bass into the backseat, he slid behind the wheel of the car and started the ignition.

"I have to tell you something," I said in a rush. It was now or never, but I hesitated, remembering the weird expression on his face when he told me I'd already brought my baggage to his doorstep. "Well, I guess I don't *have* to tell you, but I want to be totally honest with you."

Instead of saying anything, he waited patiently, hands on the steering wheel. I took a deep breath. "My ex—you know, the one I told you about? He, uh, texted me yesterday—not that we text each other on a regular basis or anything," I added quickly.

Caleb's face remained completely still.

"He asked me to have dinner with him." I paused. "For closure."

"'For closure'?" Caleb repeated.

I nodded, holding my breath.

"You should do it," he said.

I blinked. "Really?"

I thought maybe there was a slight chance he'd be annoyed, or feel threatened, but I didn't think he'd have no reaction at all.

He shrugged. "Yeah. Trust goes both ways, and I trust your judgment. I told you once, and I'll say it again: your ex clearly didn't realize what he had in front of him." His face softened. "But I do."

A cozy warmth enveloping my body, I leaned over the center console, took Caleb's face in my hands, and kissed him.

thirty

A couple days later, I stood on my tiptoes just inside Il Giardino Toscano, a high-end Italian restaurant I'd always pestered Geoff about trying. He never wanted to go, claiming it was too expensive, but when I refused to set foot in Bella Cucina, he threw it out as an alternative. My eyes swept the room and found him easily, seated at a table in the middle of the bustling restaurant. Dressed in a suit and tie as if he'd just come from an important work meeting, he tugged on his earlobe while chatting with a server.

In front of me, the maître d' opened his mouth to say something, but I held up my hand. "I found who I'm looking for."

I pulled out my phone and opened the Sensational Six group chat.

ZARA

Everyone in position?

AMBER

Yup.

> **JULES**
>
> Pinecone.

> **ZARA**
>
> I'm going in.

I tucked the phone into my purse, squared my shoulders, and strolled across the restaurant, carefully dodging the accordion-violin duo serenading an older couple at their table.

After Caleb dropped me off at my place on Tuesday—because, after all, it was a school night—I texted Geoff and told him I was willing to meet...but Bella Cucina was a no-go. I'd also told him he only had one hour—just enough time for me to order the most expensive thing on the menu, say my piece, and get the hell out of there.

I pasted on the bored expression I'd spent ten minutes perfecting in my bathroom mirror and plopped into the chair across from my ex, not even giving him the chance to stand and greet me.

He cleared his throat and offered a cautious smile. "Thank you for joining me tonight," he said stiffly.

I crossed my arms over my chest. "I'm just here so you stop bothering me."

The server he'd been speaking to earlier appeared beside our table and asked for our drink order. Instead of ordering for us both like he usually did, Geoff glanced my way, seeming almost shy.

"Do you still like California Chardonnay?"

I narrowed my eyes in suspicion. "I'll just have water. Thanks."

"Um, okay, just water for me, too."

When she left us to look over the menu, I glared at Geoff instead. "The clock starts now. Talk."

His face scrunched in consternation. "I wanted to tell you… I'm sorry."

I sat in silence, waiting for him to continue, but he said nothing more. He watched me with an earnest, hopeful look.

Seriously? That was it?

"You're sorry? *That's* why you called me here? To say you're *sorry?*"

It was almost laughable that, since receiving that life-changing DM, this was the first time Geoff had thought to apologize. It was an apology I'd once ached for—a simple, direct admission of responsibility—but no longer needed.

"I don't forgive you," I said, priding myself on sounding so calm.

Geoff nodded like a bobblehead on a car dashboard as if he'd expected as much. "I understand. I do. I was a bad partner to you, Zara. I-I disregarded your feelings. Took for granted all the things you did to keep our lives running smoothly." He scrubbed a hand over his face. "I didn't realize how good I had it with you until you were gone."

I scoffed in disbelief, but the noise was drowned out by a crash of glass. Both Geoff and I turned our heads in the direction of the sound.

Two tables away from ours, near the bathrooms, a couple of elderly women sprang up with impressive agility. In the middle of the table, a pitcher lay overturned, water soaking the white tablecloth and dripping onto the floor, which was now littered with broken glass. One of the women sported straight, ash gray hair that flowed down her back, and cat eye sunglasses with a bright purple caftan that looked like something Max's Great-Aunt Cecilia would wear.

Wait a minute.

I zeroed in on their sheepish faces. The caftan wearer had wrinkles and age spots, but the dusting of glittery blush across her cheekbones that sparkled under the restaurant's overhead lighting, was a dead giveaway. That was no old lady—that was Maxine Noelle Baldwin!

My attention shifted to the woman next to her, who wore a frumpy, ankle-length dress with a high, frilly neck. Her tall blue rinse bouffant suggested she lived by the motto "The higher the hair, the closer to God" and, oddly, made her resemble my grandma.

Jules!

When I craned my neck, I spotted Amber, Stevie, and Rosario, still seated at the table, but also wearing wigs in various shades of gray, trying to make themselves as inconspicuous as possible. Mateo's car seat perched on a high chair at the head of the table.

What the hell? I mouthed at them.

Oops, Max mouthed back with a grin.

The plan was for the girls to arrive early and be at the restaurant for moral support and backup if needed—not engage in *I Love Lucy*-style shenanigans.

Geoff squinted. "Is that...Jules? And your friend, Max? Why are they dressed like old ladies?"

"I don't know what you're talking about," I said airily, turning back to him.

For a moment longer, he kept his gaze on their table, where a server had rushed over to clean up the mess, then returned his attention to me, brow furrowed. "I suppose it's good they're here anyway."

"It is?" I asked, surprised. Jules and Geoff tolerated each other for my sake, but he'd always disapproved of Max and Ro, declaring them too over-the-top.

Our server chose that moment to reappear beside us. "Are you ready to order?"

"Give us another minute," Geoff replied, tugging on his ear.

She nodded slowly. "I'll check back in a bit."

"Do you have an ear infection or something?" I asked.

A nervous smile lit on Geoff's face. "What? No." He leaned forward in his chair. "Zara, I miss you so much."

"That's nice—"

"We were a great team."

Before I could open my mouth to list all the reasons why that wasn't even remotely true, the accordionist and violinist I'd passed earlier stopped next to our table and launched into a lively, melodic version of "Mr. Brightside" by The Killers.

Okay. Weird.

Out of the corner of my eye, I spied movement on the other side of the table. My stomach churned as Geoff knelt on the ground by my feet, fishing for something in his jacket pocket.

Oh no. No no no.

The BLT sandwich I'd eaten for lunch was clawing its way back up my throat. I was going to throw up or pass out. Maybe both.

I tore my eyes away from Geoff to see if anyone else was watching, and of course, all the people at the nearby tables were pointing and staring at us with unrestrained delight. Well, not the Sensational Six. My friends' faces beneath the old age makeup showed a mixture of horror and disgust. They looked like they were ready to vomit right along with me.

"No the fuck he isn't!" I heard Ro exclaim.

But yes the fuck he was.

"Zara Harmony Whitmore, we've spent almost a third of our lives together." Beads of sweat dotted Geoff's crisp hairline and upper lip as he opened and held out the same leather box I had found in his sock drawer many months ago. "After these last few weeks without you, I know without a doubt that you're my other half."

Even though his mouth continued to move, I didn't hear anything he said. My eyes were glued to the diamond ring winking in the box. The ring I'd yearned to slip on and never take off. The ring that said I was worthy of being loved and committed to.

For so long, I'd dreamed of this moment, and it was finally here. I thought about the mint-green album filled with all my hopes and plans for the future, what was left of it now safely stashed in the bottom drawer of my nightstand.

And then I came to my senses.

"What the hell are you doing?" I hissed. "Get up. *Get up.*"

Geoff stared at me, his forehead wrinkling. "Is that a no?"

"Of course it's a no!" I said in exasperation. Thoroughly embarrassed, I used my hand to shield my face from onlookers and glared down at the table.

Realizing things had taken a turn, the musical duo abruptly broke off the song with a sad *womp, womp,* then transitioned into something that sounded awfully close to The Human League's "Don't You Want Me."

"Oh, just stop!" Geoff exclaimed, getting to his feet. "Get out of here."

The music stopped again, followed by a disgruntled huff, and some shuffling away moments later.

Back in his seat across from me, Geoff plunked the ring down on the table between us.

"Why the hell would you do that?" I asked. "Was that your plan all along? Lure me here under false pretenses and then surprise me with a proposal?"

He blinked. "Zara, I thought this was what you wanted. The ring. The wedding. Kids—"

"But not with you!" I exploded.

His head reared back like I'd slapped him.

"You *cheated* on me and tried to make it seem like it was no big deal! How could you think I'd ever give you the chance to hurt me again? It's bad enough I've already wasted a decade and a half of my life on you." The words had weighed heavily on my heart for so long that it felt liberating to finally get them off my chest.

Geoff actually had the audacity to look hurt. "You really think our relationship was a waste?"

I took a moment before answering. Of course, it hadn't been *completely* toxic—we'd had some great moments. Like our trip to Charleston for my thirtieth birthday, where we took a horse-drawn carriage through town and had a romantic picnic near Pineapple Fountain at Waterfront Park. Or his dad's retirement party, where Geoff had proudly introduced me to his extended relatives who immediately accepted me, and I finally became part of the large, tight-knit family that I always wanted.

But I refused to give him anything he could potentially use as leverage.

Instead, I said, "You know, I want to say thank you."

He narrowed his eyes in suspicion.

I raised my voice so the surrounding tables could hear. "Thank you for fucking up so majorly that I now know what I deserve. Thank you for showing me that I deserve *so* much better than anything your feeble brain could possibly come up with. I don't need to be someone else's other half—I'm whole all on my own."

"Hell yeah!" Max shouted.

Shoving my chair away from the table, I stood up. Geoff scrambled to his feet as well.

"We're done here," I said firmly. "Don't ever contact me again unless you want Jules to castrate you with a rusty spoon."

Geoff paled, then nodded slowly.

"And that's our cue!" Jules cried.

The six biddies left their table and purposefully strode toward ours in their not-so-effective disguises, Max leading the way.

"Twatwaffle," she spat as she filed past.

Behind her, in a severe silver bun, tweed skirt suit, and

sensible loafers—not too far off from her normal wardrobe—Stevie paused to flag down their server, causing Amber to bump into her from behind. "Can you tell the chef the carpaccio was to die for? Thanks!" Then her head swung to Geoff, and the smile morphed into a grimace. "Asshole."

Amber and Rosario, who had Mateo's car seat firmly in the crook of her elbow, followed suit in their own grandma get-up, each with another colorful name for Geoff. And finally, Jules brought up the rear, shoving him with her shoulder, before winding her arm around mine. "Come on, sis."

Together we walked to the entrance, my head held high. I glanced back just once to find my ex standing beside the table, slack-jawed. I faced forward again, a satisfied smile curving my lips as we exited the restaurant. No one said anything until we stopped next to my car in the parking lot.

"What a fucking rush!" Amber crowed, rubbing her hand over her bright, floral muumuu. It was a little disconcerting to see a pregnant senior. "Did you see his face?"

"That was almost as entertaining as the breakup party! That fucker really tried to propose," Max said with a scoff.

I brought my hand to my forehead, still unable to believe what had just happened. "He really did. Wait—don't you guys need to pay?"

Stevie waved a dismissive hand. "Nah. We took care of it earlier just in case we needed to make a hasty exit."

Jules tapped her temple. "Clever, right?"

I nodded, then pointed at the girls' outfits. "What's up with the disguises? We didn't discuss that."

Amber thrust a finger at Max. "Her idea."

Max shrugged modestly. "What good is having a costume designer and stylist in the group if you never use them?"

I tugged on her caftan. "Did you raid Cecilia's closet? She's going to kill you."

"Nah," Max said. "She donated it to the cause."

Shaking my head, my gaze roved over the girls again, and when I looked down into Mateo's car seat, I did a double take. "You put a disguise on *the baby?*"

Poor Mateo wore a floppy, gunmetal gray wig clearly intended for an older child, his old man transformation complete with oversized, bushy gray eyebrows and a comically large mustache. The disguise didn't seem to bother him though, in fact, he smiled at me and giggled.

Ro grinned beneath her salt-and-pepper pixie cut. "What can we say? We're committed to the bit." She patted the fluorescent yellow fanny pack at her waist.

I stared at them, standing there with their artificial wrinkles, dressed as bumbling fugitives from a retirement home, waiting for me to announce our next move.

And then I lost it.

My body shook uncontrollably with hysterical laughter coming in wave after wave. Tears streamed down my cheeks as my breath formed clouds in the chilly February air. I doubled over, the laughter continuing so forcefully I thought I might pee myself.

"Uh, is she okay?" Ro asked.

"She's fine. I think it's a cathartic release of trapped emotion," Jules said, now apparently a psychologist.

Inhaling deeply to calm myself down, I straightened and met each woman's eyes. "I love you. Deeply. Like, seriously. You can't even begin to imagine how much you mean to me."

"Aw, back atcha," Amber said. "Group hug!"

We huddled together in the parking lot, our exhalations creating small, swirling clouds of steam that joined together to form a collective dreamy vapor around us.

"Can we get out of here? It's cold!" Jules said when we dispersed.

"I told Edgar I'd be home at nine." Rosario lifted the arm

that wasn't carrying Mateo and checked her watch. "I've still got an hour and fifteen minutes."

"That's plenty!" Jules looked around at us. "Everyone up for Cork & Vine?"

"To Cork & Vine!" Max exclaimed, pumping her fist in the air.

"Awesome sauce. I'm riding with you, sis," Jules said.

I unlocked my car and prepared to get in, while the others drifted toward theirs. But Stevie remained rooted in place. "Um, aren't we forgetting something?"

Over the roof of my car, Jules and I exchanged a puzzled glance. Amber, Ro, and Max did the same.

Stevie pointed at Mateo's car seat, the *American Gothic* bun barely staying on her head, which almost sent me into hysterics again. "We can't take a baby to a wine bar."

"Oh. That." Max frowned.

"What are you talking about? There's no baby here." Ro blinked innocently as she adjusted the carrier on her arm. "Just a tiny senior citizen who's clearly been in a time machine accident and ended up in a baby's body."

Stevie gaped at her for a moment, then said, "You're unhinged. *All* of you." Even as she shook her head, a smile spread across her face. "But I wouldn't have it any other way."

And neither would I.

epilogue

A MONTH AND A HALF LATER

"**R**emember to smile big and sing loud," I instructed my students in the wings of the school auditorium. I adjusted Rory's red sequined bow tie as he let out a sniffle. "Your nose stop bleeding yet, Walker?"

Walker flashed me a triumphant thumbs-up, two bloody, wadded-up pieces of tissue protruding from his nostrils.

"Good! Take those out and get in line behind Bronwyn."

Walker yanked the bloody tissue out of his nose and started to approach, dangling it between his fingertips. I backed up, frantically shaking my head. "Walker, we talked about this!"

"But it's not a band-aid!"

"In the trash," I commanded in my sternest voice. "Everybody else in line—it's showtime. Break a leg!"

Carissa gave me a horrified look in reply. "*Break* a *leg?*"

"It means, 'Good Luck.'" I waved at my students. "Remember, whatever happens, just keep smiling!"

After a month and a half of learning the songs, drilling choreography, rehearsing with Mrs. Alvarez's class, and practicing their entrance and exit, it was finally time for the Ellis Elephants to debut their groovy moves for the excited crowd waiting on the other side of the heavy, blue curtain. In the wings on the opposite side of the stage, Caleb conferred with the third-graders and Marjorie, Mrs. Alvarez's TA, giving them the pep talk he'd already given my class.

Over the last several weeks, our bond had only grown stronger, as had my zest for life. If Caleb and I didn't have lunch together, we grabbed dinner, trying new restaurants across the city or cooking at my place. And I'd been the recipient of breakfast in bed—complete with fresh flowers and a song—so many times that I lost count.

I proudly became the Flow State Rebels' biggest fan and even earned an honorary role in the band playing the tambourine every now and again. Caleb was trying to teach me to play guitar, but as suspected, I didn't have a musical bone in my body. Still, it was fun to share the experience with him.

And I did attend one more Alphas Unleashed show...which also happened to be my last. It was there that I realized it was one thing to *know* that your incredibly loyal and communicative boyfriend was giving other women lap dances...it was another to see it happening in front of you. But like everything else, we discussed it and figured out how to move forward in a way that made sense for us.

I slipped around the curtain into the buzzing theater where relatives and family friends were chatting and claiming seats. I scanned the room and spotted one-third of my support system seated in the far-left section, three rows from the top. They were easy to locate thanks to the impressive blonde beehive wig balanced on Max's head.

I chuckled to myself; if Max wanted to dress to match the theme of the show, more power to her. Her help in designing, fashioning, and tailoring the kids' costumes had been invaluable. As she said, what good was having a costume designer and stylist in the group if you never used her?

Grinning, I lifted my hand and waved. Jules and Max grinned

and waved back. I spied Stevie standing by the exit, too busy fiddling with the settings on her super fancy camera to notice me. When the school's photographer fell ill at the last minute, I called Stevie and she stepped in with no hesitation.

As far as the rest of The Six, Amber really wanted to come but had to go to her brother's birthday dinner, and Rosario's boys were sick. But both had called earlier to wish me good luck and sent their love in the group chat.

I dropped into a front row chair next to Susie with an exhausted sigh.

"Did Rory stop crying? And what about Jayden? Did he find his lucky shark tooth?" she asked.

"Yes and yes. I extinguished all the fires. They're going to be great, Susie."

She blew out a breath and relaxed against the back of her chair.

Caleb walked onto the stage and took his place in the center, his arrival signaling to the audience that the show was about to begin. In his dark gray blazer, slacks, and red silk tie covered with sheet music, he looked every bit the part of the cool, completely-in-control music teacher, but I knew he was battling nerves. He cleared his throat, surveying the crowd before he spoke. When his eyes landed on me, his smile grew bigger and his shoulders dropped ever so slightly.

You got this, I mouthed with a wink.

"Don't we know him from somewhere?" murmured the woman sitting just behind me.

"That's what I was thinking! I can't figure it out. Maybe we've seen him at church?" the woman behind Susie asked.

"No, I don't think so. Probably the country club."

I almost let out a snort. The country club…sure.

"Good evening, everyone, and welcome to our spring concert: Motown Mania!" Caleb said. "Your exceptionally talented students are so excited to show you all the hard work they've put into preparing for tonight's concert. I encourage you to sit back and enjoy the magic of Motown."

As the audience clapped, he replaced the microphone in the stand I had set up, then took his seat at the keyboard stage right.

And the show began.

Everything went off with barely a hitch. Sure, Duncan wouldn't stop waving at his grandpa with both hands, and Hadleigh forgot the moves to "Rockin' Robin" so she just dabbed over and over again, but I was proud of my babies. They'd come so far in the eight months since the beginning of the school year.

And Caleb—Caleb was phenomenal. There was no doubt he possessed a real gift for music and teaching. He was in his element, accompanying the kids on a couple songs with the keyboard, and then with his guitar. Reminding them of choreography from a low, crouched position in front of the front row. He offered encouragement and positive reinforcement throughout.

Roughly thirty-five minutes after our students filed onto the stage, they took their bows—and in Archie's case, turned around, bent over, and wiggled his butt. Susie's eyes shot lasers at him, her death stare so intense I worried he might spontaneously combust as the audience applauded and tittered.

Caleb shook his head, once again taking centerstage to address the room. "Fallen Oaks Preparatory Lower School family, thank you so much for coming out and supporting your little Falcons tonight. And thank you for supporting *me*—you've given me such a warm reception." He paused for a breath. "I'm really going to miss the Alvarez Astronauts and Ellis Elephants, but I know Mrs. Norman can't wait to get back and see how much they've grown."

I felt a pang in my chest. Even though I'd obviously continue seeing Caleb outside of school, I was going to miss seeing him around, not to mention sharing lunch—and a few stolen kisses —in the storage room.

He turned around to address the fidgeting students directly. "And thank *you* for being such great musicians."

"You're welcome!" Rory shouted, eliciting more laughter from the crowd.

Caleb pointed at the light booth in the rear of the auditorium. "We can't forget Coach Aaron who did a fantastic job with the lights. A round of applause for Coach Aaron!"

The room filled with polite clapping and restless shifting in seats.

"And Miss Maxine Baldwin is responsible for these stellar costumes. She's right up there; you can't miss her," Caleb joked.

Absolutely glowing, Max raised her hand and gave a slow princess wave, milking her time in the moment for all it was worth.

"Okay, okay, I know you're ready to go, but I have just one more person to thank, because there is absolutely no way I could have made this happen without her." Caleb's head swiveled in my direction, and just as I registered what was happening, Coach Aaron aimed the spotlight at me. Blushing, I forced myself to sit up straighter and not shrink away from the attention.

Caleb's eyes locked on mine. "This woman put up with my insanely high standards as we figured out what this show would look like, wrangled these little rascals during rehearsals, and somehow managed to do it all with grace, humor, and the biggest smile on her face."

Don't tear up, Zara. Don't do it, I told myself as I clutched my hands in my lap.

Caleb broke eye contact to glance behind him and whisper something to the kids. Carissa stood up and ran off into the wings, returning seconds later with a cellophane-wrapped bouquet of Gerbera daisies. When Caleb held up the flowers and we locked gazes again, his own full of adoration, I was one-hundred percent certain that every adult in that auditorium knew we were an item.

And for once in my life, I didn't care.

"Miss Whitmore, these are for you."

"Yay, Miss Whitmore!" a couple of the students yelled, leaping up from the floor to jump up and down with joy.

More polite applause sounded around the room, but loud whooping came from the area where Jules and Max sat. I even thought I heard a cheer from Stevie. I wanted to melt into a puddle in my chair, but Susie dug her elbow into my ribs. "Move it!"

Cheeks flaming, I got up and made my way to Caleb, willing myself not to trip and fall on my face in front of all these people—and more importantly, my students, if only because they'd never let me live it down. When I reached him, he gave me a chaste side-hug and whispered in my ear, away from the microphone and audience, "Remind me to show you how much I appreciate you later."

"Looking forward to it," I whispered back.

"That's *definitely* her boyfriend," Baylee said.

Carissa nodded. "Yup."

Grinning, I shook my head and took my beautiful flowers back to Susie.

"Bet you won't give those away," she said, with a knowing look.

I shrugged, unable to wipe the contented smile from my face.

"And that concludes tonight's program. Your kids don't have to go home, but they can't stay here," Caleb said into the microphone.

"I know that's right," Susie muttered.

Free at last, people stood up, collected belongings, and gathered their kids for photos. I turned to Susie, who was getting to her feet with a groan.

"See you tomorrow, dear. Don't celebrate too much." She smirked as she patted my shoulder. "I've got to hustle out of here before someone tries to ask me something. There's a pint of Butter Pecan at home with my name on it."

"Mrs. Ellis!" An elegant brunette woman dressed head to toe in designer labels, whom I recognized as Hadleigh's mom, waved her hand overhead. "Mrs. Ellis. Yoohoo!"

"Crud muffins!"

I laughed as Susie was swept away, before turning my sights on Caleb. At the moment, he was mobbed by excited students and parents.

"Well done, Zara!" Stevie's voice exclaimed.

I spun around to find my sister and friends descending the last few stairs. Stevie finished zipping her gear bag, then darted forward and wrapped me in a hug.

"On the performance or nabbing the hot music teacher?" Max asked, patting the back of her beehive.

"Both," Stevie said matter-of-factly.

Cocking her head to the side, Jules pursed her lips. "Why aren't you wearing the Bad Decisions Dress?"

I stared at her incredulously. "Well, Jules, I didn't think it would be a good idea to wear something called the *Bad Decisions Dress* to a *school music program* where at least twenty things were bound to go wrong without any added help."

She nodded. "Fair point."

Stevie wrinkled her nose. "I thought we officially changed the name to the Whatever-Zara-Needs-it-to-Be Dress?"

"I think I've gotten all I need from it," I said.

"In that case, can I borrow it?" Max asked, clasping her hands in front of her in a pleading pose. "I'm pretty sure I can put it to good use."

"I'm sure you can." I rolled my eyes. "Give me a chance to get it dry cleaned and I'll hand it over."

"Yes!" Max pointed at the other girls. "You heard that with your own ears—I asked and she said yes. I get first dibs."

"Trust me, no one else wants a Bad Decisions Dress, Max," Stevie said. "It's all yours."

Out of the corner of my eye, I saw that the auditorium had mostly cleared out, and Caleb was picking up forgotten props and leftover debris from the stage risers.

With the exception of Max and Stevie, none of the other girls had met him yet. Had I been holding out because I was afraid they would scare him away with their crazy hijinks?

Possibly.

Was I holding back because I enjoyed our private bubble and knew that once The Sensational Six found out about him, the news would spread through the city and get back to my mom in no time?

Absolutely.

But now that Caleb and I had made things official a couple of weeks ago, and it was clear he wasn't going anywhere, it was time.

I turned back to my friends with a huge smile. "Come on, girls, there's someone I want you to meet."

acknowledgments

Where to even begin? This book was a long time in the making, and so many special people contributed along the way.

Thank you my mom, my "silent partner" who believes in me enough for the both of us when I have moments of doubt. Even while battling cancer, you were still offering support. This book wouldn't exist without you.

My beloved FFGE's. If you're reading this, I hope to God it's like 2040 or something. You made me laugh and taught me something new every single day. I CANNOT WAIT to see you each grow up and chase your dreams.

Thank you Claudia for such an exquisite cover—your talent is unbelievable. Thank you Josie for your proofreading skills— love those quick turnaround times and comments.

Torie, without you this book would have no title, no cover, and would have probably just remained an abandoned file on my computer. Thank you for all of your cheerleading, the reminders to keep my eyes on my own paper, and tried-and-true publishing advice. You truly are a gem. <3

Amy, you've been a cheerleader and championed me since Day 1. The path for this book might not have been what we planned, but it's exactly what it needed to be.

Jeremy, I will NEVER NOT thank you for reading every single thing I write, even if it's not in your wheelhouse. I'm grateful for your thoughtful and insightful feedback, and for letting me peer pressure you into coworking meetings.

Clau, you get all the *besos*! Thank you for not only reading and sharing your excitement with me, but for helping me recognize the brilliance in myself and encouraging me to share it with the world. *Te aprecio mucho.*

Miranda, thank you so much for letting me borrow bits of your background (only bits!) for Rosario's life before kids. I so appreciate you reading my draft and sharing your joy with me.

Jenn, thank you for letting me yeet so many reels and ridiculous memes at you. But seriously, if I die before you, please delete my search history.

about the author

Photo by Nomad Family Photo Group

Jax McQueen began her writing journey at the UNC-Chapel Hill in the Writing for the Screen and Stage program before completing an M.A. in Interactive Media at Elon University. When she's not writing, you can find her chasing a sugar high, busting a move on the dance floor, or plotting her next big adventure.

CONNECT ONLINE

www.jaxmcqueen.com

IG: @thejaxmcqueen